S0-BXX-771

TWISTED WHISPERS

Visit us at www.boldstrokesbooks.com

By the Author

Crimson Vengeance

Burgundy Betrayal

Scarlet Revenge

Vermilion Justice

Twisted Echoes

Twisted Whispers

TWISTED WHISPERS

by

Sheri Lewis Wohl

2015

TWISTED WHISPERS
© 2015 By Sheri Lewis Wohl. All Rights Reserved.

ISBN 13: 978-1-62639-439-1

This Trade Paperback Original Is Published By
Bold Strokes Books, Inc.
P.O. Box 249
Valley Falls, NY 12185

First Edition: October 2015

THIS IS A WORK OF FICTION. NAMES, CHARACTERS, PLACES, AND INCIDENTS ARE THE PRODUCT OF THE AUTHOR'S IMAGINATION OR ARE USED FICTITIOUSLY. ANY RESEMBLANCE TO ACTUAL PERSONS, LIVING OR DEAD, BUSINESS ESTABLISHMENTS, EVENTS, OR LOCALES IS ENTIRELY COINCIDENTAL.

THIS BOOK, OR PARTS THEREOF, MAY NOT BE REPRODUCED IN ANY FORM WITHOUT PERMISSION.

CREDITS
Editor: Shelley Thrasher
Production Design: Susan Ramundo
Cover Design By Sheri (graphicartist2020@hotmail.com)

Dedication

The Lady in White
I never knew who you were
I never knew why you came
But Thank You
You made me see
You made me think
And best of all…
You gave wings to my imagination

I find hope
In the darkest of days,
And focus in the brightest.
I do not judge the universe.

—Dalai Lama

PROLOGUE

This wasn't murder. No sirree, Bob. Murder was something criminals did, and that's the last thing he was. This might be a complication that required cleanup, but that's about it. Definitely not something that might fall into the scofflaw category. He had morals as well a distinct belief in right and wrong. Criminals didn't, and that's what set him far apart from the felons.

Blood dripped from his hands as he plowed the shovel into the dirt again and again. Sweat trickled down his back and dampened the hair at the nape of his neck. The evening was deep and dark, and he didn't dare use a light. The chance of anyone coming by this time of night was slim. Still, it didn't hurt to take precautions. Besides, he didn't really need any kind of light to do his work. He was as comfortable here as if he and the darkness shared a soul. Nighttime was his favorite, which—given his mission—was good. A pansy afraid of the dark would fail miserably in his line of work.

The hole grew deeper with each shovelful of dirt he tossed out onto the blue tarp spread wide on the grass. What he was trying to accomplish needed to be right. Or more precisely, perfect. And it was. He stopped shoveling and crawled out of the hole.

The second blue tarp, this one tied with an extensive length of paracord, rolled easily into the hole. For a long moment, he stood at the edge of his carefully crafted crevasse and stared. Then he picked up the shovel and began to fill it once again with rich earth. When the dirt reached the top, was packed level, and the turf back in place, it was as if nothing had disturbed the ground. The beauty of it made him smile. His father always said, "A job worth doing is worth doing right." *Well, Daddy, I did this job right.*

Slowly he folded the tarp, taking care to ensure any loose dirt stayed within the folds. He tossed the shovel into the bed of his pickup and tucked the tarp into the diamond-plate toolbox mounted behind the cab. Keys in hand, he pulled open the driver's door and then paused. A wise man would leave now, and he considered himself a very wise man. As he debated, he tightened his grip on the door handle. *Get in. Go, before someone drives by and sees you.*

Sighing, he stepped away from the truck door, closed it, and returned to the spot where a moment before he'd worked up a sweat. Staring down at the grass he'd carefully replaced so no one would notice any kind of disturbance, he felt his heart start to beat like a freight train and his breath begin to hitch. A light rain fell from the sky, yet he still didn't return to his truck. He'd done this enough times already to know his work was good and, more importantly, his own private secret—forever.

Walking away this time was impossible, and he understood why. Understanding didn't change how he felt. This one was different from the rest. Much more personal and far more important. His head bowed and his hands in his pockets, he stood still as death. The rain picked up in intensity until it dripped down his hair and onto his face, where it mixed with his tears.

Chapter One

S on of a bitch." Lorna Dutton spit her mouthful of coffee all over the morning newspaper. With the back of her hand she wiped her mouth and then slapped the soggy paper down on the kitchen table. "When is this shit going to stop?"

Honestly, enough already. She'd moved out here on the Washington Coast to get away from people, not to end up in *The Seattle Times*, yet there she was in all her smiling—or was that grimacing—glory. Her face was front and center on page one of a newspaper with a circulation in the hundreds of thousands. Page fucking one!

All right, it just might be a pretty good story. After all, solving the mystery of a Makah woman missing for over a hundred years made for a great human-interest article. Or newscast. Or Internet video clip. That John McCafferty, the original owner of the house she now lived in, had murdered Catherine Swan, the Makah woman, then buried her in the yard, wasn't an original story, but how she'd uncovered the truth was. Good old-fashioned psychic ability, and pretty much the last thing she wanted to be known for made for a story sure to capture the reading public's attention. It didn't seem to interest anyone that she'd written training manuals for not one but three Fortune 500 companies. Now that was something she wouldn't mind seeing on the front page of the newspaper.

Didn't seem to matter what she wanted. The minute she moved into the house she inherited from her great-aunt, her latent psychic abilities began to get stronger and stronger until she solved the century-old mystery. Even as isolated as they were out here, the story still managed to work its way through just about every news outlet in the state. Instead of isolation and a chance to rest and renew, she'd morphed into a strange sort of celebrity. Not the kind that brought her technical-writing jobs either. That would be a helpful sort of celebrity status.

But no, it couldn't be that easy. Rather than connecting her name with real jobs writing books, manuals, and trade materials, all people knew about her was that she could see ghosts.

Sucked to be her.

The story did, however, have two upsides. First, she wasn't in the psychic realm all by herself. When her brother Jeremy had showed up, the old paranormal bug had managed to hit him square on too. Actually Jeremy didn't have much latent psychic ability, but he was an open type of person, which made him easy pickings for a hostile spirit. Now that they'd banished the spirit of the asshole who built the house and murdered his daughter's lover, nothing preternatural seemed to be bothering Jeremy any longer. Still, it was nice to have someone around who could relate. Most people couldn't even if they wanted to, and those that said they could were by and large the crazy ones.

The second perk, and in her opinion the best, was Renee. Lorna's heart took a big leap every time she thought about her. When Lorna inherited the house, she also inherited, so to speak, the housekeeper, Jolene Austin. Jolene's daughter Renee was a lovely woman with long dark hair and gorgeous eyes. By herself, Renee was fantastic, interesting, and beautiful. It also didn't hurt that she'd brought Clancy along with her. Probably less than a minute after he put his big head in her lap and turned his expressive eyes on her, she was a goner. Lorna loved the big German shepherd as if he'd been part of her life for years.

The whole reason Renee came to the house was tragic. A fire in the building she owned in downtown Seattle had gutted her business on the main floor and so smoke-damaged her living quarters on the second floor she couldn't live there until extensive repairs were completed. More than happy to invite her to stay at the house on the shores of the Pacific Ocean, Lorna extended a heartfelt invitation. The house was huge, with plenty of room for what turned out to be a makeshift kind of family consisting of Lorna, Jeremy, his pregnant girlfriend Merry, Jolene, and Renee. Oh, and Clancy, of course.

The truth of why she relocated so far from her childhood home was a tired old story. She came here to disappear after her long-time girlfriend, Anna, decided for both of them the relationship was over. Might have been nice if they'd talked it through first, but that's not the way it played out. Anna moved on before Lorna even knew it was over. After the relationship implosion she just wanted to hide out here all alone and train for her first Ironman triathlon. Well, train and feel sorry for herself in a way that was pretty embarrassing when she looked back on it. Somebody should have given her a big old bitch-slap alongside the head instead of allowing her to mope, whine, and cry. Luckily her self-imposed isolation was brief and she'd never been happier. Best intentions and all that.

Notwithstanding her current good feelings, right now she was sick and tired of the publicity her discovery of the body of Catherine Swan generated. She resented it, actually, for a multitude of reasons. Solitude wasn't an objective these days like it was when she first moved here, and that was okay. Privacy was a different matter. If she had her way, the whole psychic thing could disappear as quickly as it appeared. That wasn't going to happen, judging by the rabid attention her unusual talent seemed to garner.

Her reluctance to embrace her psychic ability aside, Catherine's remains were returned to her family and the Makah Tribe. A wrong perpetuated against a lovely young woman so long ago was put right. What only the inhabitants of the house knew, though, was discovering Catherine's remains also connected her spirit with the love of her life, Tiana McCafferty, the only daughter of John McCafferty. Took Lorna awhile to figure it out, but she finally realized Tiana was earthbound as she waited for someone to reunite her with Catherine. Once it happened, the spirits of both Catherine and Tiana were free at last.

She saw them together, a love so strong it defied death, and her heart ached for the travesty visited upon the two women. Until she met Renee that kind of love was an elusive dream far out of her reach. Every day she spent with Renee she understood a little more about the bond between Catherine and Tiana that kept them bound to the earth decade after decade.

Reuniting the two lovers allowed them to leave this place and go into the light, or wherever peaceful spirits go. She felt good about that, except it left the house feeling a little empty. Tiana's essence filled the place with an energy she couldn't touch but could sure as hell feel. She missed the spirit of the beautiful young woman whose only crime was to love another so deeply it enraged her father enough to propel him to commit murder.

It was time to put it all to rest, especially the part that shone the spotlight squarely on her. Lately, people were actually driving by as if trying to glimpse the *psychic*. Circus performer wasn't on her bucket list.

If she didn't have the picture staring up at her she could pretend nobody was paying any attention to her. She wadded up the newspaper and tossed it toward the trashcan just as Renee came into the kitchen.

A single eyebrow went up as she cut her gaze first to Lorna and then at the damp newspaper that missed the trash can by a pretty wide margin. "Practicing your three-point shot?" She poured herself a cup of coffee and looked at Lorna over the rim of the mug.

"Never had one," she admitted with honesty and a smile. Her heart was lighter at the sight of Renee dressed in pink-flowered flannel pants and a bright-yellow T-shirt. Unlike Lorna, who preferred primary colors, Renee embraced bright and cheerful. Her choice worked for her in a way it never would for Lorna, and it always made her smile. She pushed away from the table and got up to retrieve the wadded paper from where it landed on the floor.

"What made you want to crush the paper before anyone else could read it?"

She cocked her head and studied the missed shot. There was a reason she never made the varsity basketball team. "As my grandmother used to say, I'll give you three guesses and the first two don't count." She picked up the newspaper and stuffed it into the trash before sitting back down in her chair at the table her long legs crossed.

Renee laughed, her eyes sparkling. "Gosh, that narrows it right down. I'd have to say that something in there was about one beautiful and talented psychic. Did my first guess get close?"

"Ding, ding, ding…you're a winner." She held up her coffee mug in a mock toast.

"Sweetheart." Renee walked over and ran a hand across Lorna's hair before planting a kiss on the top of her head. "You gotta stop letting these things get to you. The truth is, whether you like it or not, God gave you a gift, and you've already used it for the greater good."

Lorna rolled her eyes as she leaned into Renee's hand where it still rested against her head. "Okay, Gandhi."

Renee's laugh was like a ray of sunshine. "I prefer Mother Theresa. But seriously, Lorna, you're unique and what you did was incredibly special. Yeah, it's kind of exploitive of journalists to keep using it to sell papers, but it doesn't diminish what you are, honey. Just roll with it for now, and as *my* grandmother used to say…this too shall pass."

"I sure as hell hope your granny was right 'cause this shit needs to pass."

"She never let me down. It will pass, I promise." She kissed the top of Lorna's head again.

❖

Thea Lynch paced the length of her office, the sick feeling in the pit of her stomach refusing to lessen. Three days, three incredibly long days, and still nothing. Not a single call, not a clue, nothing. Her sister was missing and nobody knew a goddamn thing. Worse, nobody seemed to care except her.

She glanced at the silent phone and cursed it under her breath. From the moment Grant called her, she'd been a wreck. Actually that wasn't right either; she was rattled long before that. She'd sensed before his call that something was wrong with Alida. It'd always been that way with them. Everything people said about twins was true in their case. Their connection was more than physical; it was spiritual.

Now that her worst fears appeared to be true, she didn't know what to do or where to turn for help. The company truck Alida was driving three days ago was found at a sub-station with the doors open, her backpack on the seat, and the keys in the ignition. Everything was there except her sister. How could that be? There was nothing around the sub-station, nowhere for her to go. People—her sister—didn't simply disappear.

The police checked over the truck, and searchers went out for hours to try to find her, or at least a trace of her. Nothing came of it. Alida vanished as if she were part of a magician's disappearing act.

Thea had come into work today hoping for a little distraction, but that turned out to be fruitless because so far she wasn't getting a damn thing done. How could she? Alida was in trouble, and she didn't have the first idea of how to help.

After a couple of hours she gave up and, leaving everything in the hands of her very capable staff, returned home. At least she could be here in case Alida called or, better yet, showed up. Nothing would be better than to open her front door and see her standing on the front steps. Pressing her fingers to her closed eyes she took long, deep breaths. *Please, God, bring her home.*

The ping of the doorbell made her jump and her eyes flew open. Her first thought was Alida. How she hoped God was answering her silent prayer. With her heart pounding, she ran to the front door and peered through the peephole. Her hopes crashed. It wasn't Alida standing outside but a stranger.

Slowly, she swung the door open to a policewoman. The woman standing in her doorway might be wearing plain clothes, but she screamed cop. Dark-blue cargo pants, a tan button-down shirt, and black leather boots were not the attire of the businesswomen she knew. Her dark hair brushed the collar of her shirt, the cut severe, but it worked with the sharp lines of her face. For at least a moment, Thea felt something besides fear, which wasn't totally unwelcome even if her unexpected visitor was in law enforcement.

"Theadora Lynch?" Her voice was low and a little deep, and it matched the rest of her in an interesting way that very much appealed to Thea. Her hopes ratcheted up just a little bit.

She nodded. "Yes, I'm Thea."

The vision in cop chic stepped forward and held out her hand. "I'm Deputy Sheriff Katie Carlisle from the investigations unit of the Sheriff's Department. I need to talk to you about your sister Alida. I'm sorry to bother you at home, but it's quite important. I promise not to take up too much of your time."

A couple of others had come by right after the power company Alida worked for reported her missing. At the time she was so overwhelmed by the idea Alida was gone she barely remembered what she told them. What she did recall was her disenchantment with the two men. They obviously didn't believe Alida was taken against her will. In fact, they implied she simply took off and following up on her was a waste of their time. She was glad someone else was here now—a different set of eyes and hopefully a mind more open than the last two.

She accepted the offered hand and wrapped her fingers around a warm palm. The woman's handshake was firm, confident. "Yes, please. Come on in and have a seat." Up close her eyes were a warm brown that radiated strength. Yes indeed, she was really glad the Sheriff's Department had sent someone else for this follow-up visit. Maybe she'd judged the first two unfairly when she felt they were blowing her off or not, considering they didn't come themselves. No matter, someone was here and that's what was important.

In the living room, the woman sat on the edge of the cushion in one of the club chairs. "Thank you for giving me a little of your time." She opened a small tablet she pulled from her pocket.

"What can I do for you, Deputy?" Thea sat in the chair across from her. "The other two from your office didn't seem very interested in any information I could offer that might help to find my sister."

An expression that might have been annoyance flashed quickly across the woman's face before being replaced by a look far more sympathetic. "Please, call me Katie, and I want to hear about the day your sister disappeared. I'm sorry about your prior interview, and I apologize if my colleagues gave you the impression your assistance wasn't important. I'm very interested in anything and everything you can tell me about her."

At the mention of Alida, tears pricked the back of Thea's eyes and her foot started to tap. She still couldn't fathom the reality that for three days no one had seen or heard from her. Alida just didn't do things like that. She possessed quirks, as did everyone, but that didn't mean she was a flake or that she ran away without a word to anyone, especially her. No one was ever going to convince her of that.

Once more Thea pressed her fingers against closed eyes as she took a couple of deep breaths. The possibility that Alida could be dead darted through her mind. She reminded herself not to automatically jump to the worst-case scenario. Typically she was a glass-half-full kind of woman and embraced the positive in any situation. Alida probably wasn't dead. Perhaps she was hurt and needed help. She didn't have her cell phone; that was why she didn't call for assistance. Just because three days had passed without a word didn't mean she was dead.

Except Thea couldn't shake the dread that pooled in the pit of her stomach since the first moment she learned Alida was gone. No matter how she came at it, this was different. It felt dark and desolate.

Thea opened her eyes, looked over, and met Katie's eyes. "She's just gone. One day she was there and then nothing. Her company truck was at her last stop with the doors open. She left her bag on the seat and keys in the ignition. All her stuff was there. Who walks away like that? I can tell you one thing without any doubt—not my sister."

So far Katie hadn't made notes on her tablet. Her eyes were on Thea. "I've seen both the pictures and the spot where her truck was located. Nothing jumped out at me. So, indulge me and walk me through your interactions that day. Let's see if we can come up with anything together."

Thea thought back to the morning three days ago, focusing beyond the top of Katie's head. She wanted to pick out what was different, anything that might now turn out to be a clue. The sad reality was nothing jumped out at her no matter how hard she concentrated on remembering that day. "Alida called me about two." She brought her gaze back to Katie's face. The good thing was, Katie appeared interested.

"Was that unusual?"

As much as she wanted to tell her yes, she shook her head. "No. She called me just about every day to share funny things that happened along the way. You see, I'm a graphic artist and spend so much of my time either hunched over a computer or helping one of my staff, I don't get out much. It was different for her. Alida's out all the time, every day. The things she sees are crazy, and the colorful way she describes them to me are just the adventures I need when I get wrapped up in a project."

"Nothing after that call?" Katie's head was now bent as she made notes on her tablet.

Thea's heart ached as the despair of the last three days washed over her anew. She wanted to scream and cry at the same time. Not that she intended to succumb to crippling emotion. She planned to keep it together. "I haven't heard a thing since that call. Something happened to her, Deputy. I feel it right here." She tapped her chest. It was always hard to explain to non-twins how deep the connection was. Though they looked alike, they were two distinct individuals with their own likes, dislikes, and quirks. At the same time, they were, in many ways, two halves of a whole. That's why they were so in tune with each other. That's why she knew something was very wrong.

Katie looked up from her tablet and studied her with those deep, dark eyes. "What do you think might have happened?"

God, how she wished she knew. The gut-wrenching feeling in the pit of her stomach screamed for answers, yet she possessed not a shred of helpful information. Slowly she shook her head. "I don't know, and to tell you the truth it hurts to even consider what it could be."

"What about her husband?"

"Grant?" Thea's thoughts shifted to the tall, good-looking man who worshipped his wife even if he had a wandering eye…which he did. "No way. Trust me, they had their problems, but they were the kind of couple who found a way to work things out. I don't believe he would or could ever hurt her. Cheat on her, yes. Kill her, never. He'd take a bullet for her."

Katie nodded and made a couple more notes before looking over at her again. "Okay, so for the moment we'll rule out her husband. How about other people who might have a grudge or be upset with her? Did she say anything to you in the days before she disappeared? Anything seem unusual or uncomfortable? Was somebody hanging around who made her uneasy?"

She'd expected this question and had been thinking about it since Alida vanished. She nodded slowly as she recalled Alida's concerns. "Not directly but she mentioned that it felt like someone was watching her when she was out in the field. She told me she'd never seen anyone and nothing ever happened. But it made the hairs on the back of her neck stand up."

She didn't want Katie to think her sister was paranoid because she wasn't. On the other hand, at the moment she was scared enough for Alida to throw out anything and everything to the attractive woman who was the first one who seemed to believe Alida might be in real danger. Besides, she was so emotionally involved she wasn't rational. Sharing everything she could think of with this deputy was sure to help sort out the crap from the critical.

Katie leaned toward Thea and held her eyes. "Trust me, you don't ever want to discount feelings. Sometimes they're the thread that leads us straight to the answers."

It was as if she listened to Thea's thoughts. For the first time in three days she felt a flicker of something like hope. Someone was listening and, more importantly, seemed to care. She and Grant weren't alone anymore. She almost let the tears threatening to fall burst forth.

CHAPTER TWO

The Watcher hoped that helping the souls of the two wronged women reunite would clear his path to heaven. He was mistaken. While they'd found their way from this world and into the light, he was still here. That they were home at last pleased him. That he remained tethered to the earth made his heart heavy. All he could do was watch, wait, and hope his time would come.

From the lengthening shadows, he studied the house on the bluff. Big and well-built, it had withstood the elements decade after decade while protecting those within from the ravages of Mother Nature. Tonight was no different. The wind howled and thick clouds tried to blot out the stars. The ocean waves pounding against the rocks at his back were a familiar lullaby. Cool ocean spray dampened his long black hair. It didn't matter if he was cold and wet. All that concerned him were those who lived within the big old house, and as he stood vigil, lights came on inside, pushing away the darkness.

Years ago this house was filled with sadness and death. Then she came and, together with the others, restored hope and light. But their work was not yet complete. He pinned his hopes on the other two women who were saved from limbo. However, now he understood his fate wasn't tied to the two of a century past, but to the woman of this time and place whom God had gifted with the sight.

She was reluctant. She was defiant. She was brilliant.

The Watcher stood impossibly tall in the dimming light, his nearly seven-foot frame blending with the shadows as if they were one. His fall from grace happened so long ago, and in the intervening centuries he was filled with the desire to once again walk through the gates of heaven. He tried again and again to redeem his soul, hoping God would grant him mercy.

Many times his heart was heavy and hope slipped away like the waves of the ocean that crashed against the rocks, only to then glide away into the massive eternity of the sea. Then a glimmer of something glorious would restore his faith, and he once again believed in the power of forgiveness. In her face now shone a ray of that indefinable something that swept over him like a lighthouse beacon. Together, he and this woman would right what was wrong, and one day he would leave this place and return to his home beyond the sky. She would push aside the darkness that had been his prison through the ages and open a world of light to him once more.

Tonight, however, in his soul lingered a worrisome thread of danger. Something was wrong, and she once more was the key to making it right. His vision was blurred, but somewhere in the distance, the image struggled to clear itself. A faraway cry drifted on the night air, sending chills up his arms.

At the big windows looking out over the ocean, her face suddenly appeared, pale and intent. Staring into the distance she stood motionless, searching as he did, for what exactly he did not know. Whatever it was, whoever it was, their spirit called to the two who heard the plea sighing on the wind. Neither could ignore it even if they wished to do so.

Satisfied for the moment, he stepped back and farther into the shadows. He would ready himself for the task ahead and do his best to guide her to the awaiting destiny, so that she in turn could usher him to his. His head bowed, he moved his lips in a silent prayer, speaking in a language long since wiped from the earth.

His body shook, his face blurred. Then he was gone.

❖

Katie kicked off her boots, leaving them where they landed with a thud right outside the closet door, then threw her shirt on the bed and slithered out of her cargo pants. She replaced them with a pair of shorts and a sweatshirt with cut-off sleeves. Now, that was better. Nothing facilitated the thinking process like old, comfortable clothes. For about a millisecond she thought about picking everything up. Grandma used to always remark that cleanliness was next to godliness. For her money, a certain amount of disarray and clutter made her home feel lived in and cozy. In her book, that was plenty close enough to godliness.

From the fridge she snagged a nice dark Porter and carried it to the living room. Usually she was good at leaving her work at work. Tonight wasn't one of those times when she could walk away. Actually, more than the gorgeous Theadora Lynch made her mind whirl. And Thea was most assuredly gorgeous. With thick black hair that hung down her back and eyes the color of a summer sky, the woman made Katie want to just sit there and stare. What was it about the combination of black hair and blue eyes that sent her heart pounding? She was most definitely a sucker.

Fortunately, Katie was still professional enough to keep her mind off Thea's hotness and onto the issue of her missing twin sister. The case itself intrigued her. For the most part, missing adults didn't garner a whole lot of resources, or even thought for that matter. The vast majority were people who simply didn't want to be found. Some planned their escape with great detail, while others came across a chance to disappear and simply took it.

A fair number of legitimate missing persons' cases did exist, where something went terribly wrong and harm occurred to the one who disappeared. In a great many of those cases, family or acquaintances were involved with said harm. Precisely why, despite what she told Thea, Alida's husband Grant was very high on her list of people to investigate. Law enforcement looked first to professed loved ones for a very good reason.

There was a weird feeling to this case, and Katie wanted to know why. Traditional odds were on the husband, yet her gut instinct was to look way outside the box to find the truth behind Alida's disappearance. Vanishing in broad daylight didn't feel right for this particular woman.

She wasn't about to say that to any of the other deputies. She'd earned her shield and was damn proud of it. The fact that her grandfather, father, and brother were all in law enforcement before her only meant that she had great teachers, not that they opened the door for her. Not everyone saw it that way. Escaping the "you're only here because of your family" was nearly impossible. Just because no one said it to her face didn't mean it wasn't out there. The only thing she could do was prove herself over and over. It wasn't fair but it was her reality. Slowly she was winning the battle with the guys, even though it sure as hell got old.

So in this instance, she was damn well going to keep her gut instincts to herself. At least until she could prove she was right on the money. As far as she was concerned, the family of Alida Lynch Canwell wasn't involved with her disappearance. Grant Canwell was clearly distraught, and if he was acting he should be up for an Academy Award. Even if he was still on her list of possible suspects, she didn't believe he was that good an actor. Men didn't fake the kind of emotion he displayed during her interview with him earlier today.

The sister was, like Alida's husband, so full of worry it glared from her eyes. The fact the two women were twins made Katie feel even stronger that Alida didn't simply walk away from her life. Something else had happened out there at the isolated power station, and a bad feeling the ending wasn't going to be a happy one lingered. Sometimes she really hated the knowledge that came with this job. It was hard to remain optimistic when the statistics pointed in the opposite direction. Still, she intended to give a good try.

Opening her tablet, she pulled up the electronic file. In it were jpgs of every angle of the last place Alida was seen. There was her truck, with the doors open and the bag sitting undisturbed on the seat. She didn't care how anyone came at it, this wasn't a *typical* disappearance, and Katie was going to find out what went wrong and why.

After a long pull of the beer, she rested her head against the sofa back and closed her eyes. She was given the case because no one thought it could be solved. No witnesses, no suspects, no motive. If the good old boys wanted to prove she had no business being a deputy, this could be the case that would give them the evidence they wanted to back up their belief.

Well, fuck the good old boys. Her relatives didn't get her this job. She earned it all on her own. At the same time, she wasn't stupid. She was determined to use her family's shared knowledge from decades of experience to find Alida Canwell. And when she did, all the backbiters, women haters, and chauvinists would have to shut the hell up once and for all.

❖

"Do you ever have the feeling you're being watched?" Lorna stood in the living room staring out the big windows at the inky black night. Few stars shone through the cloud-shrouded sky though for a change it wasn't raining, yet. All day she'd sensed eyes on her, though as far as she could tell nobody was around. The sensation was so strong she couldn't ignore it.

"I watch you all the time," Renee said cheerfully.

Lorna turned and smiled at her. Renee lounged on the sofa. Dressed in yoga pants and a bright-pink jersey shirt a couple sizes too big, her long hair loose and flowing, she was stretched out and obviously comfortable. She was also beautiful. Just looking at her took Lorna's breath away, and for the hundredth time she wondered how she ever got lucky enough to meet someone like her. Or that someone like Renee loved her back. It was a miracle.

"I don't mean *you*." Besides Lorna and Renee, there was Renee's mother Jolene, who'd been the housekeeper here for decades, Lorna's brother Jeremy, and his fiancée Merry. She wasn't referring to any of them. Whoever, or whatever, watched her today, it wasn't one of her peeps.

Renee tilted her head as she looked at Lorna. "Who's going to be watching you clear out here? We're not exactly on the beaten path."

Under normal circumstances Lorna would agree with her. "Couldn't tell that by all the curiosity seekers that just happen to come by lately." Since word had first circulated about Catherine and Tiana, people drove by every day and many nights. Maybe it was one of them and she was letting the irritation of being on the psychic radar get on her nerves. Except she was pretty sure that wasn't it.

"True story, baby. I grew up here and have never seen so many people out this way. This too shall pass and things will get back to normal. Once the newness of your powers fades, folks will forget all about you."

Normal? She wasn't sure she even knew what that was anymore. If she needed proof of her altered reality, today gave it to her. The curious hadn't caused her uneasiness. It was something else. "God, I hope people get tired of us soon. But that's not what I'm talking about. I stand here looking out at the ocean, and the hairs on the back of my neck stand up. I swear someone's out there in the darkness watching me, and it creeps the hell out of me."

Renee got up from the sofa and joined her at the windows, sliding an arm around her waist. "Baby, it's probably your new powers playing games with your reality. I mean, think about it. You have this phenomenal ability to see things in another dimension. It doesn't seem like it would be a stretch for your spidey senses to be in overdrive. You know, someone or *something* could be watching you…from another dimension."

Perfect, that's just what she needed, another spirit stalking her. Once was enough, thank you very much. Except Renee's take on it made sense in a lot of ways. This whole psychic thing was pretty fucking weird, and now that it was turned on, it didn't seem to intend to turn off anytime soon. She wasn't exactly sure what to do about it either. She really wanted it to turn off. One encounter with spirits from another realm was way plenty for her. It wouldn't break her heart if it never happened again.

With a sigh she turned and kissed the top of Renee's head, loving the sweet scent of vanilla that was so her. "You're probably right…at least I hope so. It bothers me to think somebody's out there skulking around the property hiding behind trees and peeking in our windows. Ghosts at least make a weird kind of sense. Stalkers don't. Who in their right mind would want to stalk me anyway? I'm pretty boring."

Renee laughed softly "I beg to differ, sweetheart. Don't sell yourself short. I think you're pretty fascinating."

"You're blinded by lust."

Renee laughed, gave her a squeeze, and let go to turn toward the windows. "True enough, my lovely." She leaned close to the glass, put her hands on either side of her face, and peered out into the darkness. "I don't see a thing. No ghosts. No stalkers. I'm thinking you're safe tonight. Now come on. Mom made one of her famous pies, and I, for one, want to get to it before Jeremy dives in."

Lorna laughed and grabbed Renee's hand. Once again this wonderful woman took her dark mood and turned it into lightness and joy. Pie it was. "Damn straight. That boy can still out eat any teenager in the county. I don't know where he puts it or why he doesn't weigh five hundred pounds."

"What boy?" Jeremy's voice came from the doorway.

Lorna and Renee looked at each other, laughed, and ran for the kitchen, Jeremy following right behind.

CHAPTER THREE

Thea was surprised by the call from the cute deputy sheriff who'd been so understanding though a little aloof. Despite that, Katie seemed to be genuinely interested in finding Alida, and that was something Thea needed desperately right now. Katie could be as distant as she wanted as long as she found her sister.

Not knowing what had happened hurt her heart. Not knowing what to do to find her was tearing her apart. She would accept any and all help.

Now after Katie called and asked her to ride along to the spot where Alida's truck was discovered abandoned, Thea felt real hope for the first time in days. Her request might be unusual, but objectionable? Not at all. In fact, her stomach fluttered a little at the idea of riding all the way out to the transfer station on the outskirts of town. The thought of standing on the ground where Alida stood caused part of it, though the other part had nothing at all to do with her sister.

Okay, face it, she thought. The deputy was hot. No. More like smoking. Two years ago Thea and her girlfriend Sue had mutually ended their three-year relationship. After that, nobody garnered more than passing interest. It wasn't that Sue broke her heart and she couldn't move past it. Not even close. It was more that the two of them simply grew apart until one day they seemed more like good friends than lovers or soul mates. They'd moved on from each other, and since then Thea had focused on her career and building her company. Romance and passion took a backseat. Who could find lifelong love when work was a seven-day-a-week endeavor? Besides, did she even have a soul mate, or was she just dreaming of something that would never be?

But yesterday when she opened the door and found Katie standing on her porch, suddenly she felt alive and tingly in all the right places. She couldn't remember the last time she felt that way or if she ever even had. The timing was insanely inappropriate, but her heart didn't care. Something about Katie Carlisle spoke to her soul.

Of course, whether Katie felt that way about her, or any woman for that matter, was currently a mystery. For all she knew, Katie could have a boyfriend or a husband, but she sure hoped not.

Outside, the sound of a car pulling into her driveway took her away from her thoughts. She grabbed her bag and headed out. Katie was halfway up the walk by the time Thea pulled the front door shut. Like yesterday, Katie was all cop in her cargo pants, dark shirt, and leather boots.

"Thanks for coming along," Katie said. Her voice and her eyes were serious, all business. That could be professional courtesy or the sign Thea hoped not to see.

At the same time, Thea appreciated her cool, professional manner. Yes, she was most definitely attracted to this tall, graceful deputy, but this wasn't about her; it was about Alida. Once her sister was found and brought home, safely, she prayed, she would have plenty of time to see if her thing for Katie might stand a chance of becoming something special.

They both turned and walked back toward the dark-blue SUV. "I appreciate your asking me to ride along," Thea told her. Even though she didn't think she could contribute much, just riding along made her feel like she was doing something, and that helped push the feeling of helplessness aside. "Is this an official vehicle?" She slid into the passenger's seat. Truthfully, it looked more like a soccer-mom car than a sheriff's cruiser. No fancy gear, no guns, no computers. Didn't all the modern police vehicles have computers these days? Was Katie a married soccer mom? Her heart sank just a little at the thought.

Katie shook her head, buckled her seatbelt, and then checked her mirrors. As she backed out of the driveway she said, "No, this is my personal vehicle. I want to go to the transfer station without drawing more attention than necessary. There's nothing on my car to alert people that I'm police. Sometimes it's better that way."

Well, maybe her car didn't scream law enforcement, but didn't she realize that one glimpse of her and people would know? She rocked the "look," for lack of a better explanation. Combine that with the handgun in a holster at her waist, and she just didn't appear to be the average gawker driving around a potential crime scene for a quick look and to snap a photo for posting to social network. No, Katie Carlisle looked all cop, and it was a look Thea liked a lot.

On the flip side, it comforted her to not be under scrutiny, so to speak. It was bad enough that Alida was gone, but she hated all the questions people threw her way. Sure, they meant to be helpful, but instead they sent daggers into her heart. "Do you think she ran away?" "Were Alida and Grant having problems?" "Do you think she's dead?"

Just the thought of answering the last one made her shudder. No way was she going there. Alida was alive. She had to be, and with Katie's help they would find her.

Keeping a positive attitude was great, except she couldn't ignore that painful nagging sensation in the pit of her stomach. She refused to give it a name, and if anyone asked, she'd pass it off as stress. This was going to turn out all right. It was. Period.

Thea watched out the window as they drove north up Highway 395. It was undoubtedly one of the most beautiful areas around here. Washington State was so diverse in its landscape, and each difference was lovely in its own way. Here the road took gentle curves and slow ascents. As they drove farther north, the trees grew thicker, the houses farther apart, and businesses thinned.

A few miles past the Wandemere Mall, the last cluster of retail businesses before the landscape turned into a combination of residential and agricultural, Katie took a right onto a rough road. She followed it about a quarter of mile before they reached a turnout where a small transfer station was surrounded by a six-foot chain-link fence. Tears pricked at the back of Thea's eyes. She hadn't been here before, but she recognized the place just the same.

The padlocked gate was just as she'd seen in the pictures. To the right of the gate stood a sign post topped by a sign that read AUTHORIZED

PERSONNEL ONLY. In her mind's eyes, she saw the dark-green Ford truck parked right in front of the sign, both the driver and passenger doors open, and scuff marks in the gravel outside the driver's door. The scene was seared into her memory as though she'd stood here when it all went down. God, how she wanted to believe that Alida was safe somewhere and that those scuff marks meant nothing heinous.

Katie brought the SUV to a stop, put it in park, and turned off the engine. Slowly Thea opened her door and got out. Equally as slowly, she walked toward the sign she'd seen only in photographs so far. A slight breeze ruffled the air, bringing with it the scent of alfalfa, plowed fields, and ranging cattle. Looking down at the parking area, she spotted the faintest hint of scuff marks in the loose gravel. Her breath caught in her throat, and she needed to give herself a moment to collect her emotions before she could walk closer.

What would Alida do if their roles were reversed? Thea always considered her to be the stronger of the two. Smart and kind as well. It took her only a second to know what Alida would do if she were standing here now. She would charge forward to reunite them, and so that's exactly what Thea planned to do. Still staring at the disturbed gravel, she kneeled and touched the drag marks with the tips of her fingers. As she did, a shot of energy soared through her body.

His power peaked when darkness blanketed the world, and yet now with the light of day still clinging, he felt the charge as though someone had hit him with a thousand volts of electricity. His body jerked and his head whipped back. With the shot came a flash of vision, and his mouth opened in a silent scream. At last he saw.

Daylight lingered, not yet fading into night, and the Watcher kept to the shadows that the thick trees created. He turned his eyes to the east and stared at the sky, today clear and blue without a hint of storm. He could almost see her. Pain tore at her heart, and fear wrapped its ugly fingers around her soul.

Evil walked the earth hundreds of miles away from this place where the ocean crashed against the rocks and the rain came too often. What it did in that place so far from here he could not see clearly, only that the one whose tears fell to the earth needed help. Not his assistance, for he was tethered to this place as surely as if he were chained to the tree he stood beneath. She needed not him but *her*.

As he'd known it would, the heavens sent him a sign. She would once again do the Lord's work, and through her, his salvation would come one step closer. He could feel her soul, and though he rarely smiled, he did so now. She would not be happy, for this was not the calling she believed in. If he could tell her, he would: the destiny God bestowed upon each was rarely what one would choose for their own life. Not chosen but exactly what each needed nonetheless. How deeply he understood that one undeniable truth.

Of course, with thousands of years to reconcile that fact within his own heart he possessed a distinct advantage in that respect. She did not have a thousand years, or a hundred, or even one. She was forced to do the same in a matter of days. Her path was not for the weak or the frightened. She was strong and pure of heart. Thus, she would do what needed to be done and use the gift God blessed her with to make this earthly world a better place. That was her destiny.

Today that meant answering the call from an old friend. With his head bowed and his hands held together, he visualized a house, a desk, and a newspaper. He nodded and opened his eyes. It wasn't much, but for now it was enough. It would set into motion that which needed to happen.

Soon, she would make a journey across the mountains, and whatever evil tried to hide, she would bring into the light.

❖

At the sound of Thea's scream, Katie raced to her side. Thea knelt in the gravel with both hands flat on the faint marks, seemingly evidence of Alida's apparent abduction. Thea's face was pasty white and her eyes were wild, as if the hounds of hell were chasing her. Katie's heart pounded, and she feared bringing Thea here was a huge mistake.

When she put her hands on Thea's shoulders, her body was shaking and cold to the touch. Definitely a big misstep. "What's wrong? What happened?"

Thea took a deep, shaky breath. "I don't know. I touched this spot, and it was like someone hit me with a Taser. My whole body started to shake and my vision began to blur. I've never felt anything like it, and right now it's all I can do not to throw up."

"This was a bad idea," Katie muttered as she put a hand under Thea's arm and helped her to her feet. To Thea she said, "I need to take you home. I'm so sorry. I don't know what the hell I was thinking."

"No," Thea snapped, standing up straight and shaking off Katie's steadying hand. "No way am I leaving. Your idea to bring me here was dead on, and I'm not letting you run me home like I'm a sick little kid. I don't know what just happened, and I don't care if I feel like crap or throw up. This is the last place my sister was, and if being here, standing where she stood, can tell me something, then I'll damned well listen."

Color was returning to Thea's face, and determination gleamed in her eyes. Admiration began to replace the panic and dismay from a moment before. Thea was right; she wasn't some delicate little flower that needed to wait in the safety of her house while other people did all the work. Even though Thea was an artist, it was clear she could handle the hard stuff. Katie was liking her more and more. She couldn't remember the last time she'd glimpsed this kind of strength in another woman.

"You're sure?" She just had to ask.

Thea nodded and met her gaze square on. "One hundred percent. Someone has hurt my sister, and I plan to find the son of a bitch sooner rather than later."

Katie looked around. The same vacant sense she got the first time she stopped here stayed with her. Usually at a crime scene something stood out, but not here. Everything screamed abduction, yet she couldn't locate a single clue. One moment Alida Canwell had been here and the next she was gone, like a puff of smoke rising into oblivion in the sky. Frustrating didn't even begin to describe how she felt.

"Did you see or even sense anything here?" Katie wasn't about to dismiss feelings, particularly when it came to twins. A lot of things in this world defied explanation, and the connection between many twins was one of those things. If Thea's scream was any indication of the closeness between the two women, Katie hoped they possessed the special connection that could be the critical link to lead them to Alida.

For at least a full minute Thea stood motionless, staring into the distance as if seeing something, except the look in her eyes spoke more of sadness than connection. Slowly she shook her head. "When I touched the ground I felt like knives were going up my arms. Pain, anger, evil, and yet I didn't even feel a flicker of *her*." She closed her eyes and seemed to collect herself. "Katie, someone hurt my sister."

The note of despair in Thea's voice tore at Katie. She wanted to say or do something to ease her heartache, but there was nothing she could offer. They weren't any closer to discovering what had happened to Alida than they were when the call first came in.

At the sound of wheels on the gravel drive, Katie turned. A dark-blue Yukon with county plates was slowly driving their way. She knew the rig. Undersheriff Vince Carl. He stopped and got out. As he walked their way, he oozed confidence and charm. At six five, with dark curly hair and sky-blue eyes, he was the kind of guy most women tripped over themselves to meet. She wasn't one of those women, and it wasn't just because she preferred women.

She knew Vince way too well. And most days, she couldn't stand him.

"Hey, Katie, what's up?"

She kept her words calm and professional, her expression neutral. His showing up here unannounced pissed her off, but she wasn't about to let him know that. "Walking through the Canwell case. What are you doing here?"

He shrugged. "Driving by and saw you, that's all." A toothpick sticking out of the corner of his mouth bobbed up and down as he talked.

She narrowed her eyes and resisted the urge to snatch the stupid toothpick out of his mouth and fling it away. He was just driving by? Of course he was. "Clear out here? Kind of out of your way, isn't it?"

Stopping next to her, he put his hands in his pockets, his stance relaxed and casual. The toothpick continued to bob. "Sure is, but this Canwell case bugs me, so I thought I'd drive around and see if anything struck me. Don't like the way this thing dead-ends."

Katie tried not to let her irritation show on her face or come out in her words. If she did, he would run straight to the boss and report how emotional she was. They were always on the alert to see if she could stay cool under pressure. "This is my case, Vince." She was proud of how even her voice sounded. *Take that, you bastard.*

"Yeah, yeah, don't get your panties in a bunch. I'm not horning in on your case. It just strikes me as too similar to an unsolved I came across, so I'm just keeping an eye out. That's all. It's what any investigator worth his salt would do. Who's the chick?" He nodded toward Thea, who was standing about ten feet away staring once more into the distance.

This time Katie's irritation flamed through, and she didn't even try to stop her anger. Where did he get off? "The *woman* is Theadora Lynch, Alida Canwell's twin sister."

"Whoa, take it down a notch or two, Deputy Carlisle." He finally tossed away the toothpick casually, as if nothing he said was worth her display of annoyance.

"Vince," she snapped. "You take it down a notch or two, or would you prefer I mention to the chief that you referred to a victim's sister as a chick?"

"You know I didn't mean anything by it." He rolled his eyes.

I know you're a dick. "Doesn't matter what you meant. It's still inappropriate language, so keep it to yourself. This isn't the fifties, and in case you missed the class, that's what's called sexual harassment. Now, perhaps you should be on your way before Ms. Lynch hears something like that come out of your mouth again and decides to report you. You go do your job and let me do mine."

He shrugged as though every word she said slid off him like raindrops. "Whatever."

She clenched her teeth against the fury she now barely managed to control. Vince was good at his job—she'd give him props for that—but he could get her back up quicker than anyone she'd ever met. The part that ticked her off the most is he did it on purpose. She just couldn't figure out whether it was because he hated her or because he wanted to see if she really was as tough as the rest of them. As she watched him walk slowly back to his car, get in, and drive away, she took several deep breaths to quiet her anger. He pulled off a pretty package, but under the wrapping, the guy was a total jerk.

Once Vince was gone, Katie turned her attention back to Thea. "Sorry about that. Vince is a colleague who unfortunately didn't have much to help us."

"A jerk," Thea said absently.

Katie laughed, and the last of her irritation flowed away. "You picked that up?" A thousand-yard stare was on Thea's face during the entire exchange with Vince. It surprised her she'd paid attention to any of their conversation.

Thea looked over at her and nodded. "His energy made me want to step back about a hundred feet or so. I've always been able to pick up people's vibes immediately. Most are good, some are creepy, and some are just plain bad."

"Well, Vince isn't a bad guy. Just a creepy one in a male-chauvinistic kind of way."

"Probably," Thea said softly as she gazed out into the distance. "But a step-back kind of guy in any event."

What about Vince made her voice so quiet and reflective? Katie tilted her head and studied Thea, who was once more focusing on the trees and hills beyond as if hoping to catch sight of her sister. What did she mean by *probably?*

CHAPTER FOUR

Thea was glad the man left. The vibes he brought to this place were dark and disturbing. Maybe she was still picking up on whatever had assaulted her when she touched the marks in the gravel, or maybe the guy was a creep. Either way, she felt better once he got in his car and drove away.

Her fingers still buzzed even as the minutes passed. It didn't surprise her to pick up some kind of vibe. After all, she and Alida shared so much. What surprised her was how desolate she felt. She'd come out here with Katie hoping for a miracle. Instead she felt worse.

"Are you okay?"

Katie's concerned words broke into her dark thoughts.

A truthful answer would be big fat no. Instead, for no rational reason she could come up with, she lied. "I'm fine."

"You don't look fine."

She let her gaze drift to Katie's face, surprised by the worry she saw there. She tried for a smile. "I'm discouraged."

"You hoped to be able to find her."

Stupid as it sounded, that was exactly right. "Yes, I did. I don't know why I thought just being here would produce some magic vision and I'd be able to do what you trained professionals couldn't."

Katie laid a hand on her shoulder, the warmth reassuring. "Nothing wrong with being hopeful."

"Unrealistic, you mean."

Katie shook her head. "No, I mean hopeful and helpful. Help breaking cases often comes in the most unexpected ways and places so don't ever sell yourself short."

Tears pricked at the back of her eyes and she blinked quickly, willing them away. "I really wanted to find her today."

"We will find her."

"Today?"

"Soon." Katie's voice was calm and steady, yet it did nothing to reassure Thea.

Suddenly, she needed to get away from here. A wave of something evil seemed to drape around her shoulders and try to cut off her breath. She whirled and headed back to Katie's SUV. Without a word, she got in and buckled her seat belt.

"Can we just go back to town?" she asked when Katie was in the driver's seat and buckled up too.

"Of course." If Thea's abrupt race for the car bothered her, Katie gave no indication.

For the first few miles she didn't say anything, grateful Katie didn't try to fill the silence. Staring out the side window, she finally said, "When we were about twelve, we did something we'd never done before. We went to different summer camps—Alida to Camp Reed up north and me to a week-long art workshop in Seattle."

"It must have been scary."

She smiled, remembering the excitement of being on her own for the first time in her young life. "You'd think so, wouldn't you? But no, we were both thrilled to be able to do what excited us the most. Alida loved all the outdoor activities, and for me, the chance to spend a week with nothing but art was like nirvana."

The memories of their excitement waned as the reality of that long-ago week settled. "Everything started off so wonderfully. On Wednesday, I woke up screaming and the counselor assigned to my group couldn't get me to calm down. They had to call my parents, and that's when they understood."

"Something happened?"

She nodded, even though she knew Katie's eyes were on the road. "Alida was always the adventurous one and would take risks. She and three other girls snuck out to go swimming in the dark. Long story short, she fell about twenty feet down an embankment, broke her arm in two places, and suffered a concussion. She was out for three days."

"You felt it over in Seattle?"

"Yes. The pain hit me first while I was sound asleep. When I woke up fully I realized it wasn't me, but I knew something was terribly wrong with Alida."

"And that's why you were so hopeful you could find her if you came out here with me today?"

"Yes."

"You did feel something."

"I did."

"And you're worried because it's how you felt when you were twelve."

It wasn't a question, and Thea felt closer to Katie because clearly she understood. Thea sat looking out the side window as she murmured, "I was scared before we came out here. Now I'm terrified."

❖

He could see it now and soon so would she. The sighs and the tears of the lost one were carried on the wind as it moved across the mountains and the deserts between the East and the West. His heart ached for yet another who cried for help and yet none came. Only he heard her pleas, and he was powerless to ease her suffering.

She alone held the power to bring her home to the family who longed to see her face. Lies told and trust betrayed, yet at her core where only God could see, she was a good person who did not deserve the fate that had come down upon her. Now that he knew and understood, it was up to him to find a way to guide her east. She was destined to help that lost soul find her way home.

He closed his eyes and concentrated. Her world was not his to touch, yet still he had to find a way not just for the lost one, but for himself as well.

To the east, storm clouds were building, the sky starting to grow dark with the familiar signs. Here along the coastal waters of the far north, lightning sliced through the gloom and thunder growled like a hungry bear. Fear shot through his body as though that bolt of lightning had struck him. Somewhere in the distance, evil flexed its muscles. Its presence sent ripples flowing unseen through the universe.

Time was once again running short. With his eyes still closed and his hands clasped tightly together, he concentrated. That was all he could do, and he prayed it was enough.

Across the mountains, three hundred and fifty miles away, a newspaper rose from where it lay in a recycle bin. For a moment it hung suspended in the air, and then slowly it floated to the floor. Against the red-quarry tile floor, a black-and-white photograph stared up at the ceiling.

❖

Lorna watched Renee walk across the massive yard and smiled. It still amazed her that someone so lovely and free-spirited would have any interest in her. She wasn't exactly what anyone would call a free spirit. Lorna liked structure, loved deadlines, and lived for challenges. If she didn't, she would never have made it as a person who successfully worked at home. Organization was the key to making a home-based career work, and she was the consummate pro.

Her career was both solid and financially sound because she was such a detail person. The quality had also put her on the path to competing in her first Ironman challenge. In three months, she would compete in the two-plus-mile swim, hundred-and-twelve-mile bike ride, and a full marathon, all in one day. The thought of what she was committed to doing often made her a little ill, and then she'd shake it off and keep training. She could hardly wait for June.

Renee, on the other hand, shook her head in disbelief every time Lorna talked with glowing anticipation of the endurance event. Like most everyone else around her, Renee thought she was crazy. Why would she want to put her body through something like that? It was hard to explain to people how empowering the race was. No, she wasn't crazy at all.

In reality she wanted to prove she could do it as much to herself as to those around her. While her family built her self-esteem, too many other people had told her she couldn't do something because she was a girl. She detested that particular line of crap. Drove her to fits of temper when she was a child, and as an adult, it hardened her resolve to do all the things people told her she couldn't. When she crossed that finish line after logging in over 140 miles in a single day, she'd see how many people tried that bullshit on her again.

For now though, she'd completed her training for today—a three-hour bike ride followed by a half-an-hour run. A brick, it was called in the triathlon world, and for good reason. Her legs felt like bricks when she got off the bike and started to run. After only a few minutes, though, she found her running rhythm and the half an hour flew by. Now her legs were a little tired but in a good way. As she put her bike away, she was already looking forward to popping the cork on a nice bottle of wine, putting her feet up, and just hanging out with Renee. It was the perfect ending to a great workout.

The house was unusually quiet considering the size of the clan that called it home these days. Jeremy and Merry were gone for the rest of the week, having decided to take a quick run up to Canada while Merry's pregnancy was still in the early stages and she could get around easily enough. Jolene, Renee's mother and their cherished housekeeper, was in her own quarters, and they wouldn't see her again until morning. Lorna loved having everyone around, though there was something to be said for a little quiet time with the woman she loved.

Lorna set the opened wine bottle on the low table in front of the sofa, along with the two stemmed glasses she'd brought in. Into one she poured the golden liquid and breathed in the aroma. With her back to the cushions and her feet on the table—something she didn't dare let Jolene catch her doing—she sipped the wine. It tasted as good as it smelled.

Renee walked into the room and smiled. "That was lovely," she said as she draped a light sweater over the back of a chair. "I know it rains here a lot and the skies are so often black and blue, but today, it was simply gorgeous. That walk on the beach was like a month's worth of therapy, and it was free!"

Lorna smiled back at her. "I know exactly what you mean. When I came here I was worried that I'd hate the weather. I mean in Spokane you have four distinct seasons complete with plenty of sunshine. Each season is fun and interesting in its own way. I didn't grow up around the dampness and storms of the ocean. I tell you what, though. Now that I've experienced this part of the country, I wouldn't trade it for the world."

Renee walked over and kissed her. "I'm so glad your aunt gave you this place."

If only she knew how glad Lorna was too, but she wasn't about to say that quite yet. Renee was smart and surely aware how much Lorna desired her and how she set her body on fire. Still, the word love hadn't actually passed her lips, nor would it anytime soon. It was that old once-bitten and all that. This time around, she was trudging along the slow and cautious road. Her heart could only take so much rejection, and if Renee turned her back on Lorna—well, she didn't want to think about that. Besides, what was the hurry?

For now, things were wonderful between them. They fit together so well, despite their differences, or maybe because of them. What was so painful during her initial days here was like ancient fading memories today. In fact it amazed her how little she thought about Anna now. When she'd first moved into the house, Anna, Anna, Anna was all she could think about. Now, she was barely a flicker in Lorna's thoughts.

Renee filled her thoughts both night and day, and in a way that made her heart light. She lit up the room whenever she walked in, and her spirited good nature was infectious. Lorna had never been around anyone quite like her. What wondrous things happened when a person least expected them.

"Wine?" Lorna asked as she kissed her back.

"You know it, sister." Renee came around the sofa and settled in next to her. Like Lorna, she propped her feet up on the table. They might all be adults around here, but when Jolene wasn't around to scold them, they tended to act like kids.

Lorna laughed, winked, and sat up to reach for the bottle. "Had a hunch you were going to say that. Two glasses, see." She held up the second glass she'd brought along with her.

She was pouring from the bottle into Renee's glass when her cell phone rang. Digging it out of her pocket with one hand, she put it to her ear, held it with her shoulder, and went back to pouring Renee's wine. "Yeah," she said a little breathlessly.

"Lorna?"

She abandoned pouring the wine and set the bottle and the glass on the table before taking hold of the phone once more. The voice seemed familiar, even if she couldn't place it, and the undertones in her caller's single word made her nerves twitch. She didn't need to twitch. "Yeah, this is Lorna. Who's this?"

"Thea."

The voice clicked into place and her momentary unease faded away. "Thea! I thought you'd dropped off the face of the earth. What's up?" She was actually glad to her from her childhood friend.

"I'm so sorry I haven't called you just to say hi and now I'm calling because I need your help. I'm a horrible friend."

Lorna smiled, thinking of the lovely Thea. She'd been a friend to both Lorna and Anna. Like so many of their friends, not knowing what to do when they broke up, Thea had kept a distance between them. At first, Lorna was hurt by the friends who stopped calling and coming by. Slowly, as the pain of the breakup started to subside, she began to understand how it must be for them. How does a person pick a side when they like both people? The hurt she felt had faded, replaced by understanding and forgiveness.

"You're not anything of the kind. I understand, Thea. I really do. Now, what can I do for you? Do you need something written?" Obviously she was calling with a project. It would be fun to work with Thea's burgeoning business. They might not see each other that often, but it didn't mean she was out of touch. She was well aware of how well Thea was doing these days.

On the other end, shuffling and the rustle of paper was all she heard. For a long moment, Thea said nothing. "It's not that kind of help."

For a second, it didn't sink in. When it did, she couldn't help the way her jaw tightened. "Not that..." Oh, crap, not Thea too.

"I'm sorry, Lorna." Tears were evident in her voice. "If I felt there was a better option, trust me, I'd take it. But I need help, any kind of help. I need you. Alida needs you."

Lorna sighed and sank back into the cushions of the sofa. She ran a hand through her hair as the tightness in her jaw relaxed and she said, "Tell me."

Twenty minutes later, Lorna set her phone down and then laid her head on Renee's shoulder. If she could, she might just stay here all night. It would be nice to simply turn off her brain because she hated to think about what Thea had just shared with her.

Renee put an arm around her shoulders and squeezed. "I caught a bit of what that call was about, but fill me in on what's going on with your friend."

"It's never going to go away." She knew how petulant she sounded and wasn't particularly proud of herself. Still, if just for ten seconds, she was going to feel sorry for herself.

"What isn't going away?" Renee kissed her on the top of her head.

Lorna bolted up and waved her arms wide. "The *thing* I can do. The goddamn psychic thing. People are never, ever going to leave me alone."

Renee nodded, her eyes gentle and full of understanding. "Oh, that thing." She reached over and took Lorna's hand, her touch soft. She brought it to her lips and kissed her palm before saying, "Tell me about the call."

And she did. "So," she asked when she finished. "Want to go to Long Lake over on the east side? Might as well get it done."

A shadow crossed Renee's face and her eyes narrowed. "Um, I can't."

Lorna twisted to get a better look at her. "You can't? Why can't you?" The tightness came back into her jaw.

Renee shook her head and bit her lip. She didn't meet Lorna's eyes. "I've been meaning to tell you that I have to be back in Seattle next week."

Her heart began to beat like a snare drum. "Next week? You're going back?" For weeks she'd tried not to think about what would happen when Renee returned to her own home. It was always there lingering in the background, and with dogged determination she always managed to avoid thinking about it. Stupid as it might seem, she opted to ignore it, hoping it would simply go away.

"Not permanently," Renee hurried to say and finally met her eyes.

She almost cried with relief at the honest emotion reflected in her gaze. "Then…"

Renee smiled and squeezed her hand. "I have to spend some time with the contractors and insurance adjuster. They're ready to really get rolling on the repairs, and I have to be there initially to guide them during the walk-through. I figured Clancy and I would spend three or four days in the city, and then if it's okay with you, we will come back here."

Okay? Hell, it was more than okay. She tried not to let the relief show on her face. Instead she opted for a soft smile that she hoped didn't give away the depth of her emotions or, more specifically, the desperation. "Absolutely. You go take care of business, and I'll run across the mountains and see what I can do for Thea, if anything. All this press tends to make people believe I can do more than I can."

Renee took her face between her hands and kissed her hard on the lips. "And I think you underestimate yourself."

She wasn't so sure about that. What had happened with the two ghosts here at the house was a fluke. Right? Or was it? She felt different these days, and it was more than just changing where she lived and finding a woman who set her body on fire. Something deep inside her was different, and she questioned whether it would ever go away.

Could she help Thea? Probably not, but what would it hurt to try? Thea and Alida had been her friends all the way through school. They looked so much alike and yet were so completely different. She was never confused about who was who. They were such distinct individuals it was always easy for her to tell them apart even if they were wearing identical clothing. And then there was the secret she and Thea had confided to each other way back in junior high. A pinky-swear secret that still made her smile. Both of them had come to understand how different they were from most of their friends, but they also knew they had each other. Having such a good friend hold her secret helped her get through the difficult times. Now, it was her turn to pay it forward.

Whether she believed she could really do anything to help didn't matter. It was time to step up and help her old friend.

"Maybe," she said, kissing Renee back. "I'll at least try."

"That's my girl."

For a little while they sat together on the sofa talking and drinking wine. It was a beautiful, relaxing afternoon. She didn't want it to end.

Renee finally stood and stretched her arms high over her head. "All this wine has made me a little tired. I think I'll be outrageously lazy and take a nap."

"It's early."

Renee shrugged and smiled. "That's what makes it outrageously lazy!" She leaned over and kissed Lorna. "You should give it a try, Miss Iron Athlete."

"I'll think about it," she said as Renee left the room.

The second Renee was out of sight, Clancy jumped up and curled up next to Lorna. With Clancy's head on her leg, Lorna absently stroked the soft fur between his ears and finished her wine. A thousand thoughts raced through her mind, and she discovered that part of her wanted to see if she could help find Alida. In fact it occurred to her she was anxious to get going. How did she move from reluctant to eager?

As the fire began to burn low she decided it required too much effort to stoke it. After her bike ride and run, she was worn out. Maybe Renee's idea of a little nap wasn't such a bad idea. She rubbed the sleeping dog's ears one more time and smiled. It was so natural to share the sofa with the big black German shepherd. The thought of him not being here hurt her heart. It hadn't been all that long, but he was part of this house, part of this family.

"Hey, you two, gonna stay out here all day? Seriously, girlfriend, I was going for subtle, but I guess I'll have to get blunt. I'm not really that tired."

Lorna's smile grew, and a tingle of excitement raced through her. "Yeah, a nap might be just what I need." She swung her legs over the sofa, disrupting Clancy. He jumped off the sofa and stalked out the door, the click, click, click of his nails sounding like gunfire as he made his way down the hallway and into Renee's room. A lovely dog bed was in there, but she'd bet a fifty that he'd walk right past it to jump up on the empty queen-sized bed.

She got up and turned toward the door, then stopped. Her heart took a leap. Renee stood in the doorway, her long, thick hair down around her shoulders, her creamy robe open to reveal her beautiful naked body. Her smile was sly, sexy.

Renee held out her hand. "I took a shower, came into the bedroom, and realized I was all alone. I just hate being in that big bed by myself."

For a moment Lorna didn't move. "Can't go to sleep?"

Renee's smile grew and her eyes sparkled. "Not tired."

❖

It was pushing nine and she'd been here way too long. Katie needed to go home yet couldn't get herself up and out of the chair. After she dropped Thea off, she'd come back to the office and had been sitting here ever since.

Vince's little impromptu visit nagged her like a bad rash that wouldn't go away. Maybe it was just because he consistently got under her skin. Or maybe it was more than that. Why would he simply happen by where they were and stop? That transfer station was far enough away from the highway to make it not observable to the casual drive-by. So why was he making an obvious effort to follow her? More than likely to check up on her because she couldn't possibly do the job right without supervision. Constantly having to prove herself got real old.

"You ever go home, Carlisle?"

Her laugh held a definite cynical edge. "About as much as you do, Roberts." Chad Roberts was about her age, two inches shorter, and with blond hair so pale, in the right light he looked bald. Unlike Vince, Chad tended to fade into the background, and people rarely gave him a second glance. All in all it was a pretty good trick for a deputy, who sometimes needed to blend in to make the case. People felt comfortable around him, a regular guy who posed no threat.

She liked him and they worked well together. He was pleasant and didn't make waves. He also didn't think he was God's gift to women or seem to think she needed a babysitter on every case she worked. If Vince could be just a little more like Chad, he'd be a hell of a lot easier to work with.

"Why are you here so late?" Things were so quiet until he spoke up she didn't even realize anyone else was around.

He shrugged. "Caught a messy case out in the Valley. Some gal holed up in that motel right off I-90 and Argonne and shot her boyfriend."

"Well, at least it sounds pretty cut and dried." She wished her case were that easy.

He sat down in the chair behind his desk. "Sounds that way, but the scene isn't playing like that. There's more to this story than little Miss Muffet is telling us."

She got up from her chair, slipped on her jacket, and put her cell phone in her pocket. "There always is, Chad. There always is. But if anybody can get her to crack, it's you."

He ran a hand through his pale hair, which left a fair amount of it standing on end. "Thanks for the vote of confidence. Now tell that to the chief."

"He giving you a hard time?"

"Naw. I just keep thinking one of these days he might actually give me a promotion or maybe even a little raise. I've done my time and proved myself, but neither seems to be working to my advantage."

Katie laughed, thinking of their very budget-conscious chief. It would take a hell of a lot more than a few words from her to make him consider giving anyone around the department a raise. "You're a dreamer, Roberts."

His smile lit up his ordinary face. "Yeah, well, a boy can dream."

She gave him a mock salute as she walked by. "Keep on doing it, my man."

Outside, Katie stopped and took a deep breath of the clear, dry air. She hoped once out here she'd feel more settled, but it wasn't happening. All day she'd been jittery and out of sorts. This wasn't a major case. Hell, it might not be a case at all. For all she knew, Alida Canwell did, in fact, run off with a boyfriend and staged the scene to look like an abduction. That line of thought was reasonable, except she didn't really believe it. Not at all. Something happened to Alida on that sunny afternoon. She could feel it in her bones, and it was bugging the shit out of her.

Figuring out where to start or who to start with would help a bunch. Taking Thea out there today might not have been the most standard police procedure or the wisest course of action, but she was struggling to find a pattern or connection that would help, and getting her twin sister's impression couldn't hurt. Unfortunately, going didn't really dredge up anything concrete that helped get them closer to the truth. It turned out to be another well-intentioned exercise in futility.

The other thing bugging the crap out of her was Vince. No way, no how was his showing up out at the transfer station coincidental. Did it have something to do with the case or with her? He had a burr under his saddle about her and wouldn't give it up.

When Vince came up against a woman who didn't want to get into his pants, he took it as a personal affront. He refused to believe Katie wasn't even slightly interested in him or that she might just be a lesbian. She could see the glint of a challenge in his eyes. He wanted to be the one who brought her to the other side. Dumb ass didn't realize it wasn't going to happen...ever.

That could be why he showed up out there. Keeping her in close proximity might be nothing more than his strategy for subtle seduction. Oh, he was a dumb ass all right, and she already had so many in her life, she didn't need another one.

But she would like a little more of Thea in her life. She was so beautiful and thoughtful and graceful. Katie just wanted to sigh and also wished they'd met under different circumstances. Thea was part of an on-going case, which meant hands off. What if, and this was a really far-off what if, Thea was actually involved in her sister's disappearance? It would do Katie's career no favors if she became more than a deputy to Thea. Something like that could very easily end her tenure with the sheriff's department, which she'd never allow to happen. She'd never disappoint her family with unbecoming behavior and never let herself down that way either. Sometimes she hated being her.

"Hey, Katie."

The sound of her name startled her and she whirled. Her hand to her chest, she said, "Jesus, Brandon, you just about gave me the big one."

"Sorry." He smiled. Tall and lean, the younger man leaned in the doorway to the IT Department, where he spent the majority of his time. He was, like Katie, a deputy sheriff, but he'd proved to be an invaluable asset when it came to all things relating to information technology.

"What are you doing here so late?"

"Helping you, of course." His blue eyes were fixed on her face, and not for the first time she had the sense he was trying to impress her.

"I don't understand." She hadn't asked him to do anything for her so it didn't make sense.

He held out several printed pages. "Background on your girl."

She shook her head. "I'm not following."

"You know, Alida Canwell. I did some background for you. Thought it might help."

She hesitantly reached out and took the papers. "Thanks."

His fingers brushed hers and his smile grew wider. "You bet. Let me know what else I can do."

"I'm headed out." She folded the pages and stuffed them into her pocket.

"See ya tomorrow." He turned and, whistling, disappeared into the IT room.

Blowing out a long, slow breath, she dug her keys out of her pants pocket and walked outside to her car. She touched the papers in her pocket, and it made her uneasy. It wasn't that she didn't appreciate Brandon performing his magic when investigating a case, but she hadn't asked him to and that bothered her.

It also wasn't the first time he'd popped up unexpectedly with helpful information. At least for her. As far as she could tell, she was the only beneficiary of his above-and-beyond efforts. She wanted to think the best of him and believe he just truly wanted to help. But that argument wasn't playing for her, and the alternatives she was left with sent dread creeping down her spine.

CHAPTER FIVE

For what seemed like hours, Thea stared out the window. Lorna called her around four thirty to say she was on the road, yet time was ticking away at the speed of light, and it seemed nobody cared, not even the tall, sexy deputy. It was probably emotion talking, but that didn't matter. A giant weight rested on Thea's shoulders, nearly breaking her back.

The terrible, unspoken sense that something bad had happened to her sister overwhelmed her. She knew Alida's heart better than anyone, including Grant. Not one single circumstance would cause her to disappear without contacting Thea. If Alida faced a problem, she confronted it with the spirit of a warrior, unlike Thea, who sometimes liked to hide and hope the problem disappeared without having to resort to confrontation. Alida was strong and assertive and fearless. She did not run and hide.

But did that keep anyone from talking or speculating that Alida ran out on Grant and the rest of her family? Not in the least. Even though everyone was polite enough not to say it out loud, she could read between the lines. They could think whatever they wanted because she knew the truth. People like Alida didn't just vanish.

Thea continued to be convinced that the location of her truck and the condition of the scene contradicted the runaway scenario. From every angle it looked like an unwilling abduction, and she wasn't about to give up until everyone could see that. Of course, several of the more skeptical law-enforcement officers still had their heels dug in deep and implied Alida might have staged the scene.

Well, they could just take their cynicism and shove it. While she did appreciate the efforts of Katie Carlisle, they weren't enough. If law enforcement wanted to wait for Alida to show up again, that was fine for them. Thea saw it differently, and she refused to wait around doing nothing until they decided to take the situation more seriously.

An article tucked into the paper about a century-old mystery solved by a psychic gave her an idea. At first glance, the article was no big deal until she saw the name of said psychic: her old friend Lorna Dutton. In less than fifteen minutes she tracked down Lorna's phone number and put in a call. People might make fun of her for going to a psychic, but she didn't care. Help was help, regardless of where it came from.

Lorna's lack of enthusiasm was a huge letdown but didn't deter her in the least. No, she wasn't above begging for assistance or using history as leverage. Her desperation worked, or at least Lorna felt sorry enough for her that their long friendship won her over.

After what seemed like a couple of days staring out the front window, Thea saw a dark-gray Honda pull up in the driveway and Lorna got out, all long legs and power. Thea smiled. She looked like the same young girl who'd been her best friend since fourth grade. Her heart leaped, and she momentarily regretted that they'd rarely seen each other over the last decade. How did something like that happen? Friends shouldn't let that much time pass between them.

She wrenched open the front door and raced out straight into Lorna's outstretched arms. Lorna's hug was so tight she knew she telegraphed her fear and relief. Tears coursed down her face as raw emotion overwhelmed her. For the first time since that horrid call she didn't feel alone. "I'm so glad you're here."

Lorna's comforting hug meant so much, as did her tears as they dampened Thea's shirt. That her friend was as caught up in the emotional reunion as she was did amazing things to her heart. "I'm so sorry," Lorna whispered against her hair. "So sorry."

Thea loosened her hold and stepped back. Lorna's watery eyes held her, and in them she could see the concern no doubt intensified by the sleepless nights and constant worry showing on Thea's face. "Come on in. I've got a lot to tell you." She turned toward the door and held Lorna's hand as they went inside. She didn't want to let go.

Though she hated to do it, she left Lorna for a few minutes to make a pot of coffee. Settled in the living room with steaming mugs of the dark roast, Thea said, "Okay, let me start at the beginning." Her heart was pounding and she was almost crying as she started to bring Lorna up to date.

As much as she'd like to gloss things over, she needed to tell Lorna how things really were, not how she wished they were. She described how Alida had been working hard but loving the freedom of her job with the utility company. How she and Grant had weathered some issues in their marriage yet were moving forward to try to work through those issues, like many couples did. Of Alida's strange feeling that something or someone was watching her and how it was the only odd thing she mentioned before she vanished.

When her words finally trailed off and then stopped, Lorna looked at her with dark, serious eyes reflecting the same hurt wrapped around her like a blanket. "We need to go where she was when she disappeared. I'll be honest, Thea. I don't know how this thing I have works. I do know that at the house, proximity seemed to play a part, so we might as well start at the beginning and work from there."

Thea was expecting and actually hoping for this exact plan of attack. The shot of adrenaline she experienced when she touched the disturbed gravel at the transfer station had tipped her off. If her connection with her twin was strong enough to affect her, what could it do for someone with true power? Lorna should be able to pick up far more. Best-case scenario: something would lead them to the truth, even if it terrified her to discover what it might be. Worst-case scenario: Lorna got nothing and they were still stuck in the same spot. Either way it was worth the drive.

Thea took one of Lorna's hands. "Are you up for the trip now? I know you've just driven for hours, and if it wasn't important I wouldn't ask."

"It's pretty late and awfully dark out, but yeah, I am if you are. I say the sooner we get started the better. I want to get Alida home." She squeezed her hand.

The tears she tried so hard not to spill again pricked at the back of her eyes. "I don't care about the dark and you're so right. We need to bring her home. She's out there somewhere cold and alone, and it's going to be dark there too. We have to find her." For days that same thought had haunted her. She couldn't sleep thinking that somewhere Alida was waiting and wondering why no one came for her.

"What about the police? Have they sent out search teams?"

The question stopped her short, and anger chased away the tears. With Lorna she could be brutally honest, and she allowed her fury to sound in her words. "For the most part, they haven't taken her disappearance seriously."

"For the most part?" Lorna's eyebrows rose.

She tightened her jaw. "The first day, they did nothing. She's an adult, they kept saying, and until she'd been gone for more than twenty-four hours, they couldn't do a whole lot, despite the truck and everything out at the transfer station screaming foul play. The second day, they finally deployed the county's volunteer search-and-rescue team, including the HRD dogs."

"HRD dogs?"

She blew out a long breath, her jaw trembling. The words were nearly impossible to say out loud. "Human-remains detection."

"Shit," Lorna muttered.

"They didn't find her body. They didn't find her, period. And more than one guy has said she might have engineered this to cover up bailing on her life. They've seen it before, blah blah blah."

Lorna was shaking her head, her lips pressed together in a thin line. "That's a crock. Alida isn't that kind of person. She's never run away from anything."

This is why she'd reached out to Lorna. She was never going to buy into the false theory that Alida ran off. "That's right. She didn't bail and wouldn't do that to Grant. And I guarantee you she would never, in a million years, do that to me. Something bad happened to her out there, Lorna, and I'm scared it may have cost her life. Somebody's hurt her."

"Has law enforcement done *any* serious investigation?"

A tiny bubble of excitement rose as she thought about Katie Carlisle. She nodded and said, "One deputy seems to be on the same sheet of music. The two of us went out to the site this afternoon, and Lorna, I have a good feeling about her. I wish she was moving things along a little faster, but by and large, she's trying to help.

That's more than anyone else from the Sheriff's Department has done so far."

Lorna stood up and grabbed the jacket she'd earlier draped across the suitcase she rolled in. "Come on. I know it's late, but let's run out there and see if I can pick up anything. Then we'll see where it takes us."

She didn't have to ask Thea twice. The relief of Lorna roaring ahead even at this time of night gave her a rush of hope. As they headed out to her car she slipped her arms into the jacket she'd grabbed out of the hall closet. She was so intent on getting to the transfer station as quickly as she could, she didn't pay much attention to the car that pulled away from the curb down the block and began to follow them as they drove north.

He didn't mean to do it, had promised himself the last one was the last one. It really wasn't his fault though. She made the first move, and all he did was say yes. It wasn't like he went looking for her or even offered anything himself. No, she offered and he accepted. It was all on her.

Thankfully, the night was deep and dark again. No rain this time, which made digging a lot easier. It was nice not to have water running down his neck and soaking his shirt, or dripping off his hair and into his eyes. It was clear and cool, perfect for this particular project. The ground was soft and easy to move.

His trusty tarp spread on the ground behind him, he moved shovel after shovel of dark, rich earth onto the wide blue surface. He was getting pretty skilled at this, and the hole was ready in no time. As he did before, he moved the other tarp, wrapped and tied with rope, into the hole. It hit with a thud, loud in the quiet night. That was okay; he was the only one for miles around. Everyone else was tucked up nice and warm in their little houses, sleeping away the best part of the night. Nobody was going to hear a thing.

He returned the dirt to the hole, then carefully replaced the sod. Shining his flashlight on the finished project, he nodded. It was good. No, it was really good. Again, no one would be the wiser. He refolded the blue tarp and returned it, along with the shovel, to the toolbox in the back of his truck. Smiling and humming, he got into the cab, turned the key in the ignition, and drove away slowly. The stars were shining and the moon was golden, a beautiful night for a drive.

As he drove along, he couldn't help but notice a familiar vehicle as it headed north. Easy to pick it out, considering they were the only two vehicles on the road for miles. He knew what had brought him out here, but it was kind of late for a scenic drive. No reason for that pretty flower to be out and about in the middle of the night. Dangers were all around, and women like her didn't have a clue. He drove to the shoulder, made a U-turn, and followed a discreet distance behind. He just intended to keep an eye on her and make sure she was safe. That was the gentlemanly thing to do, and he did consider himself a gentleman.

CHAPTER SIX

K atie sat straight up and blinked. The beer bottle was tipped over on the floor, and what was left inside now soaked the rug. *Great, just flipping great.* When she sat down with the beer earlier, she didn't realize she was so tired she'd drift off before she took more than a couple swigs. She fell asleep on the sofa, and now a slightly yeasty smell permeated the whole room.

In the kitchen she grabbed the towel hanging on the oven door. As she sopped up the brew from the rug, the towel turned brown. What a waste. Hard to see a tasty amber turned into carpet shampoo. She should really pull out the carpet cleaner and do this right, except she didn't feel like it. Blotting it up with the towel was going to have to do for tonight.

Now that she was wide-awake, she actually felt pretty good. The weariness of earlier seemed to have fled. Maybe all she needed was a little nap. Mom always said to listen to the body. Of course, she was bound to play hell sleeping the rest of the night. Not that it was all that unusual. Normal hours weren't in the job description. Such was the life of a deputy sheriff, and she accepted it when she took her oath.

Despite the energizing nap, an uneasy feeling lingered. Sleep hadn't dulled any of the intense disquiet that had settled over her the moment she took on this case. Yes, the guys thought it was a shit assignment, but not her. Whatever this was, it was going to rock some worlds when all was said and done. She just didn't know exactly whose worlds it was going to rock.

Already it'd accomplished a bit of rocking to hers. Not just because she was drawn to Thea in a way she hadn't been to any other woman, even Lucy, which was saying a lot. Back then she was deeply in love with Lucy, but then again who didn't fall head over heels for the first one. With her curly black hair, dark eyes, and infectious laugh, Lucy was the kind of girlfriend a woman dreamed of. Pretty good deal, too, for the better part of a year. As far as Katie was concerned, she would have stayed with Lucy forever.

It was a one-sided fantasy, as she was to discover. Lucy's ideas weren't the forever kind.

Oh, she loved Katie too, in her own way. But Lucy's way included loving men too. So much so that in the end, she left Katie to marry a man. And maybe, if Katie was being honest, that was one more reason she was so drawn to Lucy. She could love her unconditionally while knowing there were no conditions. Perhaps she sensed all along that ultimately it would end the way it did. They were still friends, she still loved her, but she was able to walk away without a tinge of guilt.

Until now, however, she'd kept dating totally casual. A lot of like, no love, which suited Katie just fine. Besides, her career was keeping her too busy to even consider a serious relationship, even if she met someone who intrigued her as much as Thea.

Also, maybe she was so hooked because she was mistaking fascination with a mysterious set of circumstances for attraction to a beautiful woman. Could be, except she didn't really believe that was the case. It wasn't her mode of operation.

Once she cleaned up the spilled beer, she grabbed a fresh bottle, pulled her feet up beneath her on the sofa, and opened her tablet. Tapping the screen to bring up her notes, she scanned everything she'd put down earlier. Once she read through it all, she opened the folder containing the pictures she'd taken out at the transfer station. Two words kept rolling through her mind: all wrong. Women did not go off and leave their bags, even if they were running away, and she didn't believe for a minute that Alida Canwell ran away. That bag on the seat of the truck was screaming foul play loud and clear.

And what about the deep grooves in the gravel? They were too consistent with a person being grabbed from behind and dragged. True, she could have faked the marks, but Katie's intuition told her these were real. Something happened out there at the transfer station, and it was something bad.

From another folder she clicked on pictures of the missing woman, her husband, and the rest of her family. The guys wanted to point fingers at Grant Canwell, and statistically the odds were on their side. All of Katie's training and mentoring pushed her in that direction as well. But she still wasn't buying it. Grant didn't come across as a man who would knock off his wife and proceed to stage an elaborate scene. From everything she'd gathered so far he was a relatively nice guy who loved his wife, even if he did cheat on her. Lots of guys wanted their cake and to eat it too, but that didn't make them killers.

Everything about Alida said the same for her. She loved her husband, was willing to work on her marriage, and pretty much enjoyed her life despites its ups and down. Like Grant, she strayed only to come back to the man she married. Not a bit of evidence anywhere indicated she would orchestrate her own disappearance.

No, everything pointed to the commission of a crime, and Katie intended to find out who and why. Hopefully, it wouldn't be too late to help Alida. Unfortunately, she and every other law-enforcement officer understood the clock had already ticked way past the point of hope. Those damned statistics again, and this time they said Alida Canwell was already dead.

❖

Thea had to concentrate to find the turnoff for the power station. When they left the house, it was already pretty dark. Now it was pitch black and the gravel road wasn't that easy to spot. Having Lorna here gave her a sense of hope though. It was probably an unrealistic feeling, but she didn't care. This was the most positive she'd felt since Alida went missing.

Not that she was faulting Deputy Carlisle and her attempt to locate Alida. Something about her instilled trust in Thea. She really believed Katie Carlisle planned to try to find her sister even if the rest of her squad thought something different. All she needed was one person on her side to give her hope.

At the same time, Thea wasn't stupid. Time was flying and her heart was growing heavier. Even a layperson could understand the longer Alida was missing, the less chance she was going to be found alive. The thought chilled her soul. She didn't know how to live without her other half. She'd never been alone.

Even in the blackness, she spied the turnoff when the headlights of her car swept across the tiny sign. Relief poured through her. She turned the car onto the drive and guided it toward the transfer station. The gravel road was rutted from the winter freeze and spring thaws that damaged all the roads in the area, and they bumped their way to the widened parking area. Though she was anxious to get Lorna to the spot where Alida last stood, she didn't want to shake her teeth out either.

It seemed like hours before she finally stopped and put the car in park. In reality it was less than five minutes. A single vapor light cast a dim yellow glow down on the gravel lot, and the tracks so clear in the light of day were difficult to make out.

Even without the visual cue, she could feel Alida's essence here and hoped to hell Lorna would too. She silently prayed that what Lorna had experienced in her house by the ocean wasn't a fluke. She'd never really gone in for hocus-pocus and claims of seeing into the world beyond. She was far too grounded in the here and now. But that was before Alida disappeared.

When she really thought about it, the bond between her and Alida could be called supernatural because of its intensity. If something like that could exist between sisters, why should someone like Lorna be any different? Why couldn't she possess psychic ability? Why couldn't she see beyond the everyday world? She was more than willing to open her mind and her soul if it would bring her sister home.

At first neither of them moved, just stared silently ahead absorbed in their thoughts. Lorna was squinting and gazing out into the night barely broken by the weak illumination of the vapor light and the headlights of her car. Hope threaded through Thea's heart when she turned and studied her. Thea could almost hear the wheels spinning in her head. Lorna seemed to be concentrating so hard, she didn't want to say anything to break it. Instead, she continued to wait in silence.

Lorna finally turned and met her gaze. Dashboard lights danced across her face. "I don't know," she said slowly. "When you turned off the highway, the air seemed to change, yet now that we're here, I don't really feel or see anything unusual. It's weird. I should at least feel Alida's spirit."

Thea's heart sank, but she was damned if she'd give in to despair. "Let's get out and I'll show you where her truck was parked and where it appears she was dragged away. Maybe more will come to you outside."

Lorna nodded and swung open her car door. "Yeah, that's a good idea."

Thea came around the car holding the big just-in-case flashlight she always traveled with. The drag marks were more pronounced in the directed beam of the flashlight than in daylight, and the sight sent chills up her back.

"Wow," Lorna said as she slowly walked toward them, her head bent as she studied the ground. "My first impression is pure terror." She wrapped her arms around herself as if she was suddenly very chilled.

Thea understood. She'd felt it too when she first stepped out here. "She didn't go willingly." Nobody would ever be able to convince her otherwise.

Lorna didn't look up. "No, she didn't. This is good though."

Good? How on God's green earth could this possibly be good? "I don't understand."

This time Lorna looked up and met her gaze. "It's like she left us a message. Think about it, Thea. Alida isn't that big. Somebody could have dragged her all the way to the highway and she wouldn't have left a track this distinct. She isn't that heavy."

It took a beat, and then Thea nodded as the truth of what Lorna said dawned on her. "She dug her heels in on purpose."

Lorna was nodding "That's what I'm thinking."

"She wanted to leave something behind that we could follow." Thea said a silent prayer of thanks for her sister's resourcefulness.

"She always was a quick thinker."

"Why didn't I notice that before?" If she'd thought of it days ago, maybe they'd be closer to finding Alida instead of searching out here alone in the middle of the night. Maybe law enforcement would be taking her disappearance a little more seriously.

Lorna put an arm around her shoulders and squeezed. "Don't beat yourself up. I don't think I'd have noticed either, except for the light and shadows created by the flashlight. It really seems to pop under the light."

It helped to think of it that way, but only a little. She should have realized it before. Not that it mattered at this point. Lorna was right. Beating herself up now wouldn't do a damn thing. Forward movement was the only thing that counted at present. "Can you do anything?"

Lorna's gaze left Thea's face and returned to the gravel. "I don't know if it'll work, but I'll trying touching the tracks. What happened at the house just happened whenever. I've never tried to actually kick this psychic thing into motion, so don't be disappointed if nothing happens."

She believed it would work. "Would you at least try?" Thea didn't want to sound desperate even though she was. Or maybe she did. What could it hurt? Desperation might very well spur others to action.

Lorna gave her another squeeze before stepping away. "I'll do anything I can. I just don't want you to get your hopes up. This thing I have, whatever it is, didn't come with instructions. I'm working blind here."

"I understand, Lorna, I really do, but I have nowhere else to turn and no one else to help me. I'm grasping at any straw I can find."

Lorna gave her a tiny nod. "Well, then let's try this straw." Sinking to her knees, Lorna put both hands on the drag marks. Her body stiffened and her eyes closed. A throaty "oh" passed through her lips.

"Carlisle," Katie said into her phone.

Vince's smooth voice made her grimace. "Thought you might like to know your girlfriend is back out at the transfer station."

"My girlfriend?"

"You know, the cute sister of the missing broad."

Now he did hit her last good nerve. Technically he might be her superior, but that didn't give him the right to be a sexist pig. "When was the last time you took sexual-harassment training, Vince?"

His voice took on a weary note that was so different from his usual cockiness. "Christ, Carlisle, you take everything frigging personal. Here I thought I was being a good guy letting you know she was out there again, and you give me shit."

Okay, he might have a point. She did want to know Thea had gone up north in what was essentially the middle of the night. But why was he out there again? Seemed like he was spending an awful lot of time in the vicinity of Alida's last known point, and she couldn't come up with any particular reason why he should. The case was hers, and she was accustomed to working her cases without micromanagement from him. Even for Vince this was excessive.

She didn't care to ask him to explain. He'd get defensive in a New York minute. The guy's skin was the thickness of rice paper. With that kind of sensitivity it was a miracle he'd risen to the rank of undersheriff. The politics involved there typically required the strength of hippo skin. Instead of treading on dangerous ground she shifted gears. "Thanks, Vince, I do appreciate the heads-up."

"Thought you would." The cockiness returned. The man's mood could turn on a dime, another thing that annoyed her about him.

She took a deep silent breath and counted to five. "When did you see her there?" No hint of her irritation. She was good.

"About five minutes ago."

Again, she wondered what the hell he was doing up that way this time of night. Again, she wasn't going to ask. "Thanks, I'll check it out." She clicked off and shoved her phone in her pocket. No sense in dragging the conversation out. Better to cut it off before he said something else asinine and she responded with something that would land her in the chief's office. Whether she liked it or not, he still outranked her.

Wasting no time, she put on her shoes, grabbed her jacket, and raced for the car. In the strictest sense, the transfer station wasn't considered a crime scene any longer, and nothing prevented Thea from going there whenever she wanted. Nonetheless, she wanted to know why Thea would be there at this time of night and, more importantly, alone. Even if someone hadn't committed a crime there, it wasn't a good idea to wander around late at night by herself. Thea should know better.

Unease rippled up her spine as she took the thought even further. Thea and Alida were identical twins. While they were definite individuals, they still looked amazingly alike. If this situation turned out to be a case of obsession, she worried Thea could be a target too, simply because she looked like her sister.

From her house on the north side of town, it only took about twenty minutes to make it to the turnoff leading to the transfer station. Ignoring the ruts in the gravel road, she drove quickly. The bumps were so jarring she was surely going to have a headache. She didn't have time to worry about that and pushed on. At the end of the road, just as Vince said, Thea's car was parked with the doors closed and the lights still on.

The sweep of her headlights as she brought her car around to park next to Thea's illuminated not one person but two. Her impression from the brief conversation with Vince was that Thea had come out here alone.

On the spot where Alida's empty truck had been parked and where the distinctive drag marks were worn deep into the gravel, Thea sat on the ground holding another woman in her lap. The prone woman appeared to be fairly tall with short dark hair, wearing jeans and a polar-fleece pullover. Her eyes were closed and she was still as death. This didn't look good—at all.

Jamming the car into park, she turned off the ignition, jumped out, and trotted over to Thea. "What's happened? Is she all right?"

Thea looked up, her face pale though calm. Slowly she nodded. "I think she's having a vision."

Of all the things Katie expected Thea to say, that one wasn't one of them. "A what?"

"A vision," Thea said, her eyes back on the woman in her lap.

"Thea, I don't understand."

"She's a psychic," she said softly without looking up.

Good God, not another one of *those*. Every time someone disappeared or a child was abducted, so-called psychics called or, even worse, came to her office. They always offered to help law enforcement, and some on the force felt any kind of help was help. She wasn't one of those open-minded officers. As far as she was concerned, they were all a bunch of fakes who only came out for the attention. It was never about finding the missing; it was about publicity for themselves.

Even worse, at least in her mind, was that they approached the families, who were in the middle of the gravest possible kinds of crises. These moochers offered them all sorts of unrealistic hope, but did they ever deliver? Not once, as far as she knew. These people caused immeasurable damage and heartache. They were the most horrible of narcissists.

It should be criminal for anyone to approach families and offer them something they knew damned well they couldn't produce. Like this crazy-ass woman on the ground. She wanted to kick her, drag Thea back to the car, and get her away from here as quickly as possible. This was not going to end well.

But she couldn't do any of those things, not even say a word. What a private citizen chose to do was none of her business, even given her experience. Besides, if she did say something, Thea wouldn't believe her. They never did. The false hope these imposters dangled in front of desperate families was too much to pass up.

Thea looked up at her as she stood in silence, trying to figure out what to do next. With one hand she smoothed back the hair of the woman in her lap. "It's not what you think," she said softly.

Katie tried to look neutral and lie convincingly. "I'm not thinking anything."

Thea's smile was rueful. "Your expression says the opposite."

Oops. So much for her attempt at neutrality and she never was a very good liar. "Sorry."

"No need. If I were in your shoes, I'd be thinking the same thing. That I'm crazy for listening to a psychic. That she's a fake. That I'm grasping at anything to find Alida, no matter how insane. And you'd be right, at least about trying anything and everything to find my sister, because that's exactly what I'm doing."

Her honesty surprised Katie, as did her clear understanding of what she was doing. "Then why even try this?"

Thea looked down at the woman whose eyes were beginning to flutter open. "Because she's my friend, and I know she's anything but a fake."

CHAPTER SEVEN

*I*t was dark, the moon partially obscured by clouds. The sound of an owl hooting as it soared overhead sent shivers sliding down her spine. It was cold, and the wind carried dampness that hinted rain was on the way.

In the distance, a solitary figure stood. She squinted, bringing the image into focus. It was a man, judging by his size and shape. His head was tilted up to the sky, and she wondered if he was thinking rain as well. He leaned on something, and when he stood straight, picked it up, and began to move, she realized it was a shovel. He set it aside before leaning down to pick up a bundle, long and dark. He let it slide from his arms and it disappeared at his feet. A hole, it must be a hole.

Once more he picked up the shovel. The swish of the garden tool as he shoved it into a big black pile cut across the night. Dirt, had to be. Again and again he pushed it into the mound, moving the dirt on top of the bundle until the earth was once more level. He patted it several times as if to get it just the way he wanted it before setting the shovel aside so he could place what—sod—over the hole he'd just filled. It was a grave.

Finally, he turned away, leaned down, and began to fold what she presumed was some kind of tarp. When he was done, he picked it up, grabbed the shovel, and walked to a truck parked nearby. He placed the tarp and shovel inside it, and she thought he'd get in and drive away.

He didn't. As if a second thought occurred to him, he retraced his steps to the spot where he'd shoveled the hole full of dirt. For a *long time he stood with his head down and his body shaking. Was he crying? At what? For what? Or for whom?*

After what felt like a long time, the shaking of his body calmed and his head came up. He turned his back on the grave and returned once more to his truck, where he crawled in and drove away into the gloomy might. She watched as his taillights grew smaller and dimmer until they finally disappeared altogether. Rain began to fall long before the man drove away, and coldness seeped into her bones. She wasn't sure the rain that dampened her hair and her clothes caused the chill. Step by step, she walked to the place where only moments before the man stood crying. All she saw was grass. A bit of loose dirt was the only sign that something here had been disturbed. Moisture soaked through the knees of her jeans as she kneeled down and placed her hands on the ground.

Shock sent a blood-curdling scream past her lips.

❖

Lorna cut off the scream. "Motherfucker," she said, and shot up to her feet, surprised that she was perfectly dry. No rain soaked clothes, no sopping-wet hair. No goose bumps up and down her arms.

"Motherfucker," she muttered again as she gained her bearings. Definitely a classy response to what just happened, guaranteed to impress the woman standing behind Thea. Didn't have a clue where she came from, but she did know one thing: she was a cop. It all but shouted from her pores.

"What happened?" Thea asked, her voice full of fear.

Exactly what could she tell her, or perhaps more accurately, what *should* she tell her? Either way, it was the same answer: the truth. Wasn't that always what people wanted to hear? To say anything less wasn't right. But she didn't know if what she had to say would help or hurt.

Lorna turned and nodded toward the woman, opting for diversion. "And you are?"

"Deputy Sheriff Katie Carlisle." She didn't extend her hand.

Neither did Lorna. "Deputy Sheriff?"

"Yes, and you're the psychic, I presume."

Lorna took offense at the scorn-laced delivery of the words. "I'm Thea's friend," she shot back. Fuck her if she had a problem with Lorna. She was here for her friend and could care less about some cop.

"Ladies." Thea broke in. "We're all on the same side here. Different skill sets, same objective. Pull the claws back in, please." Her eyes were pleading and Lorna knew she was right. At the same time, she didn't like the way Deputy Sheriff Katie Carlisle looked at her.

Lorna narrowed her eyes and studied the deputy, who met her gaze with narrowed eyes of her own. "If you say so."

Thea sighed loudly. "I do. Please, Lorna." She put a hand gently on her arm. "Now what did you see?"

She relented on the stare-down with the deputy. Thea was right. They needed to concentrate on what she just saw, though she'd prefer to do this when the other woman was gone. She looked between Thea and the deputy and then back again. From all appearances, Thea wasn't going to give it up so she plunged ahead. Might as well lay it all out there and see where it would lead. As clearly as she could, she gave them both a blow-by-blow of the vision. Thea's face grew paler as she spoke.

When she finished, Thea whispered, "So she's dead." It wasn't a question.

The deputy didn't waste a second, her words almost angry. "You don't know that. There's no way to know any of what she said actually happened." The look she shot Lorna's way was not friendly.

Though Deputy Sheriff Carlisle got her back up, Lorna didn't disagree with the first part of her statement. The second part, well, if her recent history was any example, she was just plain wrong on that one.

Lorna kept her own temper in check as she directed her words to Thea. "She's right about not knowing if Alida is the one I saw. What I know for sure," she cut her eyes to the deputy, "is that he buried someone there, but I have no real sense of whether it was Alida. The only thing that came to me with any amount of certainty is that he dug a grave and was burying someone in it."

Thea took Lorna's hands and held them so tight they nearly crushed her fingers. "But it has to be her. Why else would you pick up that vision from this place?"

The same thought occurred to her, and the explanation left her cold. The only other alternative left her even colder. "Because Alida is probably not the only woman this man has taken."

Thea's sharp intake of breath cut through the night, and she released her grip on Lorna's hands. "Oh, my God."

"Come on," Carlisle said at the same time. "This is a crock. You have no way of knowing any of that, and throwing out that kind of crap is just plain stupid."

Lorna shifted her head slightly so that she stared the deputy straight in the eye. "You don't have to believe me. Lord knows I didn't believe it when this shit started to happen to me. I thought I was losing my flipping mind. But you know what, sister? A whole lot of stuff in this world can't be rationally explained. What I can see is one of those things. Whoever this guy is, he killed and buried at least one person. I don't know who he is, I don't know where he buried him or her, but I know without a doubt that he did it. You can take that"—she jabbed her index finger into the air between them—"to the bank."

A subtle change came into the eyes of the deputy as she spoke. She might be wrong, but it appeared the deputy's disbelief was fading, though not completely erased. Instead, the stone wall in place moments before eased slightly. She'd take it.

"There are no real psychics."

"Yeah, six months ago I'd have been right there with you, Deputy. I've learned a lot since then, and I'm here to tell you, I can see things. You have no idea how I wish I didn't, but my wishes don't seem to matter, and since they don't, all I can do is roll with it. My friend needs my help, so here I am. I'm not asking you to believe me. All I ask is that you respect my friend and what she wants. This isn't about you or me. It's about Alida."

For a moment silence hung between them. Then Carlisle asked, "You really can see things?"

Lorna nodded. "I really can."

Sighing loudly, the deputy stared at her for another long moment. "Well, what are we waiting for? Let's figure out who this bastard is and find Thea's sister."

Lorna began to think there might be hope for this cop after all.

❖

When Lorna walked out to the deck to make a call home, Thea went into the kitchen to pour some more wine. Katie followed her.

It didn't take much more than a single invitation to get the deputy to follow them back to the house. It was too cold, too dark, and too late to stay out at the transfer station. At least here, they could do a little brainstorming, and well, the wine didn't hurt either.

Located on the bluff of Five Mile Prairie, Thea's house looked out over the city, the lights twinkling like stars in the night sky. Thea liked it here, always had. Granted, in the years since she'd built her own little bit of heaven, changes were all around her. Early on, much of the prairie was still active farmland, with acres of golden wheat waving in the gentle breezes and small herds of cattle grazing in fields of alfalfa. Sadly, most of the farmland had disappeared at the hands of greedy developers and encroaching habitation over the last decade.

Though it made her sad, it didn't quench her love for the area. No matter how much it built up, she would see the beauty that still remained and remember the beauty that was. She didn't see ever leaving this oasis she'd created for herself.

"It's a nice house," Katie said when Thea handed her the wineglass topped off with a beautiful ruby Shiraz. Their fingers touched for a fraction of a second.

She smiled. "I think so too, and I thank you for noticing."

Katie's laugh was hearty. "I love your confidence."

She shrugged. "Not confidence as much as knowing what I like. This house is me. It took me a long time to find just the right place. I knew this was it the moment I stepped inside." It was true too. She couldn't count how many homes she'd looked at or open houses she'd attended. Lots of them were dogs, quite a few really nice, and some just plain exceptional. Yet until she walked into this place none of them felt like home.

"Yeah, I agree. It suits you."

Back in the living room, Thea glanced out the French doors to where Lorna stood with her back to them, one hand holding a phone to her ear and the other gesticulating as though the person on the other end could see her. She was very animated, and she thought of when they were kids. Lorna had always talked with her hands. With her face turned away it was hard to tell if the call was going well or badly. Given it was now almost one in the morning, maybe whoever she'd called wasn't particularly happy about being awakened. None of her business really, but that didn't lessen her curiosity.

"So," Katie said as she sat down in one of the armchairs, drawing Thea's attention away from Lorna. "You think this Lorna really can see into the great beyond." The bit of sarcasm that earlier threaded through her voice was gone. It almost sounded like a legitimate question born of true curiosity. Definite progress from a mere hour ago. For a long moment she studied Katie. Her dark eyes were intelligent and direct, and she didn't flinch at Thea's steady gaze. Some might call that kind of response aggressive. Thea preferred to call it confident. She liked it quite a lot. "Yes, I do."

Katie seemed to mull over her simple answer before giving her a tiny nod. "Tell me why. I want to understand. Honestly, I'm still a skeptic. One willing to listen though."

It was the opening she hoped for, and before Katie could change her mind she leaned forward and started talking. She explained about the two women of a century past who dared to love each other and who went to their graves because of it. She told her how the beautiful Catherine from the Makah tribe was murdered and buried in a secret grave, of how the love of her life, the wealthy and privileged Tiana McCafferty, threw herself off a cliff to her own death because she couldn't bear the grief of her loss. Then she explained how they came to Lorna and how she brought them both home again. When she finished, she let out a long breath and then took a swallow of her wine.

"Wow," Katie said, setting aside her now-empty glass. "That's some crazy-ass story."

Thea shook her head. "Not a story. A fact."

Her lips pressed together, Katie seemed to be thinking. "A couple of hours ago, I'd have called it bullshit. Now, as much as I hate to admit it, I'm starting to inch over to the other side. I don't like it either. I've got a life very much grounded in the rational world. In my line of work, the simplest explanation is usually the correct explanation. Angry spouses, crazy families, jealous suitors. Definitely not spirits from beyond the grave."

Thea smiled. "Lorna has a way of making believers out of people. Including herself. The way she tells it, when this all started, she thought she was losing her mind. She wasn't. For whatever reason, she's one of the special ones graced with not only the power to see what others can't, but a generous heart as well."

"She seems like an interesting woman."

Thea laughed. "You have no idea. I've known her for years, and she's always been so full of life and adventure. Did she tell you she's training for Ironman?"

"No way."

"Oh way, indeed. I can't even begin to imagine what possesses a person to want to put their body through that. Not my cup of tea, if you know what I mean." Thea couldn't even wrap her head around the endurance event, particularly after watching it last year in Coeur d'Alene. She doubted she could even make it through the swim, let alone follow it up with a bike ride and marathon. It took a special person to make it through, and Lorna was one of those people.

Katie nodded. "I totally get that. I've gone over to Coeur d'Alene and watched a couple of them. They're pretty inspiring in a lot of ways. Not enough to make me want to do it though. I'd have a hard time finishing one leg of that race, let alone three of them back-to-back."

Thea smiled, thinking how Katie's words echoed her own thoughts. "Amen, sister." Thea put out her hand for a knuckle bump.

"Now," Katie said. "About her vision out at the transfer station."

CHAPTER EIGHT

Lorna leaned on the deck railing and waited for Jeremy to pick up, which he did after two rings. "So?" A man of few words.

"So it's messed up." She didn't have to sugarcoat anything for him.

"You got something then?"

Something was one way to put it. "Yeah, I did, and it makes me sick. Some sonofabitch is killing people and I saw him bury a body. Jesus, Jeremy, what is it about me that attracts killers?" It was bad enough she had to see dead people. It wasn't fair to be a killer magnet too.

His laugh was wry. "Whether you want to admit it or not, Lorna, it's your good soul. Something opened up inside you, and it doesn't appear to be going away. The killer part isn't so cool, but helping is, and that's what you're doing."

"In your not-so-subtle way you're trying to tell me I'm stuck with it, eh?"

"That pretty much sums it up. It's kind of sweet when you think about it. I mean, you could be this psychic detective and get your own reality show. I could be your psychic sidekick and we'd be awesome."

"That's fucked up."

"Definitely, but you could make a bundle."

"Don't care about the money." The whole idea gave her the chills. The last thing—the very last thing—in the world she would ever considering doing was a reality show. Besides, she didn't need any more people knowing about her special skills.

His voice was gentle. "I know you don't. I'm being facetious. The fact that you don't care about the money and just want to help makes you special. You have something incredible, and the way you use it is just as incredible."

"I don't want to be special," she said softly as she ran one hand through her hair.

"I get that, but you should know by now we don't always get what we want. So tell me what you saw."

She wanted to add that she rarely got what she wanted, but that was just being petty. Instead, she related the whole vision for Jeremy this time, and when she finished he whistled. "You're right, that is messed up."

"I just wish I could follow it more. She's out there somewhere and I've got to find her, but I'm having a hard time pulling all the pieces into a cohesive picture." The frustration that welled up inside her was suffocating. Surely she could do something more.

"You'll put it all together. Trust me, Lorna, you'll get it and bring Alida home."

"It would be easier if you were here too…" Despite being back in her hometown and with one of her oldest friends, she felt alone. She missed Jeremy and Merry. She missed Renee.

"Wow. Well, that was subtle."

"Not trying for subtle."

He chuckled softly. "Tell you what. As soon as I finish up the business I'm working on, Merry and I'll buzz over and see what we can do to help. You might be right. A few more heads in the mix can't hurt."

She zeroed in on one word. "Business? What are you working on?" Both Merry and Jeremy had decided to make a career change, which was great with Lorna because they'd come to live in the big estate on the ocean with her. She loved having them there. The possibility that they might leave her too made her heart hurt.

Jeremy was evasive, which didn't do much to put her mind at ease. "Can't say quite yet. Still working out the details, but as soon as it all comes together, you'll be the first to know."

She wanted to know right now. "If you say so."

"I do say so." Just like when they were kids, he wasn't about to let her in on his secret. He loved to torture her.

"Why don't you just tell me?"

"Not gonna happen so give it up. I'll tell you when I'm ready."

"Brat."

"Takes one to know one."

She smiled. He always made her feel better, even when he was being obstinate and secretive. They talked for a minute longer before she ended the call. The conversation with Jeremy left her feeling much calmer, and it would be nice now to hear Renee's voice too, but while she didn't mind dragging her little brother out of sleep, she wasn't as quick to do the same to Renee. The time on her cell phone flashed nice and bright. Way too late to bother Renee. The call would have to wait until a decent hour.

For now, she couldn't do anything more for either Thea or herself. It was a wrap for this very long day. Out front, the sound of Katie's car let her know that she was calling it a night as well. The best thing to do was to try for some sleep. Tomorrow she intended to hit the ground running, and she'd need some rest to make that happen. She just hoped she didn't dream of dead bodies, shallow graves, and faceless killers.

❖

Thea sat quietly in her bedroom, her hands in her lap. Katie was gone and Lorna was all alone in the guest room. For the last ten minutes she'd been turning over everything that had happened today. She kept coming back to Lorna. Something beyond what happened out at the transfer station was bothering her. She could see it in the tightness around Lorna's eyes and the thin set to her lips. Earlier she'd asked if she could help with anything and was met with a quiet no. Lorna was lying, of course, but she'd known Lorna a long time and realized she'd get nothing more out of her until she was ready.

Thea couldn't really blame her; she was a lot like that herself. It was hard to share with anyone except Alida. They might hold things in for a while, but in the end, they didn't have any secrets between them. What would she do if Alida didn't come home?

The thought sent chills up her arms. Why was the universe sending this her way? Had she done something terrible and now had to pay the price?

Standing, she slowly took off her clothes and carried them into the bathroom. They felt incredibly heavy. Everything felt heavy—her clothes, her arms, her thoughts, her breath. It was important to keep going, yet how in the world would she be able to do that?

After dropping her clothes into the hamper, she stepped under the warm spray of the shower. Her body ached and her head pounded. Sleep seemed as elusive now as since the day Alida went missing. Her mind was whirling and her body was wired. She could lie down but she wouldn't sleep.

The hot water did wonders for both the aches and the headache. By the time she stepped out, she figured it was time to at least try to sleep. She slipped between the sheets and stared up at the ceiling. Shadows swayed and moved as if dancing to a silent waltz. It was mesmerizing. She finally relaxed and her eyelids closed.

"Thea!"

Rain came down in buckets and she spun, trying to see her. "Alida, where are you?" Her tears mixed with the rain that chilled her skin.

"Help me."

"Where are you?" Her voice was hoarse with the force of her scream. "I can't see you."

"Please, find me. I want to come home."

Thea bolted upright in bed, her heart pounding. Disoriented for a moment, she then realized she was in her own bedroom and not somewhere out in the pouring rain. The trill of her phone had dragged her out of the dream. Tears streamed down her face as she reached for it.

"Hello," she said and knew the shakiness brought on by the dream was still there.

"Thea, are you okay?"

It took a couple of seconds before the voice registered. "Katie?"

"Yes, it's me. Sorry to call so late. I can't explain it, but after I got home I felt like I needed to check in with you even though I realize how rude it is to call this late. Are you okay? You sound shaken. Did something happen after I left?"

Thea ran a hand through her damp hair and stared out at the darkness. Despite the warmth of the shower before she lay down, the nightmare had left her cold and shaken. "Just drifted off and had a strange dream," she admitted, not really sure why she'd shared that information.

Katie sighed. "I'm so sorry."

Those words were like a warm blanket, and she was suddenly very grateful to hear Katie's voice. "I'm glad you called."

"I am too. I really debated whether I should but couldn't shake the feeling that you were in need."

She didn't miss the relief in Katie's voice. "I am glad you called. I don't have nightmares often, and lord knows I haven't slept more than a few hours since Alida disappeared. When I finally do drift off, it's like something out of a horror movie. Let's just say that dream shook me up, and hearing your voice helps." It did too, despite still hearing Alida's cries for help in her ears.

"Thea, do you need anything? Can I do anything to help?"

She closed her eyes. She needed so much. "Your call helps, believe it or not. Your taking Alida's disappearance seriously helps. I'll be fine as long as you keep doing what you do best."

"Are you sure?"

"No" was the correct answer. She didn't have the right to ask anything of Katie beyond doing her job. "Yes, I'm sure."

"Okay then, but listen. Don't hesitate to call if you need anything or if you think of anything. I'm serious, Thea. I'm here for you."

She tightened her grip on the phone. "Thank you. You have no idea how much that means to me."

She set the phone on the nightstand and lay back against the pillow once more. The call dragged her away from a horrible nightmare and made her believe at least one person in law enforcement cared about finding her sister. Maybe Katie was this thoughtful to all the people she helped, but her call still made Thea feel special and, more importantly, less alone. Right now, she really needed that.

The house was quiet, as was the street outside. No cars drove by and no one walked down the sidewalk. Far off in the distance the sound of a dog's bark wafted through the air. Soon even the dog grew quiet. As she tried to sleep once more, her mind quieted, but she could still hear the heart-wrenching sound of her sister's voice.

CHAPTER NINE

Katie punched in the code of the gray gun safe, then swung open the door. She took her Glock out and tucked it into the holster at her waist, shut the door, and pulled the handle to lock it once more. As she yawned, she stretched her arms over her head. Morning had come way too quickly and she was feeling it. Overall, last night was pretty damned strange. Enlightening to be sure, but strange nonetheless.

In her line of work so-called psychics showed up in droves every time they sniffed a big case. Not once, not one single time, during her tenure with the department, did one turn out to be legit. From her perspective they were all sad individuals looking for a place to belong and for their ten minutes to be somebody special. She wanted to be empathetic, except these people wasted time she could better use following real leads, catching real killers, or bringing home the lost, like Alida Canwell.

Last night didn't feel like one of those instances. As much as she hated to admit it, and sure as hell wouldn't out loud, Lorna wasn't like any of the crackpots she'd met over the years. In fact, if Lorna could be something besides a psychic, Katie got the distinct impression she'd grab it with both hands and run as fast as she could, and given her Ironman training that would have to be pretty fast.

Still, her foot-dragging aside, Lorna obviously wanted to help, which was admirable. She didn't just want to be on the inside of a police investigation either. Katie had dealt with more than her share of these over-eager folks too. They almost ran over the press just to be able to see their faces on the six o'clock news. The families who felt they must be front and center because the police were simply inept were also a distraction. Unlike any of them, Lorna was a hundred percent focused on finding Alida.

She ran her hands through her hair and sighed, thinking about Alida now. This whole situation made her tired, and it smelled rotten. It had nothing to do with Lorna either. Whether she'd turn out to be the real thing was questionable. Yet even if she wasn't real, at least her focus was right. From all appearances, none of it seemed to be about her, and Katie gave her points for that.

The worst part? At least part of the problem with making any real progress toward finding Alida was rooted in her own agency. A cop? She hated that thought, yet no matter how hard she tried, she couldn't shake the sick feeling in the bottom of her stomach. If she'd learned one thing from her family, it was to investigate everything regardless of how big or small it appeared. She removed emotion from the equation and considered everything—and everyone. Until she'd received the assignment, however, the investigation never got off the ground, and no matter how she looked at it, that was wrong. This was never a simple case, which was clear from day one, so why or who had tried to bury it?

Each day when she went into work, she caught herself viewing her brothers and sisters in blue with suspicious eyes. They didn't teach you this in the academy. But in reality, some cops were good and some were bad. Though law-enforcement types were held to a higher standard, they were like the folks in any other profession. Most of them fell on the side of good, but a few embraced the dark side, and they caused one hell of a lot of trouble.

When she studied those around her she didn't see anything that screamed *bad cop*. Annoying ones? Yes. Obnoxious ones? Without a doubt. Bad? No. Didn't mean he or she wasn't there. She just couldn't see anything that might tip her off.

Wouldn't it be great if evil wore a badge? Something like the red letter A in *The Scarlet Letter*? Would sure make her job a lot easier if all she needed to do was look for the E on someone's shirt. Unfortunately, evil didn't work that way. It was sneaky. It was smooth. It hid while masquerading as the next-door neighbor, a coworker, a teacher. It used subterfuge and lies to live among good people and then destroy their lives.

Just as it had in her life. At the fridge, she pulled out a bottle of orange juice. It was cold, sweet, and exactly what she needed as thoughts of another black night tried to push into her head. She didn't want to deal with those memories tonight.

Oh, hell, she didn't ever want to deal with those memories. But she could never erase them. They were seared into her brain as clearly as if they'd been tattooed on her skin. When she was tired, sad, or frustrated they barged in—cold, dark, and depressing, almost screaming "Remember!"

Crazy, considering there was no way to ever forget. It was a big reason why she was here today. No one had expected her to follow in the family business. She'd decided to go this route all by herself and chose this world, knowing it still wasn't the easiest path for a woman. When it was important, and this was, there was always a way. Besides, she was all for busting up gender roles, so it was a challenge she was ready to take on.

Her family, bless their hearts, seemed to understand with only a minimal amount of explanation. That night had changed them too, and in many ways, she wasn't taking this journey alone. How lucky she was to have a supportive family. Too many others weren't so fortunate, and she didn't take her own circumstances for granted.

She glanced up at the clock and nodded. It was almost seven— nearly nine in Omaha. Family was exactly what she needed at the moment, and her brother Kyle, a psychologist, would be in his office. Not only did he have an active practice, but he also taught at the University of Nebraska and regularly served as an expert witness in both state and federal court. She could most certainly benefit from picking his brain right now.

She grabbed her phone, hit his number, and smiled at the sound of his deep voice. "What's up, Sherlock?"

❖

Lorna leaned against the kitchen counter and sipped her coffee. From the moment she woke up this morning she'd tried to focus on how to move forward. This wasn't like solving the mystery of the two women back at her house on the ocean. For them, a hundred years had already passed and a little more time didn't matter. It all mattered for Alida, every single second, and she didn't want to waste one more. "Do you think Grant would have a problem if we looked around their house?"

Thea tipped her head from side to side for a second, her lips pressed together, then said, "I don't think so."

A user's manual for this psychic thing would be so helpful. But she didn't have one and was forced to navigate her preternatural skills all by herself. Being in Alida's space, touching her things—well, it could spark something. "I honestly have no idea if it'll make a damn bit of difference, but maybe something will speak to me, if you catch my drift."

Thea nodded. "I do, and I think it's a pretty good idea."

A decided lack of enthusiasm sounded in Thea's voice, yet it was the best idea she could come up with. "You don't sound convinced."

Thea had her arms wrapped around her body. "It's not that. I really do think it's worth a shot. I just don't think Grant had anything to do with this. He might have trouble keeping his zipper up, and I hate that about him. I don't hate him though, and I don't believe he hurt Alida. Does that make sense?"

Grant's feelings didn't matter. Lorna had never thought Grant was a bad guy either, and despite his moral failings, from everything Thea had told her so far, he sounded as though he was in genuine despair over Alida's disappearance. Maybe he was and maybe he wasn't. It remained to be seen, and she was more than willing to hurt his feelings if it would help bring her friend home. It was by far the best idea she had right now and she wanted to act on it.

"It does, and I get your hesitation. I'm not trying to poke into Grant's head. I'm trying to get a handle on what to do with the psychic thingy that seems like a bad rash I can't cure. I don't know how it works or how to make it work, so I'm trying everything. Maybe something at the house will speak to me."

Thea picked up a coffee mug and turned it around and around between her hands. "I see where you're going." She met Lorna's eyes. "I'm sure Grant will be fine with it."

"Wanna give him a call?" She didn't want to waste any time because time was working against them.

Thea nodded and, for the first time since the conversation started, looked and sounded all in. "Let's do this."

She made the call, and five minutes later they were in the car heading toward Long Lake. Lorna had a strong feeling this was the right thing to do and that something out there would help them find Alida.

❖

"So, what do you think, Kyle? What do I have on my hands?" Katie asked after she'd spent at least five minutes describing Alida's disappearance.

"You do realize you're asking me for a professional opinion without seeing any case history, files, or interviews?"

She could picture him at his desk with his red hair slightly disheveled and one hand tapping a pen. "Blah, blah, blah. You love a great puzzler, and this, my dear brother, is definitely a puzzler."

He sighed loudly, and she actually heard the plop of the pen as it dropped to the desktop. "All right, you've piqued my interest, but you knew you would the second you made the call."

Of course she knew. Kyle was a sucker for anything mystery related. The mystery of the human psyche was one of the things that drew him to his profession. Darned helpful for her too on more than one occasion. She was really hoping this would be one of those instances where he could provide assistance that would draw her closer to a resolution. "I am a deputy sheriff, after all. I've got skills. Seriously, though, Kyle. What do you think? Any bits of insight would really help. So far I've got nothing and the clock is ticking."

She could almost see the wheels turning in his head as the phone grew silent. Others might interpret his silence as rude, but she knew he was running everything she told him through the computer that was his brain. He was processing and all she had to do was wait. "Is she the only woman who's gone missing?"

She'd thought of that too and already checked her records. "The only one in my county."

"Not what I asked. Broaden your horizons, sister. What about in the city? How about Stevens County or Kootenai County? Might as well cross state lines. Killers do."

He might live halfway across the country, but he still knew his hometown geography. She was part of the Spokane County Sheriff's Department, and her jurisdiction was the county, not the city. She'd need to check with some of her pals at the Spokane Police Department. Same thing with Stevens County law enforcement. Since southern Stevens County was close enough to be a bedroom community to Spokane, it often felt like it was part of Spokane County. Kootenai County was in Idaho but just a skip and a jump from the Spokane Valley. As she knew he would, Kyle made some good points, and she was a little embarrassed she hadn't checked on those earlier.

"I'll jump on that as soon as we're done here." In fact, she was already clicking away at her keyboard while she held the phone between her ear and shoulder.

"Think about it, Katie. Your missing person might not be his only victim."

His reference was subtle, but she knew him well enough to catch it. It also echoed her own thoughts. "You don't think she's alive." She wasn't asking him a question.

"As much as I hate to say it, I don't. Anything's possible, and she could certainly still be, but I wonder if this was his one and only. Feels like he's done this before, although in all fairness, sis, I'd need to look at your files. It's hard to give you much of an expert opinion without the facts. This is all supposition."

"I know how helpful it would be if you had my files in front of you, Kyle, but it's just not possible right now. I appreciate what you're giving me, and I realize this isn't how you do things. I just wanted to get your gut feeling on this. It's the weirdest case I've ever had to investigate."

"Tell you what, email me what you can and I'll take a more in-depth look. I'll call you back with whatever else I might glean. Don't know if I can help much, but I'm happy to try."

The fact that he had her back took some weight off her shoulders. Asking Vince or one of the others for help wasn't out of the question, yet if she could possibly avoid that course, she would. "Thanks. I appreciate the help, and as soon as I can, I'll email you the info."

"Can't promise how fast I can get back to you. Between classes and sessions, I'm pretty well booked today."

"Whatever works for you. I know what an imposition this is."

"And that would be different from any other day how exactly?"

"Love you, bro." She did too. Even when they were young he'd made time for her no matter what else was going on. As adults it was the same. He was always there for her and it made her heart full.

His sigh was exaggerated. "Love you too, you little brat. Now, I've got a classroom packed with students eagerly awaiting my lecture on abnormal psych, and you've got a missing person to find."

Chapter Ten

Thea pulled into the driveway and a giant wave of emotion washed over her, nearly dragging her into a new rush of tears. Right on the water, the familiar house on Shore Drive was as beautiful as ever, especially the lush expanse of grass that flowed from the back of the house to the neatly tended beach. How many hours had she and Alida spent stretched out on the beach soaking up sunshine and sipping lemonade? They talked, they shared, and they laughed. Coming here had always filled her with joy until now.

The homes along this stretch of lake rarely came up for sale, and so when this one did, Grant and Alida rushed to pick it up. The housewarming party turned out to be delightful, and she still recalled how happy it made her that night.

What had happened along the way? She'd give anything to find a soul mate, even as corny as that sounded. She really thought that's what Grant and Alida found in each other, only that wasn't the way it appeared to have worked out. They started out with such promise only to veer onto a path littered with lies and betrayal. Now, they were both paying the price.

Grant was standing in the doorway waiting for them. He'd probably been staring out the window since she called. His normally perfect hair didn't look like it had seen a comb lately, and deep, dark circles ringed his eyes. Despite his indiscretions, she'd be shocked if he was responsible for Alida's disappearance. He might be a hound dog, but he still loved his wife. For some reason that made her feel better.

"Come in," he said as he stood back and held the door open for them. When the door was shut, he turned and looked at Lorna. "Thank you for coming."

Lorna studied him intently. "I'll try to help any way I can."

He nodded. "I appreciate that. Alida always loved you." His eyes filled with tears. "What do you need?"

With a shrug, Lorna said, "I honestly don't know. Would it be okay if I just wandered around?"

He nodded again, somberly. "Absolutely. Go anywhere. The whole house is open to you."

Thea looked at Lorna. "We'll wait for you here. It might be better if you have silence while you do this."

Lorna slowly walked around the room and then went out the door toward the kitchen. Thea moved to the window and looked out at the lake. All she could think of was how much she'd enjoyed her afternoons on the beach with Alida. How she wished they could be out there now, sitting side by side, talking and laughing.

"Do you think she'll be able to help?"

Thea turned and studied Grant. Again she was struck by the deep dark circles under his eyes. He was a handsome man who looked as though he'd aged a decade in the last few days. "What happened between you two? Why did you turn away from each other?"

His head dropped and he took several long, deep breaths. When he spoke his words were shaky. "I've asked myself that same question for days."

"And?"

He didn't look at her. "It was the baby."

The baby? "What do mean?" She must have heard him wrong. No way in hell would Alida get pregnant and not let her know.

His head came up and he studied her. "She never told you."

"I don't understand." She wasn't stupid but none of this was making sense.

Softly he explained. "A year ago, Alida was pregnant and she lost the baby."

"What!" No way. Alida would have confided in her. The idea she wouldn't didn't play for her. They were always each other's number-one confidante.

He closed his eyes and tears slid down his cheeks. "She was high risk and didn't want to say anything, even to you, until she passed the danger point." He blew out a long breath. "She didn't make it, and when she lost the baby she was devastated. I've never seen her so distraught, and I couldn't blame her because so was I. I really wanted that child."

She thought back, surprised to recall days when Alida had seemed distant. At the time she'd passed it off as the stress of a hectic job. She'd been so entrenched in her own business she didn't give it much thought. Her heart hurt to think her sister had suffered silently in so much pain and that she, the one person who should have been there for her, had been oblivious. Guilt washed over her as she realized how much her own oblivion had let her down.

Anger edged the guilt as she stared at Grant. "You blamed her for losing the baby."

Slowly he nodded. "I tried not to and yet it would come out. Intellectually I knew it was just the way things are and no one was to blame. Emotionally I lashed out at her and she at me."

She hated him at this moment, probably because it was easier to feel hate than the hurt that wanted to wrap around her. Alida had shut her out and that made her incredibly sad. "You should have been there for her."

Grant sank to the arm of the sofa and ran his hands over his face as if to rub away the deep fatigue. "Yes, I should have. We should have supported each other, but we couldn't seem to. Each of us was so wrapped up in our own pain we turned away. We both did things we weren't proud of."

"That's what prompted the affairs."

He nodded again. "We both turned to others trying to find a way to ease the pain. I'm ashamed of my behavior, and I know she was too." He took Thea's hands in his. "You have to understand. We were hurt and lost, but in the end we found our way back to each other. We were healing and we were moving forward. Then this..."

Lorna appreciated that Thea and Grant left her alone. Grant was a bit of a surprise. She'd only met him once, at Alida's wedding. Since then, the few times she'd seen Alida, he hadn't been there to dampen the free speech of three old friends.

Today she wasn't worried about censorship, though she expected it from Grant. It was his house, after all, and his wife who was missing. If he wanted to follow her around she wouldn't have objected, even if she didn't like it. This way was easier for her. She didn't know what she was looking for or what would be important. She was fishing, and it was easier to concentrate without the distraction of Thea or Grant.

After half an hour of wandering through the main floor, nothing gave her so much as a tingle. It was a tidy, comfortable space that reminded her of Alida. Though elegant, expensive homes flanked it on either side, her house was warm and inviting, like her friend. No pretense or showmanship.

Disappointed that now, of all times, her so-called psychic powers appeared to be abandoning her, she climbed the staircase to the second level. It was lovely and welcoming here as well. Three bedrooms, three bathrooms, and an open loft area that Alida used as a studio. How was it possible she'd managed to forget Alida was a painter? No matter where they went or what they were doing back when they were kids, Alida always had her sketchpad and charcoal pencils. Her talent was evident even in grade school, and Lorna was still jealous of her natural artistry. She'd kill for even a tenth of that ability, but she couldn't even draw a decent stickman.

On the easel by the big picture window sat a partially completed landscape. The colors were rich and deep, just as the sunsets here often were. Obviously her skill as an artist had grown over the years. Even partially completed the painting was gorgeous. As she stood staring at it, tears gathered in her eyes.

"Where are you, Alida? Where are you?" Her whispered questions hung in the air, and for a long moment she held her breath, waiting. But nothing happened and no voice came to her.

With a trembling hand, she reached out to touch the unfinished canvas.

The light in the studio was bright, the sun outside high and intense. Alida stood before the canvas, a paintbrush in one hand, staring at the barely started picture. Twice she dipped the brush in the paint and moved the color across the canvas. Then she stopped and closed her eyes.

"You can't be here," she said without turning or opening her eyes.

No one else was in the room, and then a voice came from the open door. "I had to see you."

"Don't."

"I can't give you up."

"I told you never to step foot in this room, and I meant it."

Still no face appeared in the doorway, just a soft male voice from the hallway beyond.

"I love you."

Her laugh was harsh. "No, you don't love anyone but yourself. You just want to possess me. Now go. I won't have you here in my home."

For a moment nothing happened, and then the whisper of retreating footsteps wafted through the air. Alida didn't move for a long time. Finally she dipped the brush into the paint once again and, as she sobbed, slashed dark-red strokes from side to side.

Lorna let her hand drop from the canvas and stood staring for a long time at the painting. The sunset that had seemed so beautiful when she first walked into the room now appeared ominous. While she'd missed it at first glance, now she could detect the strength of emotion that hijacked a soothing picture and morphed it into a scream of pain. She hadn't seen the face of the man who came to Alida that day, but something about the voice was familiar. Not one she recognized, although she might have heard it somewhere before. Even if she'd never heard it before, she would recognize it if she ever heard it again.

❖

Every time Katie tried to take ten minutes and follow up on what Kyle had posited, somebody came up with a case that needed her immediate attention or a question on procedure or help with a report. And if that wasn't bad enough, she completely forgot she was scheduled to be in court right after lunch as a prosecution witness. That was a giant pain in the ass because right now she didn't want to be bothered. Couldn't afford the time away from the Canwell case.

But not showing up wasn't an option if she wanted to keep her job, and she did. So, right after lunch she put on her jacket and headed up to her assigned courtroom. With any luck, it would go quickly and she could get back to work.

Of course it didn't. Painfully slow was an apt description, and it was almost four thirty before she got back to her desk. The case in court went well, but if she'd ever wondered how many ways the same question could be asked, her curiosity was satisfied several times over during the course of the marathon hearing. Hopefully she wouldn't have to repeat that adventure soon, and definitely not in front of that judge. Not her favorite.

Back at her desk at long last, she listened to the messages on her phone, disappointed that not one of them was from Thea. One from Vince, one from a Spokane Police Department detective, and three from Brandon. The latter made her groan. His puppy crush was getting old. Her chin resting on her palm, she stared at the phone. Why did the absence of that one call make her feel so discouraged?

No big surprise there, not if she was honest with herself. Thea was gorgeous, she was talented, and she was single. Katie liked her, which made her want to help find her sister even more than she already did. She was intrigued from the moment she saw her, and that feeling had only deepened each day since.

Right now, she had nothing to offer Thea—no words of encouragement and no leads. In fact, other than talking to her brother, she'd failed to accomplish anything on the case, which left her feeling terrible. This wasn't like her. She was a go-getter, a good investigator, and clearing cases quickly was what she did. Treading water wasn't her style and wasn't what she wanted Thea to see.

"How did it go in court today?"

Her head snapped up at the sound of Vince's voice. "Ah, fine. Jury's out, though it shouldn't take long before they come back with a guilty verdict."

"Pretty confident."

"Pretty strong case by the state."

He nodded. "Good, I hate riff-raff getting off, especially after we've done our work and then some stupid technicality lets them back on the street."

"You left me a message earlier. Something you need from me?"

With his hand he waved her off. "No biggie. Dug up the answer to my question."

She studied him. Now that she really looked he appeared a little stressed, not like his usual cocky self. This was a new one. "You all right, Vince?"

He seemed genuinely surprised by her question, but then again maybe he should be. She didn't typically ask about his well-being. Oh hell, she never asked about his well-being because he was always so full of himself she just didn't care. Today he was different, almost humble. He shrugged. "I'm fine, but thanks for asking. Makes me think you care." He winked and the Vince she knew was back.

She was shaking her head as she said, "You're a dog. You know that, right?"

He smiled, and the weariness of a moment before vanished. "I'm the best kind of dog." He was laughing as he left.

CHAPTER ELEVEN

Thea didn't speak as they drove toward home, the traffic on Highway 291 picking up as rush hour neared. Despite her vision in Alida's studio, they hadn't made any ground. She was depressed that they were stalled and heartsick about Alida's pregnancy and miscarriage. It hurt that Alida hadn't trusted her enough to tell her, and thinking of her enduring that painful experience by herself made Thea want to drop down to the floor and sob. It was all a crushing weight that threatened to flatten her.

But Lorna was trying her best to help, and Thea's hurt feelings didn't figure in at all. None of this was about her, so her bruised feelings and battered pride didn't matter. Alida would have told her to put on her big girl panties and get over it.

She smiled. Though Thea wasn't confrontational, Alida met everything head-on. How she loved that about Alida and often wished she were more like her.

But she wasn't, and never would be, so she better put on those panties and try her best. That meant working with Lorna and Katie, the thought of which made her pause. Funny, how quickly she'd become attached to Katie. She missed her today and longed to hear the sound of her voice. The day seemed to have zipped by and they'd accomplished little. She prayed Katie had done better.

It was almost nine before she gave in and picked up the phone. Looking at the business card Katie put in her hand that first day, she punched in the number and then held her breath as the phone rang. This was probably a bad idea, inching toward a schoolgirl crush. She was just getting ready to end the call when Katie picked up. Too late.

"Carlisle."

"Katie? It's Thea." Geez, was that her voice that sounded so squeaky?

"What's wrong?"

"Nothing."

"You're sure?"

"Yes, I'm sure. I, ah, just wanted to touch base since I hadn't talked to you all day. Have you made any progress?" If she talked any faster, Katie would need a translator. At least the high, squeaky voice was gone.

"I'm sorry. It was a crazy day, topped off by having to spend all afternoon in court. I wanted to work more on Alida's case but kept getting pulled away."

"So, nothing." Disappointment added to the weight on her shoulders.

"I'm sorry."

She was too, although she felt better just hearing Katie's voice. "Tomorrow then."

"Yes, tomorrow, and Thea…"

"Yes?"

"I'm glad you called."

❖

"Damn it," he muttered. She lay unmoving at his feet. He didn't need to check to see if she was breathing. What would be the point?

Despite all his best intentions, he'd gone and done it again. He'd promised himself he wouldn't go there again. The last one was the last one. It had been great too. For a little while anyway. Then something came over him. No, that wasn't quite it. It was more like she came over him.

With the best of intentions he'd gone to that lounge after work. One drink, two tops to relax, and then he'd planned to buzz on home and get a few things done around the old place. It needed it. The whole mess pissed him off. In all those years, didn't his old man do anything besides sit around drinking and bitching about his mother? From the looks of the place when he moved in, the answer was a resounding *no*. Just proved once more his opinion of him was spot on: pig.

He'd left the office with his plan set. A drink or two to mellow out after a long, stressful day at work, and then back to the old homestead for a little home improvement. That was all great until she walked in looking like…well, like they all looked: ready for him. The old man might not have been the best father around or very handy around the house, but he'd taught him some important things. Like how to shoot, how to lie, how to know when a woman is asking for him to take charge.

Each and every one gave him the signal. He looked them straight in the eye and there it was, *the tell*. It wasn't like he needed to twist their arms either. Oh no, they came with him smiling the whole way. The men who couldn't pick up women were complete losers. There was nothing to it.

The killing part, well, Pops didn't teach him that exactly. Sort of implied it, and he was smart enough to carry through with the most critical part all by himself. That's not to say Pops didn't carry through too. Damn straight. He'd found that out the night he came out to the place to find Pops in his favorite chair with a scotch in one hand and his mother bleeding at his feet, her skull crushed.

He'd cleaned up the mess, in more ways than one. The nice thing about having older parents who were damn-near hermits, nobody much asks about them. As it turned out, it worked incredibly well for him. Once Pops joined Mom he was able to give up his house in town because their social-security checks were still coming in, providing him a bump in disposable income, and he was granted all the privacy a guy could ask for.

Now, however, he had a little mess of his own to clean up. Again. He sighed and headed out to his truck. His work was never done.

The toolbox unlocked, he reached in and pulled out one of the blue tarps he kept there. When he'd purchased the first tarp he'd had no idea it would prove to be so useful. Versatile too. They kept things clean, were easy to fold up and tuck away, and, most important, were just the right size to wrap around a body. He silently patted himself on the back for having such great insight. Things really did have a way of working out.

Once he had the tarp spread out, he rolled her onto it so he could wrap her up nice and tidy. The kill was clean—no muss, no fuss. Later he would dust and vacuum just to make sure there was no evidence of her presence in his house, but he wasn't all that worried. Nobody would suspect him of anything, and the chances they'd come looking here were pretty much nil. Nobody ever came out here. His parents, who were old enough to be his grandparents at the time he was born, didn't have friends. As it turned out, neither did he.

Still, he was a careful guy, and a careful guy didn't gamble. On the outside chance something very strange happened and someone made a surprise visit to his house, he planned to be ready. He would clean his house as soon as he returned from his garden of roses. That made him smile.

He hoisted her wrapped body onto one shoulder and carried her outside, where he loaded her into the bed of his truck, making sure to conceal the rolled tarp with a bag of potting soil and a couple of shovels. Anyone glancing in the back wouldn't think a thing of the pile of stuff. Just the way he liked it.

Okay, so despite no plans for indulging himself again, especially so soon after the last one, the deed was done. Still, he admitted, he felt pretty fucking great. Like a king. It was like fate was smiling on him, and who was he to question fate? Sometimes a guy just rolled with it.

❖

Lorna sat on the edge of the bed and debated whether to call Renee. She wanted to, in the worst way, because she felt empty and scared. Though she'd called Jeremy earlier, which helped, he wasn't the one who held her when the night was dark and lonely or whispered just the right words in her ear to make her smile and believe in herself again.

Today reality hit her hard. Alida had disappeared without a trace or a clue, and the only psychic energy left behind was by someone powerful and evil. No wonder Thea had sounded so frantic and insistent Lorna come right away. With nothing else to grab onto, she chose to try a friend who perhaps might offer something no one else could. From the moment she realized what was happening to her was something along the psychic lines, she hated it. Solving the mystery of Catherine Swan's disappearance was gratifying, but she still hated seeing things. She wanted to go back to being normal. Until now. For the first time since this crazy thing started she wanted the visions to come and to see as much as she could.

Inside her was a draw to the evil permeating the parking area at the transfer station and the disembodied voice in her vision, which scared the crap out of her yet oddly gave her hope they'd find Alida. She promised herself she'd track down this guy who was, she felt certain, the same person responsible for the bad vibes at the parking lot and Alida's studio.

When an evil soul had tried to hijack Jeremy at the house, Renee was able to see the manifestation of that evil in Jeremy's aura. Renee might not have an ability to see what was or what might be, but she certainly had something special. That gift might come in handy in this instance too. But she was over three hundred miles away physically and who knew how far away emotionally.

With the phone in her hand Lorna kept staring at it as if it was a dangerous weapon that would burn the flesh from her fingers if she dared to make the call. It was just shy of two in the morning, and way too late—or too early—to call anyone, let alone someone she professed to love. Her fingers itched to make the call against her better judgment. Something had been off between her and Renee before she left to come here. And it wasn't Renee's fault. The blame rested one hundred percent on her shoulders.

She was afraid. It was easy to blame it all on Anna, and that's exactly what she'd done for months. After all, Anna had dumped her for another woman, and Lorna had run to the house on the coast Aunt Bea left her. At the time she was full of hate and fury because Anna's betrayal destroyed her. But she was over Anna and had been for quite a while. The world of denial she'd brought with her after the breakup was way too comfortable to let go of it easily. It was easier to hold on tight to anger and hurt than to open herself up to the possibility of a new life.

Then Renee and her dog had walked in, and everything had changed. She fell hard and incredibly fast. Maybe that's what made it so scary. The way she'd loved Anna didn't even touch the way she felt about Renee. So, if she was that crushed when Anna left her, what the hell would she do if Renee left her too? Or rather, when Renee left her. Her track record for maintaining a long-term relationship pretty much sucked.

It was all quite confusing. Renee had made it very clear she loved Lorna, and she believed her. That wasn't the problem. No, the real issue was geography: Renee lived in the city. She'd built an incredibly successful life there, and despite the fire that had wiped out her home and business, it's where she belonged. Every time she talked about her shop and all the unique and interesting things she carried, she lit up. Her heart was with the shop and the Emerald City.

Seattle wasn't for Lorna. It was a great place to visit, but she didn't want to live there. When she moved from Spokane she left city life behind, and she wouldn't trade the magnificent house on the shores of the Pacific Ocean to move into an even bigger city than the one she'd left. That house overlooking the ocean held her heart, especially after what had happened with Tiana McCafferty and Catherine Swan. She owed it to the two women who lost their lives on that property to give it life and love once again. No way in hell would she ever leave it behind.

Would Renee and Clancy even consider trading the life and culture of Seattle for the tranquility of the house on the ocean shore? No matter which direction she came at the question, she kept circling back around to the same answer: No. The thought of their departure tore her apart yet she was helpless to stop it.

She would have plenty of time to ponder that in the days to come, but not now. Worrying about things out of her control was a waste of time and energy better spent trying to help Alida.

The phone grew warm in her hand, and it occurred to her she should either use it or put it away and go to sleep. With a deep breath, she pressed the speed dial for Renee. Though it hurt to think about the future, it hurt more to not hear her beautiful voice. She just hoped Renee would forgive her for calling at this ungodly hour.

It rang only twice before Renee picked up. That was a good sign, right? "Hey, sexy, how's it going?"

In the dim glow of the bedside lamp Lorna smiled, and the tension in her shoulders eased. "It's going. Sorry to wake you up. You were probably sleeping."

Renee laughed, a light and magical sound that went straight to her heart. "No worries. I have plenty of time to sleep. I'd rather talk to you any time of the day or night. I miss you."

Those three simple words made her throat tighten. "I miss you too."

"Good to know. Have you come up with anything helpful for your friend?"

She shook her head even though she sat alone in the room. "No, nothing that was clear enough to figure out where Alida might be. But I'm certain it was a man who abducted her, snatched her right from her work truck. She didn't take off on her own, and it wasn't another woman."

"Oh, Lorna, that's really messed up. Were you able to see a face or enough of his features to recognize him if you ran across him?"

"No, and it's frustrating as hell. I need to see that fucker's face. Sorry…" Renee rarely cussed, but Lorna sported a regular potty mouth. Since Renee had come to stay with her, she'd tried to be more respectful and keep it clean, but more often than not her sailor's mouth just got away from her, and the obscenities rolled right off her tongue.

Renee's laughter was hearty. "All things considered, beautiful, I'd be expecting something more along the lines of 'motherfucker.'"

Hearing that kind of curse come out of Renee's mouth made her laugh in spite of her dark mood. She would have loved to see Renee's face as that word crossed her lips. "I might just corrupt you yet."

"Oh, sweetheart, you have so corrupted me, and I love it. Come to think of it, you can corrupt me anytime the urge strikes you."

Damn it, this pissed her off. She was falling hard for Renee. The tears that suddenly sprang into her eyes threatened to spill, and she blinked hard to keep them back. It was silly, considering she was sitting here all by herself. Still, she didn't want to dissolve into a lovelorn woman whether or not there were witnesses. The one thing she could cling to was her strength, and she wasn't about to abandon that now.

"Hey, did I tell you my place is looking pretty sweet? Another two weeks and it should be done. Fire inspector officially cleared me today too. It's been an awesome day except that you're clear across the state. I wish you could be here. We could celebrate my vindication with a bottle of wine."

Both joy and sadness filled her as she listened to Renee's bright voice. She missed her terribly, but the part about Renee's building in Seattle left her chilled, despite Renee's obvious joy when she answered the phone. In two weeks Renee would be gone, and Lorna would be alone again.

She forced cheerfulness into her voice and hoped it covered the chill in her heart. "That's fantastic." All things considered, she figured she'd pulled it off. Renee wouldn't have any idea she was about five seconds away from dissolving into tears.

"It's been such an ordeal. Fires suck, if I haven't mentioned it before. Thank the good Lord for insurance and astute fire investigators. I've been cleared, as I knew I would be since I didn't have anything to do with the fire, and my investment property is almost back to a hundred percent. From the ashes the Phoenix rises!"

"I'm glad for you, Renee." This time she wasn't so sure she pulled off the forced optimism.

"Lorna, are you okay? You sound down."

Again, she worked hard at pushing away the sadness. Yes, they were lovers but they'd never made any promises, and she wasn't about to push the issue. "Yeah, I'm good. It's just been a night, and after trying so hard to find Alida and failing, I'm beat."

"Look, sweetheart, get some rest and we can talk again in the morning. And Lorna…"

"Yeah?"

"I love you."

This time the tears did course down her cheeks. Fuck promises. "I love you too."

CHAPTER TWELVE

The moon was round and bright, its light a golden glow that spread across the grass. Stretched out on his back, he stared into the night sky and breathed in fresh, clean air. The smell of damp grass with just a hint of manure wafting through the breeze from a nearby pasture was comforting in its normality. He was proud of himself for keeping everything tidy. Despite his little slip earlier, everything remained nice and neat. His need to follow through on his mission grew with each passing day, but he was disciplined enough to know when it was right and when it wasn't.

After he took care of the last one, he should have gotten into his truck and driven home, except an urgent need to be close to her overwhelmed him and he succumbed to that need. For just a little while he would lie still and savor the night. Here he was as close to her as possible, under the circumstances: his precious angel. She was the special one and so much better than any of the others. In fact there was no comparison. She was all that was good and bright and clean. The others weren't. Letting go of her was impossible, and far too much to ask of him. She'd left a giant hole in his heart that another could never fill.

As he lay there, the air grew colder and moisture seeped into his clothes where they met the ground. Still he didn't move. The sensation of cool fabric against his warm skin was a little like the touch of her fingers against his flesh. He liked it. If he could stay here all night, he would.

As he closed his eyes his thoughts wandered back to the first time he saw her. There she was in her utility truck, driving by and pretending she didn't notice him. He knew a wink and a nod when he saw it, and so he followed her to the substation. Even back then it all felt so right.

When she got out of that truck she impressed him even more. In blue jeans, a button-up shirt, and work boots, she was hot at a level that sent his blood boiling. He didn't care what anybody said; a beautiful woman dressed in masculine clothing out-sexed one in an evening gown any day of the week.

She was into him, and he'd picked up on that the second she said hello. Her smile was for him alone, and he knew right then and there they were meant to be together forever. It was their shared destiny.

Now he sighed as he watched stars dot the black sky above him. Ever so slowly they shifted across the horizon like a beautiful light show put on just for him and his precious one. Despite the itch that made him want to go out and drive the streets until he found another woman, being here with her calmed him. For the time being, just spending time with her helped ease the disquiet in his soul. She gave him strength with her presence, even if it was only spiritual. It was enough because they would always have each other. Nothing and no one could ever come between them again.

Off in the distance the lights of a vehicle cut through the dark night, a signal his time with her was coming to an end. Even in the face of his compelling need to be with her he didn't care to take the chance someone would spot either him or his vehicle. Not that anyone would have a clue what drew him to this place. Still, it always paid to err on the side of caution.

He pushed up and got to his feet. His shirt was soaked and it stuck to his back, and his slacks were just as wet and sticky. It didn't matter. In fact, it was a little like he was taking a bit of her along with him, and he found a great deal of comfort in that.

In the shadow of the large weeping willow, he watched the white sedan pass by and continue down the lonely country road. The driver probably didn't even notice his black truck parked under cover of a stand of trees. Just like his father, he was drawn to dark-colored vehicles. Not only did they blend into the shadows, but in his experience, people paid little attention to them. Made it handy if he was spotted somewhere out of place. When the taillights of the passing car disappeared, he stepped away from the willow and walked to the truck.

As he pulled away, he put one arm on the open window and began to hum.

❖

Lightning cut across the sky seconds before the thunder crashed and roared. The Watcher stood at the ocean's edge and stared up at the riotous sky. Dread pooled in his heart. Evil was growing stronger and he felt powerless to help.

She was so far away, and though he could sense the impending danger, he could do little to guide her. As a fallen one, his powers were limited and his feet grounded to this place. The price for his transgressions was high indeed. If he could go back in time and undo the sin that held him captive, he would do so without a second thought.

Except he finally understood there was a second thought. How he longed to return to the time before his fall so his place in heaven could be saved, and yet he realized his place was here. She needed him, and in all his time on this planet, he had never felt needed like this. He had never experienced the desire to give of himself so freely, for his focus had always been on his own path home. At this moment it no longer mattered whether redemption would be granted. Only she mattered, and he wanted to be at her side to give her all the strength and power he could. Frustration at not being able to do so made him want to scream. He did not, for it would do him no good. No one would hear. No one would care.

Slowly he began to walk along the edge of the ocean, the wind whipping his long hair and sending salty spray across his face. His skin, already cool, turned icy. Ignoring physical discomfort he walked, his eyes focused beyond the place where his feet touched. He reached into the realm beyond the physical, searching for who or what caused such disturbance. The sight failed him, and what threatened her from across the mountains refused to reveal itself. If only he was not tethered to this place. If only he could be at her side. If. If. If. How he hated that word.

Above him the sky continued to rage, and the thread of evil was black and grim through the roiling clouds. The Watcher put his hands together and closed his eyes as tears trailed down his cheeks. "I ask you, dear Father, for this only: keep her strong and keep her safe."

❖

Thea couldn't sleep, and she wasn't the only one. She found Lorna sitting out on the deck in the dark. Though the sky was sprinkled with thousands of bright stars, the moon was a mere sliver, making the night cool and black. A couple yards over a dog barked, and as it did, a cat ran nimbly across her yard, scaling her fence in a single leap.

"Hey," she said as she lit the candle on the deck table and took the other lounger.

Lorna gave her a small smile. "Hey."

"Can't sleep?"

"Nope. You either?"

Thea blew out a long breath. She was beginning to wonder if she was ever going to be able to sleep again. "I haven't slept much since this all started. What's your excuse?"

Lorna rubbed her temples with her fingers. "I'm worried about Alida and the fact that I don't seem to be helping much. I'm letting you both down."

It bothered her Lorna would even think that. "No, Lorna, you're not. You came when I called, and I didn't have to try very hard to convince you."

"You guys have been my friends for too many years. You'd do the same for me."

She was right on that score. If Lorna was in trouble, Thea would drop everything to help her. They could go for years and not see or talk to each other. Then, five minutes together and all those years just melted away. That's what real friends did for each other.

"Yes," she said softly. "I'd come in a heartbeat."

Lorna nodded and stared out into the darkness, her arms now crossed over her chest. "So you understand why I feel so useless."

Thea swung her legs over the lounger and leaned close to Lorna so she could take her hands. "You have no idea how much help you are. Your being here has been my sanity. Without you I think I'd have lost it." She wasn't exaggerating. It was all she could do to keep it together. Panic was growing by the day, and without Lorna here to ground her, she was certain she would have cracked.

Lorna squeezed her hands. "Well, that cute deputy would probably be more than happy to help keep you sane."

Thea let go of Lorna's hands and leaned back in her lounger. The idea of a beautiful woman riding in to save the day was a great fantasy, and she so wished this was a fantasy instead of the horrible reality it was. "She's just doing her job."

"Of course she is." Lorna drew out each word.

It was a good ploy to try to take her mind off the tragedy for a few minutes, but it was misplaced. "Seriously, Lorna. There's nothing between me and the deputy."

"Maybe not right now, and that's to be expected given what's going on, but I'm telling you, Thea, there could be. She likes you."

Beyond the mere fact this wasn't the time or the place to get involved with anyone, she didn't want to get ahead of herself and didn't want to set herself up for heartache. Then again… "You think?"

"Oh yeah, I think."

Backpedaling because she didn't want to go there, not just yet, she deflected. "What really brought you out here tonight? I know you're frustrated by Alida's case, but that's not all of it."

"Nothing worth worrying about."

Apparently Lorna was forgetting how long they'd known each other. "Liar. Come on. You know you can trust me."

For what seemed like at least five minutes, silence hung between them. Thea thought that, despite their long-time friendship, she might have pushed Lorna a little too far. Then Lorna broke the silence.

"I'm worried I'm going to end up with another broken heart," she said bluntly, her words flat.

Underneath the toneless words Thea could feel the depth of emotion Lorna didn't want to expose. Despite the recent years of rare contact, she still knew her friend. They grew up together, learned about like, love, and betrayal together. Those were things one didn't forget. She could tell how deep fear ran in her friend's heart. "Okay, I don't know your Renee, but she's no Anna. That much I do know."

Lorna leaned forward and put her head in her hands. Her voice was full of the emotion she'd tried to suppress just moments before. "She's going to leave me, I just feel it. I live out there in the boonies and she's from the city. What could possibly keep her out there so far from the life she built in Seattle?"

Despite Lorna's obvious despair, Thea smiled. "Oh, my dear friend, that's an easy one: you."

CHAPTER THIRTEEN

Katie thought she was bound to be the first one in, but boy was she way off. Vince was already there, bent over his computer typing away, and Chad was coming down the hallway with a mug of coffee in his hand.

"Did I miss a meeting notice?" she asked as she dropped her bag into the bottom drawer of her desk. "I don't see you two here this bright and early very often." She was an early riser and typically at her desk well before any of the others. Chad tended to be a little early, but Vince usually walked in right on time. Early wasn't his style, although to give him credit, he was the first guy to offer to stay late.

"What are you trying to say, Carlisle? That we're slugs?"

"Your words, not mine, Chad."

He laughed and put his mug down on his desk. "Damn straight."

"You two are less than funny, and I think being here this time of morning is criminal," Vince added without looking up from his computer screen. "If this report wasn't due on the chief's desk by eight, I sure as shit wouldn't be here at the crack of dawn. This is messed up."

Now that was the Vince she knew and loved. All smiles and cockiness when things were going his way. Grumpy and whiny when they weren't. He was so thoroughly predictable. Best to leave him to his report in silence. She turned to Chad. "What's your story? You have a report due to the chief too?"

He shrugged and dropped into his desk chair. "Couldn't sleep and, since I snagged that murder out in the Valley yesterday, figured I might as well get in and work it."

Vince leaned back in his chair and looked over at Chad. "Why couldn't you sleep, Chadster? Your latest little gal pal keeping you *up* at night?"

The look Chad gave him could have curdled milk. "Fuck you, Vince."

Katie narrowed her eyes and shook her head. It was like working with children or, more likely, adolescent boys. "Really, guys. Don't care, don't want to hear about it."

Vince rolled his eyes. "We better be careful, Chadster, or Katie will run to Daddy and tell on us. Inappropriate workplace conversation."

Definitely adolescent boys. "As Chad said, fuck you, Vince."

His laughter filled the room. "Oh my, the lady does have balls."

Chad smiled. "You better not mess with her then. She can probably kick your ass." He looked over at Katie and winked. "Ignore him. You know what they say about guys like him…big mouth, little dick."

"Honest to God, you two are something else." She turned away and hit the power button on her computer to boot it up. Maybe if she ignored them they'd go away. A girl could dream.

"You know what else they say?" Vince said as he turned his attention back to his computer screen. "You can pick your friends but you can't pick your coworkers. Sucks to be you."

She corrected him. "You can't pick your family."

"Family, coworkers, it's all pretty much the same."

"Only in my nightmares," she said.

Quiet finally took over and Katie clicked on Internet Explorer to start her search. With some time to really work through Kyle's ideas she was bound to come up with something of interest. Yesterday while she was in court, he'd emailed her some additional thoughts, and she intended to use her resources to see what she might come across. She would start with searches in nearby counties to see if any cases that resembled Alida's disappearance popped up. Anything could help, even something little.

Thankfully the guys continued their own work and left her in peace. The room was pretty quiet except for the click of the computer keyboards. This was why she liked this time of day so much. It was peaceful and productive. She became quickly caught up in the information beginning to reveal itself.

Kyle wasn't too far off the mark. Less than an hour later she discovered the cases of three missing women in two nearby counties. Sonofabitch. How did she miss this before? It wasn't like law enforcement was isolated around here. Somehow, somebody should have connected the dots. By the looks of her research, obviously no one had picked up on it.

For a long time she stared at her screen while she tapped a pen on the top of her desk. After she thought it through she created a map and, taking the locations of each disappearance, marked it with a small red x. It made for a very interesting pattern. If this was, in fact, the work of one person, they went out of their way to grab victims from places where it would be hard to connect them. Very sneaky. Very effective.

She pushed back in her chair and put both hands on top of her head. This information created a completely different spin on things. She needed to adjust to this new paradigm quickly.

The hairs on the back of his neck stood up, and he whipped his head around to study the people passing him by, searching for the face that studied him back and listened in to his thoughts. It wasn't like him to react to others. Cool, collected, and unflappable, that was his style. So why all of a sudden did he have a really bad feeling that someone knew of his project? That wouldn't do. Few would understand the importance of his work.

With his left hand, he pulled sunglasses out of his pocket and slipped them on. Much better. He slowly moved his head to search faces again, confident the mirrored lenses of his glasses concealed his line of sight. Faces went past him: men, women, and children. Who or what was giving him the heebie-jeebies?

Nothing stood out. No one appeared focused on him beyond the normal glance of a passerby. It was just a regular day in the city. Cars were driving past in both directions on Broadway, always at exactly the correct speed limit, at least until well past the Public Safety

Building, aka the Spokane Police Department. People were coming and going from both the PSB and the courthouse, but no one caught his attention as being unusual. He continued down the steps and to the sidewalk, moving his gaze the whole time.

Still nothing jumped out at him, at first, anyway, and then he noticed two women making their way inside. He was certain one was the twin sister of the missing woman, Alida Canwell. They looked amazingly alike and yet there was a distinct difference between the two sisters. Though he couldn't articulate exactly what it was, he felt it in his heart. Instinct guided him to conclude this one wasn't special.

His gaze moved from the sister to the other one. Now she was interesting. There was something unusual about her, perhaps something dangerous. She was the kind he would keep his eye on.

Instead of heading straight to his car, he casually moved to one of the trees that dotted the landscaping outside the front of the building. He leaned a shoulder against it and watched the women walk to the doors. Was she going upstairs? Was she here for something with the sister? Too many questions about them, and as much as he wanted and needed to know, there was no way to answer a single one without raising other unwanted questions. That wouldn't be wise.

This unease made him jumpy, and he didn't like that either. Not knowing everything happening around him made him uncomfortable. Knowledge gave him power, and right now some of it was slipping away. Not good. But what could he do? The answer didn't please him. The word *nothing* wasn't in his arsenal.

He blamed the sister. Damn her anyway. Why couldn't she just let it go? He hated families that had a crusader. It made his job more difficult and the steps more delicate. Not that it stopped him from his important work. Nothing was impossible, even with opposition. It just created a little more work for him.

Once the women were out of sight, he pushed away from the tree and walked to the crosswalk on Broadway. The crossing sign was flashing Wait, and he did. It occurred to him as he waited that the knot in his stomach was no longer there. He glanced over his shoulder to the glass doors the two women had walked through minutes before.

The light changed and the crossing sign flashed Walk. He sauntered across the street with six other people who'd waited with him, noting that none of them gave him a second glance. He was just a regular guy heading to his car. Appearances were deceiving, especially when it came to his. He counted on it.

Down the block the neon lights of the bistro beckoned. A tall ale would be just the thing to help him relax, and unfortunately, it would also be the thing to draw attention to him. It was the middle of the workday, and he didn't need to be seen pounding down a brew. Rather than give in to temptation he walked by the bistro with a sigh of longing and headed to the sandwich shop instead. Nobody would look twice or remember a guy grabbing a sandwich.

And then he saw her, and suddenly his whole line of thinking shifted. The longing for an ale disappeared, as did his appetite. Maybe the feeling in the pit of his stomach had nothing to do with the sister and her mystery friend. Maybe, just maybe, it had everything to do with the woman in front of him waiting in line to order.

Really, it was too soon to go there, yet what could he do when God dropped her right into his lap? Her dark hair was long and shiny as it fell past her shoulders and down her back, contrasting beautifully to her bright-pink shirt. When she turned, blue eyes swept over him and a friendly smile crossed her lips. The shirt was cut low over her breasts, and a tattoo peeked out enticingly. Ink wasn't really his thing, but every once in a while an exception came along.

He was smiling too as he followed her out of the shop, his sandwich long forgotten.

❖

Thea hated coming downtown. Riddled with one-way streets, heavy traffic, and rude pedestrians, the trip was always a nightmare. Around the jail and courthouse, the parking was horrible, and that was being nice. Getting a decent spot was like winning the lottery, which of course meant she always ended up a million miles away.

Despite all the irritations associated with coming downtown, this afternoon it felt important to make the journey for a couple of reasons. First, she needed to know what was happening in Alida's case. Second, and she'd never admit it out loud, she wanted to see Katie. The more she was around her, the more she thought of her.

Yet not seeing her made her think about her even more. She couldn't shake it. Lorna wasn't too far from the mark last night.

So, instead of trying to pretend she wasn't attracted to Katie, why not just go with it? Besides, if making herself a pest helped bring her sister home, then all the better. She intended to do whatever it took to get Alida back safe and sound as soon as possible. That Katie was the key person involved just made it easier to be a pest. She squared her shoulders and held her head up, ready.

Until the instant Katie came around the counter, she thought she was pulling off cool-and-collected pretty well. Then there she was, so gorgeous in form-fitting black slacks and with a gun at her waist. Only sheer willpower kept Thea from dissolving into a jabbering ten-year-old girl. It wasn't her fault. Something about a woman cop sent her heart racing. Or maybe, if she was honest, this particular woman cop made her pulse hammer because she'd never experienced something like this before and Katie wasn't the first female officer she'd ever met.

"Come on back," Katie said as she held open a heavy security door. Thea eased by, inhaling Katie's fresh scent as she did. An urge to stop and savor the scent overpowered her, and she concentrated on the simple task of keeping her feet moving forward. Lorna followed without giving any indication she thought Thea's behavior odd. She was grateful neither Katie nor Lorna seemed to notice her inclination.

As much as Katie distracted her and her preoccupation with attempting to appear collected and calm, Thea didn't miss Lorna's expression. She noticed the change right before they walked up the last few steps of the Public Safety Building. Her body language shifted slightly, and then all of a sudden she looked around as though she believed someone was following them. Thea asked her outside what was wrong, but Lorna said it was nothing. She didn't believe her. Something kept her on edge.

Lorna wore the same cautious expression now, as they followed Katie back to a workstation surrounded by gray fabric walls about five feet high. Around them were similar workstations—some empty, some with heads bent toward computer screens or holding telephones to their ears. A low hum of activity permeated the room. In Katie's space, Thea dropped into one of two straight-back chairs, and Lorna took the other one. Katie sat in a black task chair and swiveled around until she faced them. Nobody said a word for at least a full minute, the sounds of the squad room a continuous thread of voices and movement.

Katie broke the tense silence, her face grim. "I have some good news and some bad news."

Thea's heart began to hammer for a different reason now. "You have a lead?" She didn't dare to hope, yet she did.

Chewing her lip a little, Katie nodded slightly. Thea liked the nod but wished the expression on her face was more optimistic. "In a sense, yes, I do. Unfortunately it's not in a good way, and that's the good news."

Now she understood the look on Katie's face. Her heart sank, and she bit her lip to keep it from trembling. "And what's the bad news?" Maybe if she got the bad news details first, the good news might sound better. She glanced over at Lorna, who stared intently at Katie as if soaking everything in. A frown line creased her forehead and shadows ringed her eyes.

Leaning forward in her chair and putting her elbows on her knees, Katie looked first at Lorna and then at Thea. "I don't know how to say this."

Just spit it out is what she wanted to scream. Instead, Thea put a hand on Katie's arm and forced her words to remain calm. "Please, just tell us."

Blowing out a breath, Katie spoke in a rush. "All right. I'm beginning to believe we have a serial killer on our hands and that Alida probably came into contact with him."

Serial killer was just about the last thing Thea was expecting Katie to say. She struggled to process those two horrible words. "Serial killer?" she whispered. Over the last twenty-four hours her thoughts had drifted in all sorts of directions, some of them very dark. This was something she'd never considered.

Katie nodded and blew out another breath. "It didn't occur to me either until I called my brother in Omaha. He's a neuro-psychologist, an expert in criminal cases, and he suggested that Alida's disappearance might not be an isolated instance."

Thea took some deep breaths and tried to quell the nausea that was setting in. "He was right?" Saying the words nearly made her throw up.

Katie's eyes were sad. "Looks like it. I considered it before I called him and actually ran some local checks. After talking with him, I widened my search parameters. That's when I hit pay dirt. Three other missing women with similar stories popped up. I didn't catch them because they were too spread out."

Three other missing women? How could this be? How could they miss something like that? "Alida was the only one local?"

"Sort of. One woman disappeared from Grant County, which is only about a hundred miles away. Another woman went missing from King County in the Seattle area, and the final one was from Kootenai County, just across the border in Idaho. The last one was very close, and I didn't catch it at first because I didn't run my search query across state lines."

With her right hand, Thea massaged the back of her neck. A dull ache was beginning to run up it and into the back of her head. Katie was right; the good news wasn't particularly good, even if it was a weak lead. Then again, it was progress, and there was much to be said for that. "So you have something to work with?"

Alida had been gone too long, and Thea wasn't dumb. The longer she was missing, the less likely they'd find her alive. The thought cut through her heart like a knife, yet she was forced to be realistic. She might never see her twin sister alive again. Even if that turned out to be true, finding her was still critical. She was out there somewhere, cold and alone. That wasn't something she could live with.

"Not a lead exactly, but it gives me a new avenue to explore, and I'm hoping like hell it points me to your sister." Katie sat back in her chair and clasped her hands together.

"I hope so too." Thea turned and looked at Lorna. "It's something, don't you think?" The hope in her voice made her sound like a little girl on Christmas morning.

Lorna nodded, but her eyes weren't focused on either Katie or Thea. They were scanning the room as though searching for some threat. She seemed far from engaged in the conversation that had just occurred.

"Lorna?" she asked again.

Lorna's eyes shifted until they connected with Thea. "Sorry," she said. "You were saying?"

As Thea suspected, Lorna hadn't caught a word of the conversation between her and Katie.

"It's encouraging that Katie has something to work with, don't you think?"

"Yeah." Lorna squeezed her hand. "Yeah, I do." For the first time since they got here, Lorna seemed engaged, though Thea wasn't confident Lorna knew what she was agreeing with.

"We're going to find her soon." Thea spoke with far more confidence than she felt. Maybe if she put voice to it, she could make it true. Again she was showing that little-girl optimism and she wasn't embarrassed about it.

Katie echoed her. "We will find her."

This is the kind of attitude Thea had hoped for from day one and was so grateful someone finally got it.

For five more minutes they talked about what Katie had discovered and where she was going next. Finally, the conversation trailed off until silence fell between them. There didn't appear to be anything left to say. Her hesitation to leave was twofold—she wanted to be here to know immediately about anything that could lead them to Alida, and she simply wanted to be near Katie. She didn't put voice to either one, so instead Thea and Lorna got up and left Katie to continue her work. It was the right thing to do even if it was the exact opposite of what she preferred.

Once they were outside, Thea turned and put a hand on Lorna's arm. She still wasn't engaged a hundred percent and Thea wanted to know why. Lorna wasn't the type to check out, or at least she never was before. "What was up with you in there? You were a thousand miles away."

Lorna rolled her head slowly as if trying to make sense of something. "Yeah, I was. It was really weird. About the time we hit the front doors it was like somebody was pouring ice water down my back. The oddest sensation hit me from the top of the stairs all the way through the door, and then inside, it was still like ghostly fingers were poking at me."

That explained a lot in a frightening sort of way. She didn't want to ask and couldn't keep herself from doing just that. "What do you think it means?"

Lorna was shaking her head now with conviction. "Damned if I know. It's not like what's happened to me before. Keep in mind I'm still pretty new to this psychic thing, and so far I've had visions or felt like I'm channeling vivid movies that show me what I need to see. This wasn't like that. It was a feeling but in a cold, rather icky way, to put it in technical terms."

That was plenty technical for her. Her desperation to find Alida had driven her to beg Lorna to come help. In reality Thea didn't know the first thing about psychics or what they could do. Even given her profound lack of knowledge, this didn't sound good. "I don't like it."

Running both hands through her short hair, Lorna leaned her head back and stared at the clear sky. "Back atcha, sister. Didn't light me up either. Something or somebody left a really black pall on this place. If I couldn't see the big blue sky up there I'd swear on a Bible a big black cloud covered everything. "

She wrapped her arms over her chest and let her gaze move across the faces of the people coming in and out of the building. "Maybe so many bad people have walked this ground it left traces of bad energy behind."

Lorna's eyes met hers and she didn't like what she saw there. "I'd agree with you, except I've been in two other police stations since this thing manifested itself, and nothing even remotely like this happened."

Her heart constricted and it felt a little like her air was being cut. She was the one responsible for asking Lorna to use her gift to find Alida, and she was doing exactly that. There were no rules, no guarantees, and no timelines. She got it and the fact that all they could do was keep going forward and, corny as it might sound, leave no stone unturned. One way or the other, they would find Alida and bring her home. Thea just wished the terrible feeling in the pit of her stomach would go away.

CHAPTER FOURTEEN

Well, this was a new and most decidedly unwelcome wrinkle. Were surprises going to just keep coming? It was bad enough Lorna could see dead people. Now she was being hit with the heebie-jeebies too. Some days it just didn't pay to get out of bed.

It surely had something to do with Alida, because nothing else made any sense. Since she got back to Spokane she'd focused all her energy on locating her, and in a weird kind of psychic way it made sense. Funny how six months ago this never would have occurred to her and now it was the new normal. Considering possibilities outside of the physical realm was becoming an everyday kind of thing. She wasn't thinking inside the box any more. She was way outside it these days.

As she thought about the weird feelings washing over her as she stepped up to the doors of the Public Safety Building, every nerve ending tingled as if it was happening again. This was different from the way Tiana McCafferty had asked for help. It was more like a bad, itchy rash that no matter how hard she scratched wouldn't go away.

God, this whole psychic thing really was crazy or, at the very least, making her crazy. She wanted to help, but so far she felt like she was running through peanut butter. Somewhere a clock was ticking and the minutes were passing much faster than she was moving.

Something needed to change except she was lost as to what it was. She had no clue where to look or what to do. When she was working on a particularly difficult project and got stuck, it was usually best to walk away and take some quiet time to focus. Then, suddenly, the brick wall she'd been running into again and again would crumble.

Maybe it was time for something like that now. It couldn't hurt and it just might help.

At the curb where Thea had parked the car at a three-hour meter, Lorna paused. Not wanting to hurt Thea's feelings by bailing on her for a while made her hesitate. She almost got in the car and abandoned her idea, except she needed to do something to bring things into clearer focus. "Thea, if you don't mind, I'd like to take a walk."

Thea, who looked tired and near defeat, pulled her hand back from the door handle and studied her. Whatever was going through her mind at this moment, it wasn't optimism. Lorna wanted to give her assurance but didn't want to lie. There was nothing she could offer to help ease her mind.

Thea started to put her car keys back in her pocket. "Sure. We can take a walk if you think that'll help."

Lorna shook her head. Clearly, Thea needed sleep more than a walk, and she wanted to be alone. "No, you don't understand. I need to think and I need to be alone to do that. Do you understand?"

A flicker of hurt crossed Thea's face. "Of course…"

She didn't understand and guilt tugged at Lorna's heart. If she didn't sense how important it was to try to jump-start her new skills, she'd cave and stay with Thea so she didn't feel as though she was being abandoned. "Please, it's nothing about you. I mean, I'm just getting in touch with this thing I have, whatever it is, and to be honest, I'm struggling. Right now I need to turn inward to plug into it. I can do that better all by myself."

Thea held her gaze, then nodded before once more reaching for the door handle. The hurt in her eyes was gone, and resignation seemed to drop down on her like a curtain call. Her voice echoed the weariness in her eyes and her body. "Give me a call when you're ready to head back to the house." She got into the driver's seat and fastened her seatbelt, the door still open. The sunglasses she slipped on hid the charcoal circles beneath her eyes.

Lorna tapped the top of the car. "You go try to get some rest. I'll hop a bus in a little bit."

Thea smiled and shook her head. "No, you will not. No reason for you to ride a bus when I'm just hanging around waiting for something to happen."

She shrugged and decided Thea probably wouldn't rest anyway. "Gotta admit, I'd rather not ride a bus all the way up north. It's not that I don't like public transportation, but I always end with a heavy smoker sitting next to me, and I hate that."

"Call me when you're ready and I'll come pick you up."

Lorna leaned down and gave her shoulder a squeeze. For the first time she noticed how thin Thea was. She was always lean but this felt like more than that. She made a note to make sure she got some food in her tonight. "You know I love you, right?"

Thea rested her head against the hand Lorna still had on her shoulder. "You say that to all the girls."

She winked and kissed the top of her head. "Only the pretty ones." She shut the car door. "Go get some rest. I'll call you in a little while."

After Thea pulled away, Lorna put her hands in her pockets and began to walk toward the river. As much as she loved the ocean and the rambling house she now called home, this place had something special that she missed. It took her five minutes to walk from the PSB to the center of the Monroe Street Bridge. With her arms resting on the concrete banister, she leaned out and stared at the river flowing strong and clear a hundred feet below. The air carried the fresh scent of the water and just a hint of moisture from the spray of the rapidly running water as it crashed over the basalt rocks. She was mesmerized.

Amazing how something so simple as standing in the middle of a bridge could clear her mind. Even with four lanes of steady traffic going north and south across the bridge creating a subtle vibration beneath her feet, the spot was soothing. She closed her eyes and breathed in the scent of her childhood home. The sweet familiarity of it eased the tension in her shoulders. She let her thoughts wander and reached out with her spirit. *Show me, Alida. Show me where you are.*

She waited, hoping, like with Tiana, something would come to her. It was a total bust. Nothing hit her beyond the feel of the cool spray of the water against her face. Not a single damn thing. She wanted to scream, maybe stomp her feet like a little kid.

Except she was pretty sure neither one would help her. And even worse, it would draw attention of the unwanted kind from those passing by. This bridge was infamous for being a favorite spot for jumpers. Throwing a tantrum would most certainly draw the attention of the Spokane Police Department, if not mental-health officials.

Opting not to draw unwanted notice, she instead settled for swearing under her breath. This thing the universe had cursed her with possessed its own mind about how it worked. Would be nice if she was privy to the how and why, but apparently the universe deigned to keep that little secret close to the vest.

Before someone decided she was considering jumping, she opened her eyes and walked south to the lights at Main and Monroe. Another block down and she was on Riverside Avenue. The main drag of the city, it was lined by many historic old buildings, the most beautiful of which was the Review Building with its corner tower. The building was home to the local newspaper and had been standing guard over the corner of Riverside and Monroe for over a hundred years. She meandered down Riverside until she hit the Spokane Transit bus station. It made her smile.

Like the Review Building, its permanence spoke to her. Some things never change, and she found a certain amount of comfort in that fact. The transit station covered an entire block, and the busses pulled into marked stops on the north and south sides. Groups of people clustered around the signs designating the different routes and waited for the bus doors to open. The people were interesting and ranged from students with backpacks to young mothers with strollers to businessmen carrying messenger bags. She could easily lean against the building and watch the dynamics of the various groups for hours. Instead, she walked through the automatic glass doors that opened as she stepped close. Inside, she rode the escalator to the second floor. The ride up the moving steps was her favorite because of the bronze cougar sculptures that stood in the beautiful waterfall feature separating the up and down escalators.

The majority of the folks milling around both the ground floor and the second story were curious: a mixture of young and old, clean-shaven and bearded, tattooed and pierced. It was the melting pot of the city. It had always fascinated her, and today it brought a bit of longing into her heart. But then a familiar voice caught her attention.

"Lorna!"

No, no, no. The fates wouldn't be that cruel. As the sensation of being watched grew, her back stiffened and if she could, she would have walked the other direction, pretending she didn't hear. It wouldn't work. She was cornered. Slowly she turned and smiled while pretending her teeth weren't grinding so hard her jaw hurt. Addy Courtland wasn't exactly her favorite person. Worse than the simple misfortune of being in the wrong place at the wrong time, Addy and Anna were pals. Good pals.

What she was doing here? It didn't make sense for a number of reasons, not the least of which was Addy drove a Mercedes and would never, in this lifetime, consider riding public transportation. In fact, Addy would consider taking public transportation far beneath her.

With her smile pasted on as convincingly as she could make it, Lorna said, "Hey, Addy." The woman enveloped her in a giant hug that almost pushed the breath out of her. She smelled of expensive perfume. "What on earth are you doing at the STA Plaza?"

"I just got out of a meeting with the director about a project we're partnering with them on." She pushed Lorna away but held onto her as she swept her gaze up and down. It was a bit like being checked out by a horny guy. Not comfortable and not welcome. "God, you look fantastic. It's so wonderful to see you."

"Nice to see you too." The words were nothing more than lip service. It wasn't nice to see her. It was frankly a pain in the ass. Truth be told, she could go the rest of her life without running into Addy, and it would be just fine and dandy.

Addy batted her expensive false eyelashes as she fixed her gaze on Lorna. As always her skin was flawless and her makeup perfect. Money could buy the best of everything. "Why are you here? Have you seen Anna? What do you think of her new place? It's gorgeous, don't you think?"

It was coming back to her in an uncomfortable rush of memory, the rapid-fire way Addy liked to talk. She always wondered how she managed to breathe amidst the nonstop barrage of words. The woman could talk this way for hours, and the best way to handle Addy was to simply wait her out. So that's what she did, and when Addy finally trailed off, Lorna unclenched her jaw.

"I'm here helping a friend." Keep it short. Keep it sweet, and do not let her know how unhappy she was about seeing her.

"Helping a friend?" Addy's brow wrinkled, and Lorna could imagine the wheels turning in her head. Most of the friends from before were *their* friends. Hers and Anna's. Addy would be thinking that as well, while wondering how Lorna could possibly be here helping one of them without Addy knowing about it. Funny how she conveniently forgot Lorna was born and raised here, which meant she had a great many friends long before she ever laid eyes on Anna. In Addy's world, that simply didn't make for a good story. Way too boring. It was much more interesting to throw in drama that would connect her back to Anna.

"Yes," she said, working to keep her voice calm and trying not to roll her eyes. "An old friend of mine."

"Oh, I see." But Lorna was pretty sure she didn't. Not interesting enough if the friend was only Lorna's, and she wasn't going to leave it be. Addy opened her mouth to say more and undoubtedly push for more details about whether Lorna was planning to see Anna, but she cut her off. She was not going there. She wouldn't do it for people she liked, and she sure as hell didn't intend to do it for someone she barely tolerated. Addy needed to butt out.

"I'd love to catch up, Addy." The lies just kept coming. "Unfortunately, I simply can't today. Thea is waiting for me and..." She made a point of looking at her watch. "I'm already late." Without giving Addy even a second to respond she turned and fled down the curving stairs that took her to the ground floor.

Not to be thwarted by Lorna's hasty escape, Addy made sure to have the last word. Some people never change. "I'll be sure to tell Anna I bumped into you."

Great. Just. Fucking. Great.

❖

Once more Katie stood on the last known place Alida had been before she disappeared. Why this one bothered her so much was a bit of a mystery. She totally got that at least part of it had something to do with the twin sister. No matter how professional she tried to keep it, her thoughts turned to Thea. She was beautiful, interesting, and talented. Any woman in her right mind would be attracted to someone like her. If it was all about Thea, it would at least make sense, but it felt like there was so more to it than that.

Or maybe she was totally off base and it really was all about Thea. Something about her tugged at Katie's heart. When she closed her eyes, she saw her face. When she sat in silence, she heard her voice. She swore she could smell the light sweet scent of perfume even when she was on the other side of the city. It was like she was in love, only she was the complete opposite of a love-at-first-sight kind of woman. In fact she had no problem admitting she felt that kind of thing was a crock of shit.

Worse than that, it was dangerous. Who knew what kind of pervert or criminal lurked inside the disguise of a beauty who made the heart flutter? More than once she'd witnessed the tragic result of a relationship based on pure lightning-fast emotion. She was so not going to be one of those women who took an emotional leap only to discover the reality was miles away from the pretty picture. No, she believed in the old-fashioned get-to-know-someone philosophy before she even came close to opening up her heart.

Then again, her style wasn't working out so well. She was chronically single. Almost, some might say, obsessively single. She preferred the term cautious. Or maybe it was scared. Yeah, definitely scared.

Her brother was oh so subtle in hinting she should perhaps seek some assistance in dealing with her commitment issues. She always told him he was way too much a shrink and that he couldn't turn it off even when he was with family. Deflection was one of the sharper tools in her bag of skills. Despite what she might say to her brother, in her heart, she got what made her tick and wasn't oblivious when it came to her own over-abundance of caution. But life moved so quickly, and she never got around to taking the time to learn to let go. Her job, her friends, her family—that was enough.

Or was it?

For the first time, the flutter that hit her heart felt totally different. Thea made her want to believe in more, and that was something no one else had brought out in her. But was Thea even interested in her?

Or for that matter was Thea even interested in women? The short answer? She didn't know, and therein resided the major source of her issues. It was hard for her to step outside her comfort zone when her mind was flooded with unanswerable questions. Not a place she liked to be. To trust and to put herself out there was an important step her brother would wholeheartedly approve of. In short, take a risk, and that's where she always found herself pulling back. Just like now.

This train of thought was getting her nowhere. Instead of focusing on her attraction to Thea, she turned instead to the work of finding Alida. The whole case so far frustrated the hell out of her and, in an odd way, motivated her as well. Dad had taught her well, and she went into every case intending to do the best job possible and help people who really needed her assistance. In that respect, this case was no different from the hundred others she'd handled to date. Despite her dedication to every case, this one was different. She was determined to solve it no matter what. No way did she plan to let Thea down.

Why? Pretty simple really. She wanted to impress Thea. No way could she get around the truth of that one, even if she tried lying to herself. Certainly she wanted to bring Alida home. That went without saying. It was always about the victim, regardless of what might be going on in the periphery. Like with all the families she worked with, she wanted to give Thea closure and, if at all possible, peace.

But what would they ultimately find? Her years in law enforcement gave her a leg up on how things like this worked. Unfortunately for Alida, the odds weren't in her favor. Katie wasn't telling her yet the chance of Alida coming home alive grew fainter with each passing hour. Statistically speaking, this would more likely be a case of recovery, not a reunion.

She was heartsick for Thea and her friend Lorna, who was trying in her own strange way to help. Though Katie didn't put much store in psychics, she couldn't deny what she'd seen with her own two eyes. Lorna possessed something otherworldly, and with her back up against the wall, what could they lose by giving her a shot? If Lorna could help in any way, she'd take it and, at this point, even hoped Lorna did come up with a lead.

The sound of an approaching vehicle made her turn. Surprise, surprise, it was another unmarked. Undoubtedly it was Vince…again.

He seemed to have some weird territorial connection to this place. She wouldn't be surprised if he'd already walked around and peed on everything to mark his territory. Why did he have to know every time someone came here? She narrowed her eyes as the car stopped. Maybe it was time for a little point-blank questioning. He might be the undersheriff, but that didn't excuse or explain odd behavior. She didn't like to consider the possibility that one of her brothers in blue might be involved. Then again, it wouldn't be the first time a cop went bad. Her daddy didn't raise a dummy…it didn't pay to be naive.

When Chad stepped out, she was shocked. She sure didn't expect to see him out here. He typically kept a pretty low profile and quietly went about working his own cases. Unlike Vince, Chad was calm and personable. His easy way with both victims and suspects made him a valuable resource to the department. Granted, she didn't know him well and didn't think anyone at the department did either. He was the kind of guy who did his work well and then went home. It wasn't a big deal. Some were just more reserved and private than others, which was an accurate characterization of Chad. She couldn't fault him for keeping to himself because she practiced the same philosophy.

All that said, it still surprised her to see him here. This was her case, and while Vince apparently took it upon himself to be her partner of sorts, no one else appeared to be overly interested in the case, or her, if she was being honest. Despite her family connections, she was still a woman, and many of her colleagues viewed that as a handicap and not the first choice for a partner. Every time she turned around lately, there Vince was, as though he'd appointed himself her unofficial partner. He was like a bad ache that wouldn't go away. But Chad was the complete opposite, making today's appearance all the more puzzling.

"Hey, Chad. What's up?"

He stuffed his hands in his pockets as he walked her way. "Curious," he said as he stopped next to her and studied the gravel parking area. "What do you and your partner find so interesting about this patch of land? You think if you stand here long enough, new evidence will magically appear?"

She barely heard the second question. "Vince isn't my partner."

He gave a wry chuckle. "Yeah, try telling him that. He's on your six whether you want him there or not."

She shook her head and tried not to sound like a bitch. "Trust me, I've tried to be very clear that I don't need his help. From what I can tell, he's deaf."

"So seriously, what's up out here? What have you found?"

"Nothing, Chad. God damn nothing. It's the definition of stupid."

"What?"

"You know, doing the same thing over and over again and expecting a different result. I keep coming back here hoping something will lead me to Alida. Nothing changes, and I'm no closer than on the first day."

He put a hand on her shoulder. "I think we've all been there a time or two. You'll figure it out, Katie. You always do."

She let out a long breath as she swept her gaze over the place where Alida's empty truck was discovered. "Yeah, I will this time too, but I have a sick feeling I'll be bringing home a body."

❖

"Tell me that one more time," Thea said to Grant as she sat at the table in her kitchen, an untouched mug of coffee growing cold in front of her.

Tears were running down Grant's pale cheeks, and his head was in his hands. "I couldn't sleep and I couldn't sit around doing nothing, so I started tearing the house apart. It was crazy to act that way but I couldn't seem to stop."

"You found the cell phone?"

"Yes, under the mattress." His words were barely audible.

"Jesus, Grant."

"She was cheating on me, and I guess she was still trying to keep it secret even though I was cheating on her too. It was so stupid. I knew what she was doing and she knew about me too. We were seriously messed up."

She rubbed the bridge of her nose with her thumb and forefinger. How did she not see what was happening to her sister's marriage? She knew things were far from perfect, just not quite how far. Again the knifing pain sliced through her heart at the realization Alida hadn't come to her. All along she thought they were as close as ever, but Grant was being straight with her. There was no point in lies.

Grant was running his hands through his hair, and his red-rimmed eyes were still filled with tears. How she wanted to hate him and blame him for what happened. It wasn't in her, and her anger would be misplaced. The marriage was obviously in big trouble, and the story most decidedly had two sides. He owned up to his, and the pain he was experiencing now was as real as it got. He, like Thea, was hurting to his soul. The betrayal and lies, those were things to deal with later. Right now, they had bigger issues to concentrate on.

"Okay, Grant, this might at least give us something to go on. Have you called the sheriff's department yet?"

He closed his eyes and shook his head. "I couldn't."

The small phone lay in the center of the table between them, and she resisted the urge to pick it up and dig into the call history. She stared at it for a moment, then looked over at him. "What do you mean, you couldn't? For God's sake, Grant, this is huge."

His words were heavy with weariness. "Yes, it is huge, but I don't know if I can handle what's inside it, and they'll probably start looking at me as a suspect again."

She let out a big breath and counted to ten. Calmly she said, "It doesn't matter how you feel, and that's the sorry truth of it. Think about it, Grant. This might lead them straight to a person of interest. You? Well, you have to realize they're going to be interested in you with or without a little girlfriend on the side. They always look at those closest—" the word victim flashed in her mind but no way in hell was that word passing her lips "—first."

He didn't seem to notice the hitch, or if he did, he wasn't going there either. Instead, he seemed tuned into the ramifications of his own actions. "True enough, but this makes it worse. It's so fucking real, and they'll think I hid the phone from them."

"Grant," she snapped. God, this whole conversation made her sick to her stomach, all of it, said and unsaid. What they'd done, what they'd done to each other. How they took what she always believed was a fantastic, loving partnership and turned it into something ugly and, worse, dirty. "Pull your head out. You have to call the deputy. If you don't, I will, and that'll make it look even more like you've done something to Alida."

His head snapped up and he blinked. "Jesus, Thea, I would never, ever hurt her. You might not believe this, but I loved her more than anything."

Thea just stared at him. *Keep telling yourself that.*

He closed his eyes and slowly opened them again. "Okay." He held up his hand as if to ward off any words of reproach that might come his way. "I mean I wouldn't hurt her physically. Ever. I know I've hurt her heart, and damn it, she hurt mine too. We should have been there for each other when it got bad. Instead we turned to others to fill whatever it was we couldn't fill ourselves. We were wrong and we both knew it. We can find a way to fix it, we can. You and I just need to bring her home safe." He tilted his head as he stared at the phone. "What about your friend?"

"Lorna?"

"Yeah, she's a psychic, right?" He didn't wait for an answer. "She could maybe get something off the phone."

It was a good thought, and she considered holding onto the phone until Lorna got back. Except she didn't know when that might be. She'd told Lorna to call her when she was ready for a ride back. Hours had ticked by without hearing from her. On the way here, she tried calling her, only it went right to voice mail. Now, she took out her own phone and tried one more time. Again, it went to voice mail. As much as she wanted to wait for Lorna it seemed wrong. This was something important and Katie needed to know about it now, not later.

"She might be able to, but we can't wait around to find out. We have to turn this over to the police. Sooner rather than later."

Tears welled up in his eyes again. "I need her to come home."

"Well, if you don't talk to Katie, I mean Deputy Carlisle, you're sure as hell not helping, and she won't be coming home." She was compelled to say the words, though they left a bitter taste in her mouth.

"Don't say that. She's coming home...she has to."

His voice broke and something in her broke as well. She wondered if it would ever be fixed.

❖

Thea was most likely going to be pissed that Lorna opted for the bus ride home. At the time it seemed like the right thing to do, and it turned out to be interesting, if nothing else. The elderly woman who sat next to her and talked nonstop until it was her time to disembark at Garland Street reminded her a bit of her grandmother. Lorna stayed on the bus and got off at the Five Mile Park & Ride lot. Again she opted not to call Thea and instead walked up the long ascending road from the Park & Ride to Thea's house. The day was beautiful, the air warm and sweet. It cleared her head, and by the time she reached the top of the hill she felt more energized. Thea might very well be angry with her, but she was confident the decision was the right one.

She reached out for the front door just as her cell rang. Rather than going in, she stepped back down to the lawn and looked at the display. As she saw the name that popped up, her heart leapt.

"Hey," she said, and smiled.

"Miss you," Renee said in a breathy voice. "Do you intend to come back here soon?"

She closed her eyes and pictured Renee's beautiful face. God, how she wanted to be there right now. "Soon, I hope." As much as she longed to be with Renee, her commitment to being here was solid. She couldn't walk away.

"Have you made any progress?"

The joy of hearing Renee's sweet voice was overshadowed by the despair filling her at the thought of Alida out there somewhere alone and afraid. She wanted, no, needed, to bring her home. Alive or…

"No, still nothing."

"You're going to find her. I have faith in you."

"I appreciate that, and I'm glad somebody does."

Renee's voice went quiet. "I've had faith in you since the minute I laid eyes on you, all sleepy-eyed and in your best sweats. You were pretty hot that morning, just in case I've never told you."

Despite the heaviness in her heart, she smiled. "How is it that no matter how down I'm feeling, you bring me up?"

"You don't really understand, do you?"

"Understand what?" She wasn't stupid yet wasn't following where Renee was going with this.

"Precisely."

Sometimes they really did speak different languages. "You're being cryptic again."

Renee laughed lightly. "Maybe, but I don't plan to explain it to you."

"So you plan to leave me hanging?"

"No, I'm going to leave you thinking. Once again, I have faith that you'll figure it out."

"You drive me crazy, woman."

"I know. Isn't it fun?"

The smile spreading across her face spoke to the truth of Renee's words. Fun was an understatement. Every day was an adventure filled with playful banter, encouragement, and love. It was fun and frightening all at the same time.

Lorna leaned against the doorframe and looked out into the distance. The neighborhood was lovely, the sky blue and clear, the traffic light. This was a wonderful place to live. Once not so long ago this city was her home and she'd been content. Now, she was a visitor, and surprisingly it didn't bother her. Instead of feeling sad, she couldn't wait to get back across the mountains to her house, to Clancy, to Renee.

CHAPTER FIFTEEN

The Watcher's head came up and he studied the blue sky. Was it in the sun? Or perhaps in the clouds that floated above him in shapes that shifted and changed? What?

Whatever it was, unease settled like a massive ache in his bones. How he wished he were not anchored to this place. She needed him. Of that he was most certain. She was lost and trying to find that place between this world and the next, where the answers she searched lay nearly hidden. Her struggle reached him in a wave of frustration. If he were there, he could gently guide her to vision.

A bold breeze blew in from the ocean waters, making him shiver. The waves crashed against the rocks in a symphony of rhythmic chaos. It wasn't the cold that rippled uneasily across his skin; it was something much darker. He'd felt it here in this place in the time before she came and banished the darkness that had lived in this place for so many years. The change here was dramatic, and for the first time in decades, light penetrated the gloom. Until today, and once again the darkness tried to intrude. It was faint, as if coming from a long way off, and indeed he believed it did.

Though grounded by the boundaries of this place, he was nonetheless tuned into her as if they were physically connected. Never before was his connection to another so deep and all-consuming. What tried to touch her touched him as well. What tried to hurt her hurt him. With each passing day the oneness he felt with her grew stronger, and that was why he now paced back and forth along the lonely beach, his big feet sinking into damp sand. Waves washed ashore erasing his footprints as if they were never there, as if he was never there.

Her search pulled at her soul, and something evil pushed back. That's what he was feeling now, and that he was stuck here, unable to give her strength, made him want to curse. He did not for it was not his way, and there would be no point for no one would hear him.

Solitude. Isolation. Silence. All were part of his sentence. Every day he prayed for release and redemption. Every day he tried to redeem himself in the eyes of his God.

Every day he failed.

This day was no different. She needed him, and he was unable to do anything except let her down. Alone and searching, she had no one to guide her to the truth. Another of the tests blocking his way home and he refused to fail. It went beyond his desire for personal redemption. She was special. She deserved more from him than failure. If he held power at all in the moment, it was in the words etched into his soul from Psalm 37. His lips moved as he quietly repeated, "Though the wicked draw his sword and bend his bow to slaughter the honest and bring down the poor and needy, his sword will pierce his own heart…"

❖

Lorna almost said good-bye, and then Renee said the three words guaranteed to melt her heart. "I miss you." She was such a goner, and she could tell herself different all day long, but it wouldn't change a thing.

"You have no idea how much I miss you and Clancy," she admitted.

Renee's laugh was light and cheerful. "I should be jealous because it's very clear he misses you too. He keeps going to your room trying to find you."

That made her smile. She could see the big dog trotting into her room and jumping up on her bed. One thing about a German shepherd, they don't ask permission. He decided her bed was his shortly after he arrived with Renee. Funny how it didn't bother her at all. She liked to see him stretched out on it.

"Anything new on your place?" A sick lump settled in the pit of her stomach. Sure, they both shared those all-important big three words. They didn't change things much. Lorna lived in the big house by the sea, and Renee lived and worked in Seattle.

Lorna had already proved she couldn't sustain a relationship when she lived in the same house with a woman, so how in the hell would she make one work long-distance? The bitter answer to that question was she couldn't.

"Well, now that you mention it, beautiful, as a matter of fact there is."

A light note in Renee's voice made the sick lump spread and grow. Here it comes...she hoped she didn't throw up on Thea's front porch. "Oh," she said as lightly as she could, given the inevitable bad news about to come her way.

"The repairs are nearly done and the place looks fantastic. I can't believe the beautiful work they've accomplished. As big a pain as it's been dealing with the insurance company, I have to hand it to them. The contractor they pointed me to is a magic man. He's turned a lump of coal into a diamond."

"That's great," she said. That sucks, she thought.

"Oh, it's better than great. I'm so amazed and happy."

"When are you moving back?" She couldn't believe she actually forced the words to pass her lips and managed not to sound like a pissy little kid.

There was a pause before Renee said, "About that..."

"Yeah?" Here it comes, the easy letdown. The *let's always be friends.*

"I've had an offer to sell the whole building."

She opened her mouth to try to say something gracious but then snapped it shut as the words hit her brain. What? Did she really hear that right? "Sell?"

"Yes, ma'am, and it's an unbelievable offer. I knew I was in the right place at the right time when I bought the building after my divorce. But I didn't know how right until a commercial real-estate agent approached me yesterday." She spoke more quickly and excitedly.

"Are you thinking about selling?" That really didn't make any sense. Whenever she talked about the store and the home she'd created from the shell of the building, her love for it was clear. Selling and walking away just didn't ring true.

"Well." Renee's voice held a note of hesitation. "Kinda depends."

"On?" She knew there was a catch.

"You, actually."

That wasn't quite what she expected to hear. What did she have to do with Renee's business or the decision to sell it? Giving financial advice wasn't her strong suit either. She was a damn good technical writer, and if she wanted advice on formatting a manual, well, then she'd come to the right person. Whether or not to sell a valuable asset? Not so much.

"I can't tell you whether you should sell your building."

Renee's words slowed down and so, too, it sounded like, did her earlier enthusiasm. "I wouldn't put you in that position, but here's the deal. If I sell, I want to take some time to figure out what to do next. I mean, the shop has been my life for quite a while, and where I take my life if I accept the offer is a giant mystery. "

Comprehension dawned and a flicker of hope began to bloom. Tears pricked at her eyes, and she pressed her fingers against her closed eyelids. The last thing she wanted to do was let her expectations get ahead of her. "You need a place to stay while thinking things through?"

"Why, yes, I would."

"I have a place." She said the words softly, hoping her voice didn't echo her desperation.

"Why, yes, you do." Lorna could hear the joy in Renee's words.

For a long moment she just took in deep breaths, and then she summoned her strength. "I love you, Renee."

Renee's laughter was light, tinkling silver bells. "I was really hoping that's what you'd say. Then it's okay with you if I take the offer and stay with you a bit longer?"

"More than okay. You can stay as long as you want." With all her heart she wanted to say, forever.

"I can't tell you how happy that makes me."

That made two of them. As happy as she was about this turn of events, she was equally interested in the real-world stuff. She might not be the financial guru, but the business end of things intrigued her.

"I'm curious. How much were you offered for the building, if you don't mind me asking? You won't hurt my feelings if you tell me it's none of my business."

Renee didn't even hesitate. "Oh, baby, you're not going to believe this. I had to see it in writing before I would."

"And?" Now she was even more curious.

"A cool million."

❖

Katie turned off her digital recorder and put it to the side, along with her note pad. For a moment she sat at the interview table and stared at her hands. She wanted to say she wasn't surprised, but honestly she was, a little. Same old song and dance she'd heard a hundred times in domestic situations, except for a little twist in this one. Usually only one spouse was having an affair. The fact both of them were, or had been if she could believe Grant, made it unique. Talk about two messed-up people.

It also put a different spin on the investigation. From day one Grant was a person of interest, which was nothing out of the ordinary. The spouse was typically number one on the list, for good reason. More often than not, they were the responsible party. Like anything, though, there were always exceptions, and Grant could very likely be one of them. She sure wasn't ruling it out, just as she wasn't ruling him out as the one responsible for Alida's MIA status.

Even so, Grant was different from the typical cheating spouse. He'd come across from the very beginning as straight up, and he wasn't faking his distress at his wife's disappearance. Through the years she'd seen enough forced emotion to detect the difference in a heartbeat. While it didn't get him off the hook, it lent weight to his words. He was still on her suspect list because sometimes that very real emotion created fatal violence.

What made this one different was she hadn't expected to find out the victim was also playing the field. That knowledge widened her field of suspects by a lot. The problem was, the husband professed to have no clue as to the identity of his wife's lover. He only knew there was one.

"What do you think?" Thea asked her after Grant left with another deputy, who escorted him out.

She looked at Thea, who'd showed up at her office for the second visit today, only this time with Grant in tow rather than Lorna. When Grant finished explaining how he discovered the cell phone, he looked completely defeated and asked to leave, while Thea asked to stay behind for a few minutes. That was just fine with Katie.

She blew out a breath and met Thea's eyes. "This phone could help a great deal or not at all. Obviously the secret phone meant Alida and her friend were being careful. Once we have a chance to go through the phone, we'll know exactly how careful. Thea, you really didn't know about this?"

Darkness flowed over Thea's lovely face and she felt a little bad for putting it there, but really, how does a person not know her twin sister is keeping a giant secret? She figured all twins were too close for secrets, even if that was painting the twin relationship with a brush a little too broad.

"No, I really didn't. I can't believe she kept this from me. It's like I didn't know her at all."

Judging by the sorrow that seemed to physically press down on Thea's shoulders, apparently this set of twins might not have been that close. "It happens," Katie said gently.

"Not to me and Alida. We've always been open and honest with each other." Thea's words were bitter.

"Don't beat yourself up over it." Katie put a hand on Thea's arm. "We all have our secrets, and just because you two are twins, human nature is still the same. Some secrets are little. Some are big. But we all have them. What's important is what we do with this one now that it's out in the open."

Tears welled in Thea's eyes. "That's the problem. What do we do with it?"

Good question. "We start digging deeper, beginning with this phone."

"I should have waited for Lorna," Thea said as she stared past Katie and out the window behind her. "I should have let her try before we brought it to you."

Part of her thought that might not have been a bad plan. Then the cop part of her dismissed the idea just as fast. It was amazing what their lab could do with electronic equipment these days, and the sooner they got started on the phone, the better.

As if he was standing outside listening to them—and that wasn't out of the realm of possibility—Vince opened the door and stepped inside. "What do you have, Carlisle?"

She resisted the urge to tell him she'd handled it and opted for being professional instead. Technically he was her boss, so good politics told her to play nice, especially with a civilian in the room. Daddy had taught her how to deal with the politics, even if it did gall her more often than not. She handed him the phone, which she'd placed in an evidence bag as soon as she got it out of Grant's hands, then explained how and where it was discovered.

Vince was nodding and turning the bag over in his hands. "This is good. I'll take it and have it checked."

It was her case and the phone had been brought to her. It was all she could do to keep the resentment out of her voice. She hated when one of the guys tried to step into a case she was lead on. "I can—"

"I got it, Carlisle. You finish up here."

He almost made it out with the phone, and then vindication was hers. She managed to keep the smile off her face when Brandon sauntered into the room looking, well, looking like typical Brandon in tight jeans, a bright-orange shirt, and Chuck Taylor tennis shoes. Funny thing was, he actually made it all look good. He was a strange one, but he was a cute strange one.

"You rang, Detective Carlisle? Something about a phone you need me to dissect."

Vince spun and glared at the younger man. "I got it."

Brandon raised an eyebrow. "Whatever you say, Boss. I got the impression my mad skills were needed for this one."

Katie was pleased to see the look of frustration that passed over Vince's face. He was a seasoned law-enforcement officer and possessed mad skills of his own, just not the kind they needed to reveal the secrets within the cell phone. Even Vince knew it; she could see it on his face.

For a moment no one said a word, and then Vince slapped the phone into Brandon's hand and said, "Fine. Get it done." He paused before leaving, and she sensed he was waiting for her to react. He left, apparently satisfied that she was going to play nice and not make any snide remarks.

Katie turned back to Thea and hoped her irritation didn't show. But Thea wasn't looking at her; she was staring at the open door Vince just walked through. "Is he always like that?" Thea asked.

Katie almost laughed. "Afraid so."

"Oh yeah, man," Brandon said. "He can be so shitty."

She raised an eyebrow as she ever-so-slightly shook her head. Brandon had the good sense to look sheepish.

Thea was still staring at the doorway Vince had just disappeared through. "I sure hope he's good."

Vince pissed her off on a regular basis, and today was just one in a string of those days. Another thing her dad had taught her was to see things as they really were, and that included Vince. So, even as irritated as she was by him, she had to be honest. "Yes, he is, and trust me, Thea, he'll help us figure this out."

"Dude didn't want to give it up though, did he?" Brandon was looking at the phone through the clear plastic evidence bag he held up to the light.

Katie agreed. For whatever reason, Vince seemed intent on inserting himself in every aspect of this investigation and the small phone his personal piece of evidence. "You know how he is, Brandon."

Nodding his head enthusiastically, he backed her up. "Yup. Guy's got a serious control-freak thing going on. Not cool, if you know what I mean. Hey, I'm Brandon." He held his hand out to Thea. "You're the sister."

Thea nodded and accepted his outstretched hand. "Yes, I'm Thea."

Brandon's head bobbed and his eyes searched her face. "Freaky how much you look like her. Well, not exactly like her." His head tilted. "Your eyes are different, and she had that little scar right here." He touched a spot on his chin.

Thea's eyes narrowed, and she seemed to put a little more distance between her and Brandon. "How would you know that?"

The tone in Thea's voice mirrored her own reaction to Brandon's breezy statement. His words were light and quick, yet they had a level of detail that didn't make sense.

Brandon shrugged. "Easy, the pictures." He tapped a finger to his chest. "I'm the go-to guy for all things techy around here, and I put together the digital file. Takes hours to really do those files right, and by the time it's done, I'm real familiar with the faces I work with, like your sis. Then I see you sitting here and it's whoa, twin city. Hits me how freaky alike you are until you look real close. Then you see the differences. You're both real pretty though."

The lines around Thea's eyes eased, and Katie sensed she was appraising him as the character everyone in the department knew him to be. Brandon was the kind of guy who was true to his own individuality.

Thea bit her lip, then said, "Thanks, I think."

With a slight nod, he turned to leave. "I'll get this thing picked apart, and you'll get the goods as soon as I know."

"Thanks, Brandon. Call me when you know something."

"Copy that," he said with a wave as he walked through the door.

Katie turned her eyes to Thea. "Brandon's good, Thea. This phone gives us another avenue to follow, and he'll make sure we get anything and everything we can from it. Don't let his quirky personality fool you."

A shadow crossed Thea's face, and she could tell Brandon's earlier words about how much she and Alida looked alike bothered her. Sometimes crap just rolled out of his mouth years before his brain engaged. There was a very good reason he wasn't a field guy. His room full of computers was the perfect place for a guy whose interpersonal skills constantly required tutoring.

"That's good, and if you're comfortable with him, I am too."

"He'll pull whatever there is to find out of the phone."

"Even so, we still don't know who she was seeing. What his name is. Where he's from. Even with that phone we have nothing, and she's still as lost as before." Despair colored her words.

Katie wanted to tell her she was wrong, except she wasn't. The best thing she could do, however, was try to keep things on a positive note. "Someone will know something. We just have to dig a little harder to find what we need. There's a trail somewhere and we'll discover it. It could very well start with this phone."

Abruptly, Thea stood up from the table. "You want to get a drink?"

Katie cocked her head. The question was pretty random. "A drink?"

"Yeah, you know, ice in a glass, booze over the ice, nice and relaxing." Then she stopped and looked a little sheepish. "Oh, wait, you're probably on duty for a while, and this was a very inappropriate invitation. I'm sorry."

Katie shrugged. Why not? Random could be good. "Actually, I'm off duty. I was just about to head home when you guys got here. So, sure, a drink would be nice. Where would you like to go?"

"My place."

❖

Lorna was surprised to find the front door locked. Or maybe not. A woman who lived alone really shouldn't leave her front door unlocked, even if she did have a guest staying with her. She walked around the house and tried the back door. It was open, though once inside she realized pretty quickly that she was alone. Back in the empty kitchen she wondered where Thea might have gone. Could they have found Alida? Only then did she think to check her messages, and sure as the world, there was a text from Thea saying she was heading downtown to talk with Katie again.

One mystery solved and a new one created. Why did she need to go back down to the sheriff's department? What hadn't they covered this morning that was so urgent now it required a second trip? Or had something happened while Lorna was downtown wandering around like a nomad? The latter made her angry at herself for being so selfish she'd left Thea to handle potentially bad news alone. As a so-called good friend she sucked.

She punched in Thea's number, surprised to hear the ring right outside the back door. A second later Thea walked in, and Lorna's calm demeanor put her worst fears to rest. Whatever had taken her back to Katie's office, it wasn't worst-case scenario.

"You rang?" Thea said as she put her bag on the kitchen counter.

"Freaked me out when you weren't here. What's up? Did they find her?"

A frown shadowed Thea's face and she shook her head. "No, nothing like that."

"Then why go back down to the sheriff's department? Your text scared the crap out of me."

Thea sighed. "Grant found a cell phone between the mattress and box springs."

"A cell phone?" She was so entrenched in thoughts of bad news, it took a second for Thea's explanation to sink in.

"It was Alida's, and she'd taken some pains to conceal it from Grant."

"But…" And then it hit her. "Oh."

"We think she used it to call him."

"Why didn't you wait for me? I would really like to have held it to see if I could pick anything up."

Thea gave her a long look. "How many missed calls do you have on your phone?"

"What?" Lorna fumbled with her phone and hit the button showing the missed calls. "Crap."

"I tried you over and over." She looked up and met Thea's eyes. "I'm so sorry. I wasn't paying attention."

"I would have waited, but I thought we needed to get the phone to the police as soon as possible to try and figure out who she was calling."

"Do we know who he is yet? Were they able to track any of the calls to the secret guy?"

Thea shook her head again. "Not yet. They're checking it now. As soon as Katie knows, we'll know."

That the police had a possible new lead was good. She only wished she'd had a chance to handle it before they took it in. Tactile contact sometimes triggered knowledge, and missing the chance to give it a shot made her sad. Not that she blamed Thea. If she'd given Thea a call to come get her like she said she would, she wouldn't have blown her chance to hold the phone first. The fault rested squarely on her own shoulders. "I hope it helps."

"So do I." Thea walked over and patted her on the back. "Now, did your walk help?"

Kind of hard to say whether her detour this afternoon did much good. The interlude with Addy certainly didn't. Still, she did feel a little clearer and more focused. Her sixth sense wasn't quite up to the same speed she'd experienced back at her house, but this was all new. Maybe she wasn't giving herself enough time to let it all jell. Or, and right now she hoped it wasn't so, maybe what had happened with Catherine and Tiana was a fluke. Perhaps she wasn't some kind of psychic after all and she wasn't going to be able to do a damn thing to help Alida.

Actually she was feeling a little different. Her body sort of buzzed, and the sharpness she felt couldn't be a coincidence. Despite her doubts, she really didn't think her *powers* were a fluke. If there was a veil between the worlds of seen and unseen, it was parted for her. All she needed to do was figure out how to part it when she needed to. "Yeah, I actually think it did."

Now Thea hugged her with one arm. "I'm glad, though I'm a little less glad my cell didn't ring with a call from my dear friend saying she was ready for a ride home."

Lorna put an arm around Thea's waist and hugged her back. "About that."

"Yes, indeed, about that."

She told her about running into Addy and how she'd jumped on a bus to get away from her. "It was a chicken-shit move, but it worked. I should have called you. Should have been here when you needed me. I'm so sorry."

"Oh, Lorna, I'm the one who's sorry. If not for me and Alida, you wouldn't even be here to have to deal with uncomfortable situations with so-called old friends. I call myself one of your friends, and yet I impose on you. On so many levels it's not right."

That Thea was apologizing to her under these circumstances made her feel ashamed of herself for all the self-pity. Big fucking deal if she was uncomfortable because of a chance meeting. In the big picture it didn't mean a damn thing. "I'm a tough bitch," she said as she placed a kiss on the side of Thea's head. "And nobody, not even Addy, can keep me from being here with you."

❖

Earlier, Katie had sent Thea on ahead with the promise to be there shortly. She wanted to take the high road and leave the cell phone with Brandon while keeping Vince in the loop. Screw the high road. It was her case, she was lead, and he was butting in. It seemed like every time she turned around, there he was. He didn't need to be in the loop at all.

Downstairs, her bad luck held. Vince was leaning over Brandon's shoulder. The phone was connected to one of Brandon's computers with a cable. On the screen were half a dozen numbers.

Brandon looked up and smiled. "Hey, Katie. Just in time to take a little look-see."

"Anything?" she asked, her gaze on Brandon while at the same time she pretended Vince's continued presence didn't piss her off.

Vince glanced over at her and shook his head. "Nothing helpful."

"Dude, I've pulled up more helpful information than you have." Brandon rolled his eyes.

"But all the calls?" It was obvious by what was up on the monitor that Alida had made a lot of calls, and the string of numbers was identical. Surely there was something in that.

Brandon leaned back in his chair. "She was a chatty thing."

"Maybe so. Still doesn't give us squat since they all went to the same burner phone. Canwell and her squeeze were apparently very careful." Vince sounded disgusted.

Damn it, another dead end. She hadn't realized how much she was hoping the phone would be the key to finding Alida. When were they going to get a break on this case? "There's nothing we can use?"

Vince stood and stuffed his hands into his pants pockets. "No prints from any unidentified person, no calls other than to the untraceable burner phone. I'd say we're in exactly the same place we were before the hubby brought this in."

"I was really hoping it'd tell us something."

"Typical nothing. You're chasing ghosts here, Carlisle. It's the husband. It's always the husband."

She took a deep breath and let it out before answering. "So you've already solved the case, is that it, Vince?"

He shrugged. "Don't let a pretty face sidetrack your good sense. I've seen the way you look at the sister. You and I both know the perp is most likely someone very close to her, like her husband. So just because the sister doesn't think it's the husband doesn't mean it isn't."

Fury roiled inside and she wanted to snap back at Vince. One more lesson from Dad...don't react, even when you're sure you're right. "I know my job, Vince, and I'll grant there's merit to your position. I also know that if we focus only on the husband, we could very likely miss the real killer. Sometimes these things aren't cut-and-dried."

"And most times they are."

She studied him for a long moment. Why he was so intent on laying the blame at the feet of Alida's husband? Despite how she felt about Vince, he really was a good cop, and good cops didn't get fixated on a single person before ruling out all possibilities. They hadn't even come close to ruling out everyone close to Alida.

"Just let me do my job, Vince, and if it turns out you were right all along, I'll bow to your expertise."

Again he shrugged and turned to walk away. "Whatever you think you need to do, Carlisle. It *is* your case."

"Man, that guy is such a dick," Brandon said after Vince was out of earshot.

"Be careful, Brandon. I swear he has our offices wired."

His head tipped up and his gaze moved over the ceiling. "Naw, I sweep the place for bugs every day."

Good old Brandon. He had a way of making her smile regardless of how pissed off she was. Helped, too, at least until she got in her car. As soon as she was inside with the door shut, the quiet settled over her and her mind zoomed back to Vince and the way he pushed to take the cell phone. It would be so much easier if he'd just butt out and leave her to work her case the way she always did.

In the end, she fumed all the way to Thea's house. At least until the moment she opened the door, and then all her distress fled. Just seeing Thea's face took the sting out of everything that happened before she got here. She stepped through the doorway feeling suddenly better. Inside, the house was comfortable and inviting. Thea still looked tired, but at least here she seemed calm.

"What's your poison?" Thea asked, pointing to an array of bottles inside a glass-fronted cabinet.

She swept her gaze over the bottles until it settled on a familiar label. "Scotch."

"Rocks?"

The woman caught on quick. "Yes indeed." Good liquor. Good instincts. Good company. Didn't get much better than that.

Thea smiled, and for a moment, the sadness fled from her face. The effect was dazzling and breathtaking. "A girl after my own heart."

She watched as Thea pulled the bottle from the cabinet and poured the golden liquid into two crystal glasses. After Thea handed her one of the drinks they walked out to the paver-brick patio. Outside, Thea built a fire in the raised pit. The fragrant wood crackled and popped as the fire took hold. Warmth and the scent of tamarack floated through the night air. It was beautiful and peaceful and, if not for the reason that had brought them together in the first place, romantic.

"Tell me about you and your sister," Katie said as they settled next to each other on the padded patio sofa.

She softly tapped her fingers against the ice-filled glass with the expensive scotch. Thea knew how to buy her booze, and, after the exchange with Vince down in the lab, it was very much appreciated. She leaned back against the cushions and looked around. This was space designed for comfortable entertaining. The back of the house opened onto a large deck created from the kind of decking material designed to last for decades. A glass-topped patio table surrounded by six matching chairs was perfect for outdoor dining. Five steps down and an expansive brick patio spread out below the deck. In the center was the custom-built fire pit they sat around now. The yard was obviously designed for privacy, with trees, flowering bushes, and flowers planted along the six-foot perimeter fence. It was clear Thea spent a fair amount of time and money creating her own private oasis.

Out here on the attractive and comfortable patio, sitting on the wicker sofa with its deep, comfortable cushions, it was nice. Despite that, she could barely sit still. It had nothing to do with the location and everything to do with the woman seated next to her sipping from her own glass of scotch.

Funny how she could go along with her life, as her grandmother liked to say, fat, dumb, and happy, and then boom, one woman walks into it and stirs things up. That's how she felt right now: stirred up.

Her mind whirled with the possibilities that Grant's discovery of the secret cell phone brought up and the web of lies he and his wife had been spinning for everyone around them. She'd follow those threads and hope something in there would lead her to Alida, even if at the moment the cell-phone lead appeared to be a bust.

She was also caught up in the aura of the woman next to her. She couldn't help it. Thea was interesting and beautiful and alluring. It had been a really long time since anyone had captured her attention like this, and never once had it happened in the blink of an eye. Crazy as it seemed, she'd been infatuated the moment she laid eyes on the dark-haired beauty, and that wasn't the way a good cop reacted in life or especially in the line of duty.

What really bothered her even more than the unusual speed of her attraction to Thea was that she had no idea how Thea felt. So far she'd been nothing except gracious, forthcoming, and always available for Katie's on-going questions. Not surprising, given how much she wanted to find her sister. Katie didn't want to mistake her quickness to make time for Katie as anything more than a family member helping law enforcement to the best of her ability.

She could tell herself to keep it on a professional level all she wanted, but her heart longed for it to be deeper. Her mind cautioned her not to make it out to be more than it was. But she wanted it to be a heartfelt connection, and the truth of it surprised her as much as it would anybody who knew her well. She wasn't the kind of woman who jumped first and asked questions later. Oh no, she always asked questions first, and jump? No, she never jumped.

She took a sip of the drink, loving the smoothness of the liquor and appreciating the way it soothed her jumping nerves. Given that she was the cop and expected to be the calm and rational one, it wouldn't do for Thea to know how twitchy she really was at the moment. After one more healthy sip, she turned to study Thea.

Holding her drink between her hands, Thea was focused on the firelight glowing through the amber liquid. She didn't turn Katie's way as she said, "I always thought we were the perfect siblings. We were tight in a way only other twins can understand, and I never minded the fact there were two of us. I know some twins resent that they have to share everything, but not me. I don't believe Alida did either. It was the two of us against the world, and it was great. There's something really special about the feeling that you're never alone."

An echo of something sad filled her words. "I hear a *but* in there."

"I suppose you do, and really, it's a brand-new one. I'm still reeling from everything I've learned. I want to close my eyes to shut it all out and convince myself there's no way Alida wouldn't come to me when she found out she was pregnant or when she was hurting at the loss of her baby. There's no way she'd get involved with another man and not tell me. Except I can't deny any of those things because I feel the truth of them all the way into my bones. She shut me out."

"She didn't tell you any of it, did she?"

Thea shook her head. "I wish she'd felt she could trust me, but obviously she didn't."

"How do you feel about it?" As soon as the words were out of her mouth she thought of how stupid they sounded.

"Hurt. Sad. Disappointed." She looked over at Katie with tears in her eyes. "Like I'd somehow betrayed her, and she didn't trust me anymore."

Katie pressed her lips together and felt bad about even asking because it was clear how painful this was to Thea. All she could do now was damage control. "I don't think that was it at all. I didn't know her, but from everything I've discovered so far, she didn't seem like a person who kept secrets without a really good reason. I don't believe she'd hurt you if she could avoid it."

Tears fell from Thea's eyes. If Katie didn't feel awful before, she sure as hell did now. Some kind of cop she was to bring someone she was supposed to be helping to tears.

Thea turned her tear-stained face to Katie. "God, you have no idea how much I want to believe that. All of it seems so unlike her. Maybe Alida and Grant were having issues, but it just doesn't feel right that they would risk throwing away a relationship with more ups than downs. Neither one of them is that flaky. Losing the baby had to be devastating, and despite the strain of their loss I still believe they were a solid couple. They were the kind who could make it through whatever happened."

Katie didn't know why, but she reached over and put her hand over Thea's. It was cool, as if she were standing in a windstorm instead of sitting next to the warmth put off by the crackling fire pit. She fully expected Thea to pull away, but she didn't. Instead, her fingers wrapped around hers accepting, perhaps welcoming, the comfort she offered.

"Even those closest to us sometimes feel lost and alone. Losing a baby is hard, and people work through loss in different ways. Hers was apparently to turn inward. As to the boyfriend, maybe she was working up the courage to tell you because she was less than proud of what she'd done."

Thea bent her head in Katie's direction, giving Katie's fingers a light squeeze. "It hurts my heart to think she'd hesitate to tell me anything. I'm the one person who would never judge her and would always have her back. At the same time, what you say makes sense. In time she probably would have told me about the child. The only reason she'd keep something from me is if she was ashamed. Or at least that's the only thing that makes sense."

Katie took her hand away, sorry to lose the warmth that had begun to return to Thea's flesh. Still, for her anyway, it seemed like the right thing to do. She might be off duty, but any way she looked at it, this was more official than social. Hand-holding wasn't particularly official, even if it was infinitely pleasurable.

Thea glanced up into her eyes when she took her hand away, and the expression reflected there sent a flutter into Katie's heart. What she saw in the depths of her beautiful eyes hardened her resolve. She was compelled to help this woman and would push through every obstacle to find her sister.

Katie couldn't look away. "All this information gives us a little bit of something more to work on, so don't let it hurt you. Instead, think of it as arrows pointing us in the direction we need to go to find her."

"You're good at your job, you know that?"

The warmth she was already feeling by just being near Thea spread. Compliments from a pretty woman could do that. Compliments from this particular pretty woman were even better, the warmth even deeper. "I appreciate your kind words."

"No, I mean it," she said with vehemence, the tears gone and her eyes now bright. "Whenever I talk to you, the hopeless feeling fades.

I'm not stupid, Katie. I realize the longer this goes on, the more likely the ending isn't going to be good. I hate it so much you can't even imagine, yet when you're around, some of the pain eases. You have a gift with what you do and how you make people feel."

She couldn't help it; she took Thea's hand again. "I may not have walked in your shoes, but I see what happens to people day in and day out. I feel for what you have to go through and will try my best to do what I can to ease your suffering. It's what any good cop should do."

Thea brought their joined hands to her lips and kissed the back of Katie's. She almost moaned and silently said a prayer that she could manage to maintain a little self-control.

"Thank you," Thea said as she released Katie's hand.

"We'll find her," Katie promised and hoped she wasn't lying.

Chapter Sixteen

From the shadows he stood and watched through narrowed eyes. He *wasn't* imagining it. For days now he hadn't been able to shake the feeling someone was watching him and, even worse, following him. Now he knew it for a certainty.

He didn't understand how or why. He was careful. Nothing he'd done could be traced. He'd left no bit of evidence anywhere that could or would lead back to him and timed and implemented each move perfectly.

So why was that fool watching him?

Of course, he caught on quickly enough. It was, after all, part of his extraordinary gift. Time to turn the tables on whoever was tailing him. Now that he'd spotted the person following him, he planned to simply try to get a read on the reason behind the surveillance. Why would someone be interested in him? He'd done nothing to bring attention to himself. Several cars drove down the quiet street without pausing or looking at him as he leaned casually against the brick wall. Their lights flowed across the black SUV parked half a block away, its occupant keeping a low profile as if he believed he was invisible.

Maybe that was true for everyone else, but not for him. The guy might as well have a flashing light on top of his rig. Leaning against the tree he wondered how long he should wait before leaving. Or would it be better to just walk up and confront him? That would be rich, and the temptation was almost too much to pass up. If he marched up and knocked on the car window, what could the guy say to him? No way would he be able to explain why he was here. The truth wasn't an option, and a lie, well, that wouldn't play so well either, considering where they were. This just wouldn't be a good place to be for certain folks with certain reputations.

It didn't bother him. Granted, this wasn't the kind of place he typically went to when he felt like hanging out, but at the moment, it served a very real purpose. First, it was nice and in a good location. Secondly, he didn't care what anyone thought about his going into this particular establishment for a drink. The talk it would likely generate could prove to be very amusing. Others might not think so, and that was exactly the point behind going in for a drink.

He kept his spot on the wall, continuing to watch couples, all men, walk inside. With a backward glance at the SUV, he pushed away and followed yet another couple as they walked hand-in-hand through the door. He happened to know the bar served some really great microbrew, and since he was thirsty he might as well avail himself.

Smiling, he opened the glass door and strode inside the Gilded Goose. The lights were low, and he took an empty stool at the bar next to a good-looking young man in tight jeans and an equally tight shirt. Just because this wasn't his usual scene didn't mean he couldn't appreciate some of what the place had to offer. Fact was, the guy was easy on the eyes, and pretending to be interested was no big stretch.

"No-Li," he told the bartender and waited for the draft. He glanced at his bar mate and winked. The iced glass in his hand, he spun on the stool so he could see the doors. Before he finished the beer he held in his hand, he'd know which way his shadow was going to jump. He vaguely wondered how long he'd have to wait.

❖

Lorna closed her laptop and lay back against the stack of pillows on the bed. Here she was in someone else's home and a long way from home for very tragic reasons and, despite all that, was feeling great. Not a big surprise considering she'd just successfully completed a well-paying project for one of her best clients. A satisfying finish always made her feel fantastic.

That wasn't actually the reason her spirits were so buoyed. It was one hundred percent the result of the call from Renee. When she moved into Aunt Bea's house, the very last thing she intended to do was fall in love. The very last thing and yet that's precisely what happened. What fell into a person's lap when they weren't looking was amazing. Considering how wrapped up she was in her own misery at the time, and her obsession with Anna doing her wrong, it was a miracle she'd even noticed Renee at all.

Fate brought them together. In fact, fate had brought each of them to that house on the shores of the Pacific Ocean and changed all their lives. If that wasn't a higher power at work, she didn't know what was. It was truly a special kind of magic.

Of course she always questioned everything, especially herself. As much as she loved Renee, she'd second-guessed every little aspect of their relationship, including Renee's depth of emotion toward her. Each day she'd awaken fully expecting Renee to pack up her dog along with her few belongings and head back to Seattle. Or, run back to Seattle. The fact that she wanted to stay with Lorna was almost too good to believe. She wasn't that kind of lucky, or at least she never was before.

Now, if the fates would smile on Merry and Jeremy, her world would be complete. She knew her brother. He'd sold his interest in the company he helped build to his partner and would now be on the lookout for the next great adventure. When she'd first heard what he did she couldn't help but think he'd made a big mistake. His company was crazy successful, and he loved the process involved with developing it into something so viable. To walk away like that wasn't him, and at the time she was very worried about him.

For a week or so anyway, and then she came to see that what he did was absolutely the right thing for him. As he grew more rested and relaxed, a wonderful change came over him. He was calmer, he was happier, and he was more focused than she'd seen him for a long time.

That was all fine and dandy, except as he restored himself, she also realized his mind would once again start spinning, and he wouldn't be happy just hanging around the house with his big sister. As delighted as she was about Renee, she felt sad knowing that, before too long, Jeremy and Merry would likely be gone. The house wouldn't just seem empty without them; it would be empty. Not something she wanted to think about right now. This strange new world of hers worked in an odd and exciting way. She dreaded the idea it could all disappear as quickly as it came to be.

Before she lost her pleasant buzz to melancholy, she picked up her phone. "Hey, bro," she said when Jeremy answered.

"What's up?" His tone was happy, upbeat. No need to dwell on what might be. Live in the moment.

"I wish I could tell you things are going well here and I'm helping Thea, but that's not so. I can't seem to tap into anything helpful here like I did with Tiana. I think my so-called gift is a dud on this side of the mountains. Maybe it only works on the west side."

"Hmm, there's got to be something you can do. I don't care what side of the mountains you're on, you've got the touch, sister. You're a little touched too, so one or the other should help."

She couldn't help smiling. "You are so funny."

"Yeah, I am a funny guy, aren't I?"

"Pain in the ass, actually."

"You been talking to Merry again?"

"Speaking of Merry, how's she doing?"

His voice sobered. "Oh, man, she's been throwing up like the flu on steroids."

"Seriously, Jeremy, is she okay?" She didn't have any firsthand experience with pregnancy and worried about her sister-in-law to be. Merry had been looking a little pale before Lorna left.

"I actually talked to the doctor in town, and he told me some women have a first trimester filled with nausea. She should be fine."

"Should be?" Lorna wasn't all that fond of the word should. She liked firm, concrete answers.

"Gotta say, after talking with him I felt a lot better. He was honest and said there are always risks, but the majority of the time it all works out. He seemed pretty certain that's the case with Merry. Me, I'm just trying to be there for her and help her through since there's not much else I can do."

"You're a good guy, Jeremy." She was proud of him and couldn't imagine him doing a thing to change her opinion.

"I don't know about that. I mean I'm an unemployed dad-to-be with no prospects in sight. How good is that?" It was the first time she'd heard a note of defeat in his voice.

"I thought you told me you were working on something?"

"I am, but who knows if it'll turn into something or be a total bust and I'll be living off your largesse forever."

Not in a million years is what she wanted to tell him. He wasn't that kind of guy. "Make you a bet."

"I love bets." His words were a little more upbeat.

"Geez, how did I know that?"

"You're psychic."

"Ha ha. Here's the thing. I bet you a hundred bucks you'll have something new lined up inside of thirty days."

His laugh was more of a snort. "Out here in never-never land? Are you kidding me? What am I gonna do, take up commercial fishing? I'm a horrible fisherman."

"A hundred bucks," Lorna repeated.

"You're on, big sister. Besides, in a month I'll probably need that hundred bucks."

❖

Thea watched out the front window until long after Katie's car disappeared from sight. Since the first day Alida disappeared, she'd felt adrift, lost in a tidal wave of despair and fear. Tonight, for the first time, she felt different. Safe.

It was more than just feeling safe, and she knew it. Deputy Sheriff Katie Carlisle was interesting and intelligent. Having a brain combined with her dark and attractive good looks was incredibly alluring, so it was no wonder she felt such a draw to her. She'd been single for a couple of years and so busy it was fine to be alone. Her career as a graphics artist took off about the same time things ended between her and Sue. They were still friends, and Sue remained a very vocal supporter of her art and the company she created.

Since the breakup with Sue she'd had a date or two, but no one had lit her fire. Until now, that is. It was nice to feel the tug of attraction and desire again, and it was scary as all get-out.

With her right hand she rotated the control to close the blinds, shutting out the soft glow of lights from neighboring porches. Then she turned away from the window and stared into the shadowy darkness of the room. Sleep would be a good thing, except it wouldn't come. She'd managed very little of it in the last few days, and she held no hope tonight would be different. No matter how hard she tried, she couldn't turn off her mind or her worry. A couple of well-meaning friends had suggested meds to help her sleep, but she didn't care to take that route. Insomnia was going to be an intimate acquaintance until she and Alida were reunited, and she could live with that.

If she were inclined to walk down the hall and knock on the guest room door, Lorna wouldn't hesitate to talk with her if she was awake. She was sure to be asleep by now, and she didn't want to bother her. It was bad enough she'd dragged her away from her own life and into the chaos of the investigation concerning Alida's disappearance. Disrupting her night just to keep her company wasn't right.

Instead, she made a cup of tea and took it down the hallway to her home studio. Her day job was graphic arts, but just like her sister, her heart was painting. Since she was old enough to hold a paintbrush, she'd found escape and salvation on the canvas. It was another bond between them, and right now it would help her feel closer to Alida.

Usually she worked in the daytime when the light was brilliant and warming. It helped her breathe life into her work, something that made her paintings distinctive and personal. Right now she didn't need the light because she felt only darkness.

The paints she filled her palette with were shades of blue, cerulean, cobalt, and black. A single dab of yellow was the only bit of brightness. A new canvas on her easel, Thea began to work. Her brush moved, guided by emotion rather than thought. Tears blurred her vision as the image took shape. Outside, the night grew darker and the moon rose high and bright in the sky. She kept moving her brush across the canvas.

Several hours later, her cup of tea long forgotten, she laid down the palette and brush. Her tears had long since subsided, and now a bone-deep tiredness descended on her. Sleep would come now, but she still hesitated before leaving the studio. The painting tore at her heart. It encompassed all she was feeling, the darkness and despair, as well as the tiny bit of hope that both Katie and Lorna gave her. She might not be able to articulate her feelings, but she could paint them.

"That's really something."

She jumped at the same time a small scream burst from her. Whirling around, her hand on her chest, she said, "You just took about five years off my life."

Lorna was leaning against the doorway dressed in old sweats and a baggy T-shirt. "What are you still doing up? You need some sleep."

"Couldn't turn my mind off." Might as well be honest. Lorna would see right through a lie anyway.

Lorna nodded toward the painting. "That help?"

Thea turned to look at the painting and nodded. "Yes, a great deal, and now I think I can sleep."

"Good. You look like you're about ready to drop. Let me help you put this stuff away, and then you need to lie down." Lorna walked into the room and started to screw lids on open tubes of paint.

Five minutes of working in silence and everything was tidied up, or as tidy as it got in her creative den. She flipped the lights off as they walked out together. "Why are you up? I thought you'd gone to bed hours ago."

Lorna nodded as she walked. "I was asleep. Weird dreams woke me up, and I saw the lights in your studio when I got up to use the bathroom."

"I'm sorry."

"For what? You didn't come in my room and wake me up."

"I sent you the bad dreams."

Lorna stopped and took Thea by the shoulders, turning her so they were face to face. "That's crazy. You didn't do any such thing. This psychic gig is the culprit. Ever since it hit, my life and my sleep have been crazy. None of it's your fault."

"But if I hadn't asked you to come over and help—"

"Then I'd be having crazy-assed dreams at home."

"It'd be different."

"You didn't drag me over here. I came of my own free will. Look, Thea, I love Alida, always have, and if this psychic thing that seems to be taking over my life isn't good for helping someone I love, then what the hell is it all for?"

Tears pricked at her eyes again, and weariness almost buckled her knees. "Thank you," she whispered on a sob.

Lorna let go of her shoulders and kissed her on the cheek. "Let's get some sleep, and tomorrow, we'll make something happen. I feel it right here." She tapped her index finger on her heart.

How Thea wanted to believe that was true.

CHAPTER SEVENTEEN

Lorna laced up her running shoes and headed outside. She couldn't have asked for a nicer morning to run. On top of that it was a really good way to get her thoughts in order. After she and Thea had gone to bed, she'd slept without the interruption of dreams and woke up feeling gratefully rested. It was still quiet when she made it to the kitchen, and rather than hang out while Thea slept, she decided a run would help her focus her energies on finding Alida. Besides, the longer Thea could sleep without someone rattling around her house, the better.

Up here on the prairie the roads weren't very runner-friendly, and watching for traffic moving too fast destroyed the relaxing element, so she jumped in her car and drove the back roads down to Indian Trail. A couple minutes from there and she was at Aubrey White Parkway, a lovely, quiet road that wound along the east side of the Spokane River in Riverside State Park. For her the best part was the river. When she lived in Spokane she often came here to run and drink in its quiet beauty.

Today she hoped the run would kick-start her preternatural talents. Her stalled powers didn't make sense. Why could she help Tiana and Catherine when they were not just strangers but ghosts? If she could use it to assist those she would never know, she should be able to use it to help those she loved. That it wasn't working out that way pissed her off more than she could say.

Cool air kissed her skin and the sun warmed her face as she ran along the curving road. As always, her muscles screamed and her breath hurt as she pushed herself to keep putting miles beneath her feet. Just as she did during every other run, she wished she were a natural runner. She wasn't. Never had been and never would be. For Lorna, making herself a runner took hard work and a great deal of determination. It was important to prove to herself she could do it even as the pain and exertion took its toll. The beginning of every run made her question her ability to complete her upcoming endurance race.

After the first couple of painful miles, though, she always found her rhythm, and her stride became smooth and easy. Then her mind could turn away from the pain in her body while her breathing evened out and her pace became steady. This was the point when she realized her dream of completing her Ironman race could actually become a reality. Twenty-six point two miles seemed impossible when she wasn't running. Once she got going and settled into her pace, she gained confidence.

Now as the sun continued to warm her skin and the scent of fresh air filled her lungs, she let her mind turn to Alida. She went over everything she'd seen so far and what she knew about her lifelong friend. What was she missing? It was there right at her fingertips, yet she couldn't touch it. She definitely couldn't see it. Little wonder she was frustrated.

Ahead of her a coyote ran across the road, heading down from the hillside brush toward the river below. She loved to run here because she never knew what she'd see. Sometimes it was fawns. Once a porcupine waddled down the road in front of her, and on a particularly good day, a bald eagle soared above her head. The random beauty of nature and wildlife nourished her soul.

Around the bend she reached the area known as the Bowl and Pitcher because of the huge basalt rock formations in the river. The temptation to detour was too great, and she veered off the road and followed the path leading down to the swinging bridge. In the center of the bridge, she stopped and savored its sway as she gazed out over the water. It was clear and fresh, rushing across the rocks beneath the bridge. She loved the way it made the bridge sway gently. From where she stood, she could easily see how the rocks had earned their names. A cave formed what looked like a sugar bowl tipped on its side, while the pitcher was a tall basalt pillar with a pouring spout jutting from the side. The amazing work of the glacial floods that once carved the landscape was breathtaking.

No one else was around, and she stood alone on the bridge for a long time. The beauty of what she saw, no matter which way she turned her head, filled her with peace. And then it hit her.

The truck.

❖

"You want to do what?" Katie was holding the phone to her ear and thinking she'd just heard Thea wrong because what she'd just heard didn't make sense.

"Not me. Lorna. She wants to sit in Alida's truck. Please. She really feels it's important."

Katie ran a hand through her hair and tried to think. The cop part of her was screaming *hell no*. The woman part, the same one undeniably attracted to Thea, was leaning the other way. The woman part trumped the cop. Besides, why not let her try? At this point what could it hurt?

Of course the truck was in the impound lot and had already been searched from top to bottom by evidence technicians. How in the world Lorna thought she could glean anything else was beyond her. Then again, what did she really know about how a psychic worked? It wasn't like she'd ever used one before. Wasn't like she truly believed in them. Although, if pushed, she might have to admit that the more she was around Lorna, the less she thought she was a flake.

More importantly than her own fading reluctance, if it would make Thea feel better, then she was okay with it. Her own lack of progress certainly wasn't doing much, and it was frustrating, particularly when considering her bold promise to find Alida. So far she wasn't making good on that promise, which was totally unlike her. When she made a promise, she kept it. When she made this particular promise to this particular beautiful woman, it was set in stone.

It was far more than the simple fact Thea was gorgeous and she was drawn to be close to her every time she saw her. It was this case, period. The reality of a woman out doing her job and then vanishing was driving her crazy. No way in hell was she going to let this case go cold. Didn't matter it wasn't as high a priority with the rest of the department; it was on the top of her list. Whatever the outcome, she would find Alida.

So, if Thea wanted Lorna to sit in the truck, Katie didn't have a thing to lose by letting her try. Chances were good they'd still be in the same place afterward, but she was game. Nothing ventured, nothing gained.

"All right, if you think it might help."

"Lorna thinks it will, and that's good enough for me." Thea sounded excited.

"Okay, Thea, then bring her to the impound lot at one o'clock, and I'll meet you there. We'll give your psychic another shot." She ended the call and shook her head. If any of her colleagues got wind of what she was about to do, she was never going to hear the end of it. When others in the department had opened up their investigations to psychics, she was the first in line to give them grief. Payback was going to be a bitch.

At five minutes to one when Thea came around the corner of the gated lot, Katie wasn't shocked. Dark circles were half-moons under her eyes, but they did nothing to lessen her beauty. She could show up in ripped sweats with dirty hair and broken nails and still outshine any other woman in the room. Made her heart race.

Lorna was right behind Thea, and though she too looked tired, she didn't radiate the soul-deep exhaustion written all over Thea's face. And her step was sure and energetic. For someone who claimed not to really "get the psychic thing," she exuded confidence and, more importantly, power. A flash of something like belief blew through Katie, and she suddenly realized how much she wanted Lorna to be able to help. Well, wasn't that a fine turn of events?

At the same time frustration, fear, hope, and desperation roiled within her, fighting for domination. It took a tremendous amount of effort to keep calm and focused and not let the tiny voice in her head start screaming failure! She needed to remember this was an added tool to help in their search. The success or failure of what happened here wasn't defining. A tool, it was only a tool.

For a lot of reasons, not the least of which was the promise she'd made Thea, she was going to stay strong. It was incredibly important to keep her promise. But it wasn't just giving her word to Thea. Many eyes were on her. She was trying to carve out a career in a male-dominated world. Many of the men accepted her and worked side-by-side with her as though she were just another one of them. Others in her chosen profession, not so much. The resentment or outright hostility reminded her of the fifties. That mentality amazed her more than it irritated her. Sad for them, really. Times were moving on and they weren't. In the end, they would be the ones hurt.

Still, a failure, any failure, would stock ammunition in their belts. They would love to point fingers and remind the powers that be how this was a man's job and women just weren't cut out for it. A bullshit attitude, to be sure, and most of those in the upper echelons knew better than to buy in. Giving them a chance to voice those ugly sentiments, however, was something she'd do anything to avoid.

Her final reason was the most important. Once she had been the victim, and for no reason other than because of who she was. What she was. It could have crushed her and destroyed her future. It didn't, and she had many to thank for that, not the least of which were family and friends who stood by her and lifted her up. They gave her courage to be as the phoenix and rise from the ashes. She couldn't walk away and not find another victim. It simply wasn't in her and would be a disservice to those who were always on her six.

Now, she motioned for Lorna and Thea to follow her into the impound office where they signed in as guests and were given laminated badges to clip to their shirts. Once the administrative duties were behind them, they stepped out into the yard packed with vehicles of every make, model, and year. The one they searched for was in the south corner of the front row.

"What do you think this will do?" she asked Lorna when they were out of earshot of the personnel assigned to the impound lot.

Lorna looked at her and shrugged. "Honestly, I don't know. I just think it's worth a shot. The psychic thing was strongest back at the house when I wrapped my fingers around a necklace that belonged to one of the victims. I'm thinking if I touch something Alida was holding around the time she disappeared...well, who knows what might happen. It could work."

"What did you see before?" Despite her lingering skepticism Katie was curious. More than curious though, she wanted to believe this approach would work, even if her lifelong disbelief still held her back from vocalizing as much. What she wouldn't give to find Alida Canwell right now.

Again Lorna shrugged. "At first it was like I was watching through the window and seeing things as they happened outside. In the end, things shifted and suddenly it was like Tiana McCafferty and I shared a single body. Let me tell you, that was pretty damned weird, and I really hope it doesn't happen again. It's work enough just being me. Sharing the mind, body, and spirit of another person is freaky, especially when that person has been dead for about a century."

A little shiver went down Katie's back. It was beyond her to even imagine what it was like to have a ghost inside. If that's what really happened, the skeptic in her added. Still, Lorna's face was devoid of anything resembling deceit. Katie's years of experience with people who lied told her Lorna was being truthful. The issue wasn't whether the shared body experience did or didn't happen. Lorna believed it did, and whether Katie believed it happened or not didn't change the fact Lorna was able to solve a mystery.

The crunch of their footsteps on the gravel lot stopped when they reached the utility-company pickup truck involved with Alida's disappearance. It looked exactly as it did the day it was towed here and top-notch crime-scene techs did their work. Katie had been disappointed when the techs' report reached her desk, but she hadn't questioned their inability to find anything. If there had been anything to find, they would have found it. She didn't hold out much hope Lorna would have any better luck.

For a minute or so they all stood looking at the truck, nobody moving any closer to the sturdy four-wheel drive vehicle that had served as Alida's rolling office. It was as if all three of them were afraid to touch it. Actually, Katie wasn't afraid to touch the truck. She just knew in her case it wouldn't make a damn bit of difference. For Lorna and Thea, it was different. A shadow of fear drifted across each of their faces. Finally, Lorna took in a big breath and then let it out slowly.

"Okay, ladies, waiting isn't going to make this any easier, so I might as well give it a try. You ready, Thea?" Lorna asked.

Quiet and pale since the minute they reached the truck, Thea seemed a little lost and uncomfortable, as if she wished she was anywhere but here. Katie wanted to reach over and take her hand, but it wouldn't have been either proper or professional. At a personal level she couldn't help thinking it would have been very much the right thing to do. Her professional training won out, however, and she kept her hands to herself, clenched and tight to her sides, digging her short nails into the skin of her palms.

With a nod to Lorna, Thea answered her in a low, strained voice. "I'm ready if you are."

Lorna gave a single nod in answer. "Let's get it done."

With purpose, Lorna walked to the driver's side door and pulled it open. From Katie's perspective the only sign something might be happening was the tightening around Lorna's lips, which were now pressed together in a grim line. She didn't pause, though, and pulled herself into the cab and behind the wheel. With both hands on the steering wheel, for a moment she didn't seem to be experiencing anything, but then her eyes rolled back in her head and she slumped sideways in the seat.

Thea jumped in the direction of the pickup's cab at the same time she grabbed Katie's hand in a death grip.

❖

It wasn't like he was following her. Not like the dumb ass following him last night. No, this was a classic case of being in the right place at the right time. Well, that and his incredible skills of observation. Not that he was bragging, but he was always aware of what was going on around him, which is why he was able to spot them right away.

Why were the three women going into the impound lot? At first it made little sense to him why they'd be here. Then it hit him. This was all about the truck. They were going to check out the pickup.

He smiled as he watched them walk across the lot, two of them tall and athletic, one slender and willowy. All attractive in their unique way, though only one could make him look twice. So much like her sister and not like her at the same time. His angel was special, and not even a twin sister could ever come close to stepping into her shoes. His angel was one of a kind, and she was all his forever. The other woman was simply a shallow imitation.

His gaze stayed on the women as they headed to the back of the lot and to where the truck sat still and dust covered. What they thought they could possibly glean from the hunk of metal, he couldn't imagine. It was a stupid waste of time, and if the deputy possessed any experience at all, she'd know that. He'd never touched it. Not that he ever did. It wasn't like he was stupid. He was smarter than the whole lot of them, and by now, they should be catching on. For a long time he'd performed his important work quietly and efficiently, and no one even came close to connecting him to any of it. They wouldn't, either, because he was simply that good and always ten steps ahead.

Today he would love to follow them behind the tall chain-link fence and watch their futile efforts to discover his identity. He wouldn't. As much fun as it would undoubtedly be, it just wasn't a good idea. Tempting, nonetheless, and he found himself inching closer to the gate. Maybe just a peek and he'd be on his way. What could a brief bit of intel hurt?

Halfway across the parking lot, his eyes on the gate, he jumped when a hand on his shoulder stopped him. Involuntarily he stiffened and forced himself to be calm.

"Hey, dude, haven't seen your smiling face for a while."

It was a testament to his skills that he managed not to appear shocked. The fact he didn't hear the person walk up behind him was more disconcerting than being spotted out here. It wasn't like him to be so oblivious. He heard and saw everything all the time. Today he was so focused on the three women, he was in the zone and everything else around him was filtered out. He made a mental note to be more careful. No one else was going to catch him unaware again.

"Back atcha, Cowboy." The nickname was well earned, for this colleague always sported a pair of high-end cowboy boots, Wrangler jeans, and an array of belt buckles from rodeos all across the Pacific Northwest. Born and raised in Omak, a small town near the Canadian border in northeast Washington, Cowboy had spent all his formative years on horses, and that legacy stayed with him after he moved into the city. He'd been here for years now, but he still carried his Omak heritage like a badge. It granted him a certain amount of respect for being dedicated to his roots.

"Yeah, true story. Don't know if you heard, but I got loaned out to the feds. Just finished up that little project and am back home now. Quite the ride with the federal boys and we kicked some serious ass. Probably get my butt hauled into federal court to testify against the fuckers we busted." He rolled his eyes. "Anything interesting in your wheelhouse these days?" He shoved his hands in his jeans pockets and appeared to be settling in for a lengthy chat.

Oh, plenty interesting in his wheelhouse though he wasn't about to share those details. Besides, if he knew Cowboy he wasn't really interested in what was going on in his world. He really only wanted to boast about his foray into the world of federal law enforcement. Rather than share anything of substance, he shrugged and said, "Same old shit, different day."

Laughing, Cowboy smacked him on the shoulder. "I hear that, brother. Let's grab a beer one of these days and talk about the good work we do keeping scum off the streets."

If he only knew how true that was in his case. "Count on it." Thank God he wasn't going into one of his lengthy shoot-the-shit sessions right now. Cowboy was famous for his nonstop ramble, and he didn't have the time or inclination to join in today. It would be a long forever before he'd go out for a beer with him.

When Cowboy decided he was done sharing for the day and walked off, so did he. As relieved as he was to get away clean, any chance at sliding into the impound lot unnoticed had just gone up in a fiery blaze. Good old Cowboy was waving to everyone he knew—and everyone else for that matter—as he headed toward the PSB. The risk of being seen was too great now. Cowboy talked a lot, and the chance he'd mention running into him was a sucker's bet.

His step was quick and sharp as he walked in the opposite direction from the lot. Pissed him off when someone derailed his plans. Sure, this was a spur-of-the-moment thing, but it didn't matter. The idea came to him in a minute. From the moment he decided on his course of action, he was invested, and when Cowboy shot it all to hell he'd wanted nothing more than to put a bullet in his chest. It wasn't that he disliked Cowboy. Actually, he liked him about as much as he did anybody, even if he didn't want to sit around some bar drinking beer with him. Cowboy still embodied the Wild West sort of approach to getting things done, and he admired that about him. The always-by-the-rules bunch—which was most of them—got on his nerves. The guys who knew the difference between good and bad and then did what it took to eliminate the bad were the ones he could relate to. That was Cowboy.

That was him.

❖

Fear washed over her like a tidal wave of rancid water. The day turned black, the clouds overhead threatening to burst forth in torrential rain. She was no longer in the truck. Instead, she was standing next to the tall chain-link fence surrounding the dangerous equipment at the transfer station or, in the words of her search-and-rescue friends, the PLS...point last seen.

The truck was parked in the gravel lot. The waning daylight had caused the automatic headlights to come on, and they now cast shafts of lights to laser toward the thick pine trees in the distance. The driver's side door was open, and standing next to it, bending into the truck, was Alida. She appeared to be working on an electronic tablet of some kind, her attention focused on the task she was trying to complete. Whatever she was working on, it held her attention.

The sound of an approaching vehicle broke her concentration. Alida set the tablet on the seat of the truck and turned to look at the crew-cab pickup truck bumping down the road with an expression of interest on her face. That quickly changed as the truck drove closer. Even in the waning light the unhappiness shadowing her face was crystal clear. She was not pleased to see that truck.

The man didn't even have a chance to get out of the truck before she was moving like an angry cat. Alida marched to the driver's side door of the black, late-model half-ton and smacked the window with the palm of her right hand. The window whirred down and she leaned in, tension clear in her rigid stance.

"You can't keep showing up," she snapped. "This has got to stop."

"I can go wherever I please and I will." The man's voice was calm and without a ghost of emotion present. "You don't have anything to say about it."

Alida's voice was nowhere near calm. Emotion rang through the night air like the bells from the church tower. "It's over. Why can't you accept that?" Frustration seemed to bring her words to a chilling high note.

"It's over when I say it's over." Again the icy calm.

"God damn it," Alida nearly screamed. "I can't keep doing this with you. What can I say to get it through your thick head? I made a mistake, a huge fucking mistake, and God help me, I won't make it again. We are over!" Her knuckles were white where they gripped the open window frame.

His hand reached up to cover Alida's where it rested on the driver's side doorframe. "That's where you're wrong, beautiful. This magic between you and me was never a mistake. It was destiny, and that's why it will never be over. We are meant for each other. Always have been, and nothing you can say or do will change it."

"Go away," she said in a voice choked with raw emotion. "Go away. Go away. Go away." She turned her back on him and started toward her truck again.

"Never." His single word was as quiet as hers were loud.

The driver's door of his truck flew open so fast it startled Alida, who tripped backward and went down hard on her behind. Pain covered her face and tears welled up in her eyes. The man came out of the truck, a blur of motion. He grabbed her by the back of her shirt, pulled her up, and put an arm around her neck as if he intended to choke her. Her feet kicked and her hands clawed at the arm around her neck. Alida fought like a tiger to free herself. It didn't work. His grip never appeared to loosen as he held her against his body and backed toward his truck. The heels of her boots dug into the gravel, leaving trenches as he pulled her along. What seemed like an hour later and was more than likely only a minute or two, her body went slack, her head lolling to the side until it rested against his arm.

As though she weighed nothing, he continued to drag her until he reached the back door of his truck. He opened the door and shoved her into the crew-cab seat. For a moment he stood still and stared at her sprawled across the seat, and then he slammed the door. The fact that her truck was wide open and all her things were still inside didn't appear to concern him. Without even glancing at her vehicle, he climbed into the driver's seat of his own, turned it around, and drove toward the highway. The whole thing happened in the space of a few minutes. One second he was there and Alida was alive. The next he was gone and so was Alida.

Never once during the entire interlude did she glimpse his face.

CHAPTER EIGHTEEN

Thea's heart pounded so hard she thought it might literally come out of her chest. Instinct pushed her to grab Katie's hand. She was compelled to hold on to something...someone, and the fact it was Katie was not unpleasant. What surprised her was the silent acceptance of her gesture because she fully expected Katie to pull away. After all, they were standing in full daylight and in the middle of the sheriff's department's vehicle-impound lot. One of her coworkers or her boss could be here. Or one of the public watchdogs who were constantly waiting around to catch a public servant doing something so egregious it would make great material for a viral video. Katie most likely wouldn't want a single one of them to see her holding hands with a woman.

Well, anyone for that matter. Public displays of affection were undoubtedly frowned on during working hours, particularly on work premises. Or at least she supposed they were. This was different though. She couldn't control her reaction. It had just happened in what felt like a completely natural way.

And that's what made it really weird. Not only was open affection way outside of her comfort zone, but so was reaching out for comfort from someone else. Well, someone besides Alida, that is. Her entire life Alida had been her one and only sounding board. Alida, always the open and free-spirited one, had been consistently able to express her feelings in a healthy way. Or, perhaps in the case of the affair she'd apparently been involved in, in unhealthy ways too.

Not so for Thea. She might be Alida's twin in looks but definitely not in temperament. In that respect they were worlds apart. Thea was as insular as Alida was open, and not just because she was a lesbian. Even if she were straight, she'd react the same way. She simply wasn't comfortable depending on others or openly showing emotion. Her art was as open as she got when it came to expressing herself publicly, and as far as she was concerned, that was plenty open enough.

For the first time she decided to take Alida's lead in the vulnerability department. The ghostly pale cast to Lorna's skin as she sat as still as stone behind the wheel of the truck made her want to scream. If she hadn't seen the rhythmic rise and fall of Lorna's chest, she would have probably raced in to drag her out of the cab. Something unspoken told her to leave Lorna be, and so as hard as it was, that's what she did.

Katie must have sensed much the same thing. Instead of taking offense at Thea's desperate reaction, she squeezed her hand and said quietly, "Give her a few minutes."

"Look at her face," Thea said worriedly, and hated how her voice trembled. "I don't like how white she is."

"She is pretty pale but let's give her a minute or two. As much as I hate to admit this, she might actually be picking something up."

Thea turned to look at Katie, who kept her eyes focused on the cab of the truck and Lorna's pale face. Katie didn't let go of her hand, and neither did she move to interrupt whatever was happening with Lorna.

As Thea turned her gaze away from Katie and back to the truck, she saw intense concentration on Lorna's face. Whatever was going on in Lorna's head, it was more powerful and having far more of an effect on her friend than what she'd seen before out at the transfer station. A wave of guilt ripped through her heart because she was the one who'd asked—begged—Lorna to come help. Now she wasn't so sure it was a good idea.

"I don't like what this is doing to her."

Katie shook her head slightly. "I think she's okay. She's pale, but her breathing is stable."

Thea's heart was pounding and her own breathing neared panic level. "It's not good enough, and it's not right to let this happen to her. I know I asked her to do it, but I'm changing my mind really fast. We've got to get her out of there."

Katie squeezed her hand again and turned to look at her. "Thea, I didn't believe your friend was anything but a nut job until we took her to that parking area. I wouldn't admit it to anyone besides you but I started to believe then that she might have something special. Right now, I'm all on board. She's not a fake, and trust me, that's something I've never said before and probably never will again."

Thea took in a deep breath and let it out slowly, hoping she could keep the panic at bay. That Katie finally believed in Lorna helped a ton. "No, she's never been a fake at anything, and she's always had my back no matter what. She would never lie to me, and if she says she can see things we can't, I believe her one hundred percent."

"Then let her have it now. Let's give her a chance to do what she does."

Even though she believed in Lorna, Thea didn't like what this was doing to her. She also couldn't really argue Katie's point. She nodded and they both turned back to watch Lorna.

In the few seconds their attention was turned away from her, something changed. Her eyes were open now, and she was running her hands through her hair. Color was beginning to return to her cheeks and her lips were pressed together in a thin line. She turned to look at them and then said matter-of-factly, "Well, that was fucked up."

Lorna wouldn't say anything until the three of them were back in Katie's office. Even then it was as if she searched hard for the right words, and Katie had a terrible feeling she understood why. What she suspected Lorna saw in those fugue-like minutes behind the wheel of Alida's truck probably wasn't anything definitive, but it might very well confirm what Katie was afraid of: Alida was dead. She sensed Lorna hesitated to share because she wanted to be very careful what she said to Thea.

In the end, Lorna put it all out there, and though her words were thoughtful, they were equally honest. It was clear to Katie that the two of them were on the same wavelength. To Thea's credit, she took what

Lorna offered with calm acceptance and didn't dwell on the more frightening aspects of the vision. Neither did she or Lorna, and all three of them avoided the word dead, focusing instead on what they could do to find Alida and bring her home.

Lorna's vision didn't yield a ton of concrete information, yet it did give Katie a couple of things to work with she didn't have before. After Lorna finished filling them in on her experience in the truck, they talked for another twenty minutes or so before she sent Lorna and Thea back home. Even considering using a psychic was outside her standard operating procedures, and going beyond what they already did was out of the question. From here, she'd take what Lorna gave her and use good old-fashioned techniques to roll with it. As soon as they left, she immediately started on a new line of investigation.

Two things Lorna said gave her a touch of hope. One was the description of the pickup. A black, late-model Ford, crew cab with a diamond-plate toolbox mounted in the rear. The second was a partial plate. Lorna explained that as it was driving away, she was able to see a Washington plate reading A85. A complete license plate number would have been gold, except she wasn't able to get the rest. Still, three numbers was three more than she had an hour ago, and she could work with that.

Katie was just reaching to pick up the phone when Vince plopped down in the chair next to her desk. "What's up?"

Big surprise. Leaning back in her chair, Katie studied him as she took the opportunity to push away the irritation his presence brought on. She wanted to believe he possessed the potential to be an okay guy. If only she could get past his annoying façade. It grated on her and now was no exception. She had a lot of work to do and his presence just got in the way.

"Still treading water on the Alida Canwell case." She hedged, not wanting to get into a lengthy conversation about what she was following up on right now or why. Vince was an expert at offering unsolicited advice on how to work a case. How he'd react to her use of a psychic was not something she felt like getting into today.

He shook his head and his eyes darkened. "Too bad. This one bothers me, Carlisle. Something isn't right, and the longer it goes on the easier it'll be for this to get away from us. Can't let that happen."

She stared at him. Us? Since when was there an us? Did he think she was too inept to work the case herself and needed his help? It took supreme effort not to let him know he was pissing her off. He just needed to leave her alone and let her handle this her way. "I realize that, Vince. I'm turning over every stone and looking at everyone who knew her. I want to find this woman, and I want to find the bastard who did this to her."

He nodded slowly while pulling on his lower lip with his teeth. "Yeah, I know you do. I'm not sure what has me twitchy on this one. Why don't you tell me what you've got so far?"

She tapped her fingers on her desk, trying to figure out how to make it short and sweet. If she didn't give him something, he'd hang here for hours. Chad wasn't far off the mark when he called Vince her unofficial partner.

So far, she hadn't shared with anyone that Thea's friend was a psychic, and explaining that to Vince now didn't feel right. She didn't trust him. A little, maybe…the brothers and sisters in blue and all that. Trust at the heart and soul level was something altogether different, and well, it wasn't in her heart or her soul yet. Not even close.

After mulling over her options, she decided to go at it a bit sideways. A little truth, a little omission—not exactly a lie. "I have a witness who saw a dark-colored crew-cab pickup leave the area around the time we believe Alida was taken."

He stiffened. "Taken? When did we nail that down? Have you ruled out that Ms. Canwell didn't just walk away?"

She wanted to snap at him and caught herself. Whether she agreed with it or not, his question wasn't actually out of line. Hard evidence didn't exist. "No, I have nothing definitive saying she didn't take off. On the other hand, we haven't exactly ruled out abduction either, and given this witness, I'm leaning hard toward that."

"Leaning toward what?"

Great, just flipping great. It was bad enough she was forced to explain her every move to Vince. Now Chad was jumping in too. She flicked her gaze up to where he stood in the doorway. The guy was like a goddamn ghost. She never heard him coming. Usually it didn't bother her. Lately everything the guys did—Vince, Chad, Brandon—rubbed her the wrong way.

Vince answered for her. "Carlisle here doesn't want to consider the possibility Alida Canwell just ran out on her life."

"Could have happened," Chad said and raised an eyebrow. "Wouldn't be the first time an unhappy wife hit the road."

"Of course it *could* have happened," she snapped. For God's sake, how stupid did they think she was? Was it so hard for them to believe she could actually think through the various possible scenarios all by herself? Apparently, if she was to judge by this conversation.

Chad tapped his fingers on the doorframe, his eyes narrow as they studied her face. Her vocalized irritation seemed to flow right past him without ever touching down. "You don't think so."

"No, I don't." She gave Vince a pointed look. At least Chad was considering her theory.

Vince nodded slowly, his eyes on her face. "Okay, Carlisle, so if you don't really believe that's a possibility, what's your gut telling you?" He was finally waving the white flag.

She looked first at Chad and then turned to meet Vince's eyes. "She was taken…against her will."

❖

Lorna lagged behind Thea once they returned to the house. Thea pulled into the garage and was out the side door heading toward the house before she even got her car door open. Earlier she was filled with vigor and momentum. Now, she was wiped out. The interlude at the truck had just plain kicked her ass. Beyond zapping her energy, it also weighed heavily on her heart. What she saw in those minutes of clarity didn't leave her feeling good at all. It was hard to gather the energy to stand up and head inside.

Thea's scream got her moving and she was out and running in a flash. Racing out the door and toward the back deck of the house, she was up the first of five steps before she halted as if she'd just literally run into a brick wall. What the…

Sitting around the patio table were Renee, Jeremy, and Merry. Thea was standing at the top of the steps, a big smile spread across her face. "Sorry," she said as Lorna finished climbing the steps at a slow and easy pace. "They scared me. I wasn't expecting to see anyone sitting out on the deck, let alone this particular crew."

Renee pushed up from her seat and came to Lorna. She wrapped her arms tightly around her and kissed her quickly on the lips. She tasted like sunshine and honey. "Missed you, gorgeous." Apparently, so did Clancy, who appeared from around the corner of the house to hit her side with a spirited leap. Her first thought was "that's gonna leave a mark," and her second was simple joy at the touch of the big dog.

Of their own accord, Lorna's arms went around Renee and her heart all but sang. The idea was so corny it almost made her laugh. Singing hearts were in the movies; they weren't for tough-as-nails women like her. Still…"I missed you too," she whispered into her ear. Then she reached down to rub Clancy's ears. "Missed you too, handsome."

Renee stepped out of the embrace and took her hand. "Come on, you two. Sit down and have a glass of wine. We all need to catch up."

It was only then that Lorna noticed the bottle of wine. She cocked her head and studied the bottle, the glasses, and the people around the table. "How did you get in the house?"

"We didn't," Jeremy said, holding up a plastic glass. "Dollar store, sister."

That made her laugh, and some of the dread that had nagged at her since the truck experience eased away. He was indeed holding a cheap plastic wineglass that would break in an instant if it was held too tight. She should have guessed as much. Her brother was creative and inventive. With a grimace she said, "I hope the wine didn't come from the dollar store, too."

Jeremy gave her his patented grin and squared his shoulders. "No chance. We stole that from your wine cellar and brought it with us."

She should have guessed that as well. If there were a wine cellar in his house, she'd steal his wine too. It's simply what one does to one's little brother and vice versa. "I still can't believe you're here."

"Didn't you see Jeremy's car out by the curb?" Merry asked.

The question about the car bounced right off her as she looked at the glass Merry held in her hand. This wasn't good and she didn't intend to be quiet about it. "Merry?" The snap in her voice was like a schoolteacher chastising a bad student.

Merry's gaze followed hers to the glass and she laughed with cheerful gusto. "Oh, Lorna, you're sweet to be concerned about me... or us, I should say. It's apple juice and I do appreciate the worry. You've always got my back, and since I don't have a sister, it's awesome to have you."

Relief was sweet. Apple juice, not wine. Considering Merry was pregnant with Lorna's first niece or nephew the idea she was drinking a glass of wine made her stomach roll. In all fairness to Merry, Lorna never should have doubted her. Her sister-in-law-to-be was smart, capable and full of common sense. She would never put her unborn child at risk.

"I'll take the wine," she said then and sank into the chair next to Renee. Clancy plopped down at her feet, his head on her knees. Dark, soulful eyes looked up at her as if to say, "Pet me." So, of course, she did. She rubbed his head, loving the silky feel of his fur against her fingertips. The simple touch sent tension flowing out of her body like a tidal wave.

"Make it two," Thea said as she also took a seat. Unlike Lorna, though, her body continued to radiate fatigue.

A plastic glass of wine in one hand, holding Renee's hand with the other, she asked what was sure to be an obvious question. "What the hell are you three doing here?"

Jeremy raised an eyebrow and looked at Thea. "She doesn't sound pleased to see us. You're pleased to see us, aren't you?"

Thea pointed her glass of wine at Jeremy. "I'm delighted to see you. I'd be happy to see you any day of the week, but even more right now. At this point I can use all the positive energy I can get."

"See." Jeremy looked pointedly at Lorna, a bit of a smile on his lips. "Somebody appreciates us."

She shook her head and rolled her eyes. "You didn't answer my question."

Renee squeezed her hand. Softly she said to both Lorna and Thea, "We're here to help."

"Help how?" She didn't mean to sound so churlish; it just came out that way. In her defense, it wasn't like any of them were psychic, and given what she saw earlier, she wondered if anybody could help. Besides the medical examiner, that is.

Renee didn't sound as though she took offense at Lorna's snarky question, another one of the things she loved about her. "Think about what transpired with Tiana and Catherine. True, you were able to see them and Tiana was able to bodily connect with you, but we were together when it all came to a resolution. You said you felt as though you were treading water. So, we figured for it to work here, perhaps you need us. Needed our life force to fully open the veil between this world and wherever it is you go."

She intended to say no but then gave herself a moment to think about it. Maybe it wasn't a bad idea. Back at the house when it all started to happen, she'd been alone at first. Yet when it all opened up and the truth was finally revealed, it was when they were all at the house together. Besides, what could it hurt? Having Renee next to her, sleeping with her, and touching her could only give her more strength, and before this was all said and done she'd probably be able to use every last ounce of power she could get.

Her gaze traveled to Jeremy as he leaned back comfortably in the deck chair, his wineglass in one hand and his other resting on Merry's shoulder. The love flowing between the two was impossible to miss. It made her happy to see him so content. His professional life might be in flux at the moment but his heart was not, and the heart was by far more important than anything else. The rest were just details.

As she studied him now, she thought back on how it went down not so long ago. He'd played an important part in revealing the secrets hidden in the estate on the ocean shores—a scary but critical one. Having an evil spirit come for him was harrowing but also incredibly important in bringing Tiana and Catherine together. Whatever Jeremy possessed might help them here too. Why she hadn't thought of it earlier made her wonder, except that true to form she figured she could do it all by herself. Some day she might actually grow up enough to admit she needed others like Jeremy and Merry…like Renee. Knowing her, it wouldn't be anytime soon.

In this instance, it was way past time to find Alida and bring her home, so if the three most important people in her life wanted to help, she'd take it. She looked at each of them before nodding. "Okay."

Then she turned to Thea. "We can stay at a hotel." She refused to inflict a cast of four and a dog on a woman already under more stress than one person should have to endure.

Thea protested. "There's plenty of room here."

She was right, but this was taking a toll on Thea, who'd always needed space to recharge. Quiet space, which meant she didn't need the lot of them invading her home.

"I know, and I think I speak for all of us when I say we appreciate your offer. Just the same, there's a lovely Marriott just down the road, and I'm pretty sure a couple rooms there have our names on them."

"Just one room," Jeremy told them with a small grin. "Merry and I plan to crash at her brother's house. Merry and his wife want to talk weddings and babies and all kinds of cool shit. I can hardly wait."

Merry smacked him in the arm. "You mean really important things."

"Yeah, right, that's what I meant."

"Okay then, it's settled. Renee, Clancy, and I are headed to the Marriott, Jeremy and Merry to her brother's. You," Lorna pointed to Thea, "are going to get some uninterrupted rest."

"Ah, Renee," Merry said with a hint of hesitation in her voice. "Would it be okay if Clancy came with us?"

Renee looked at Merry in surprise. "You want to take Clancy?"

Merry's grin was wide and bright. "I do. I've told my brother all about him, and he adores German shepherds. If Clancy could come for the night the whole family would be pleased."

Renee looked at Lorna and shrugged. "Okay with you?"

She wanted to say no because since she'd left home she was missing Clancy more than she would have believed possible. On the other hand, it also meant the entire night would be theirs, uninterrupted by the need to take Clancy out for a stroll through the pet area. "Sure. Even a dog needs a sleepover now and again."

Merry was still grinning. "That's awesome. My brother's family is going to be so excited, and don't be surprised if they try to keep him."

"Well." Renee hedged. "In that case…"

"No worries. I'll bring him home."

"All right then." Renee rubbed him between the ears and stared into his big dark eyes. "You be a good boy." Clancy wagged his tail and bounded after Jeremy and Merry as they headed toward the car. She looked over at Lorna and raised an eyebrow. "I guess we don't have to worry about whether he's going to miss us."

Her thoughts exactly. Lorna and Renee helped tidy up the now-empty glasses by throwing the dollar-store chic into the trash and putting the empty wine bottle in the recycle bin. Lorna might have felt bad about leaving Thea alone except for the deep lines of exhaustion that shadowed her face. She wished for a good night's sleep for her friend but had a feeling that wasn't likely to happen. Not after what she'd told her back at Katie's office.

Chapter Nineteen

After Lorna and Renee were on their way to the hotel and she was all alone, Thea found the stillness in her house both disquieting and comforting. Having Lorna here was good for her soul. Having her house to herself again was also good for her soul.

When she'd made her call she so hoped Lorna would come here and use her newly developed power to lead them directly to Alida. She envisioned finding her sister tired and hungry but alive and well, with a wild story to tell them all. Slowly, her hopes for a happy reunion were beginning to fade. She was a bright woman who did well for herself. The agency she'd started from the ground up had grown into something magical and far more successful than she'd ever imagined. So much so she had employees capable of handling the business while she stepped out to attend to this emergency. In many ways it was humbling.

She might not be as outgoing as her sister, yet she'd managed to put together a thriving business in an industry that liked to crush all but the strongest. From inside herself she'd discovered courage and it took her to new heights. Tonight, however, she felt anything but strong. Reality had always been her strong point and her comfort zone. Alida loved to see the bright side of everything. Thea always accused her of wearing the proverbial rose-colored glasses.

But then Alida went missing, and on that day Thea grabbed those rose-colored glasses and held on to them as tight as she could. If she just believed in something hard enough it was bound to come true. Now, though, her grip was beginning to fail and her true nature was rolling in like the tide. God, how she hated reality. It might have helped her become a success in her field, but it was horrible when it came to the kind of tragedy spread out in front of her now. She wanted to slam those glasses on her face and see roses. Lots and lots of roses.

In the kitchen she seriously considered opening another bottle of wine. After all, she'd only indulged in one small glass of the nice pinot Jeremy brought from Lorna's wine cellar. What was in her kitchen was nowhere near as nice, but it boasted a high alcohol content, and at the moment that counted for a lot. In fact, it was the only thing that counted. She grabbed the nifty corkscrew that made opening wine bottles a breeze and popped the cork.

She'd just taken the newly poured glass of wine into the living room when the doorbell rang. So much for a nice, quiet night of getting drunk and passing out—even that plan was a bust. She set the glass and bottle on the low table in front of the sofa and went to the door. On the way there she glanced out the window, surprised to see Katie's car in the driveway.

One part of her was happy to see who it was. She couldn't help it. She liked her, which became clearer each time they were together. Another part of her dreaded why Katie was here. The fear she would bring more bad news was a truth she couldn't avoid.

She swung the door open and leaned against it. "Hey," she said. "What brings you out so late?"

Katie's hands were in her pockets and her face was serious. "On my way home and thought I'd bring you up to date."

Every part of her screamed no, shut the door, don't listen. She stepped back and waved her in. If she hid behind the door, bad news would still be waiting for her on the other side no matter how long she tried to hide from it. At least this way, she would have some time with Katie, and that was worth something. "You on duty or off?"

"Officially, I'm off."

Thea held the door open wide. "Good. Then you can help me polish off the bottle of wine I just opened." Passing out might not be out of the question after all.

Katie grinned. "All right. Anything I can do to help."

Thea patted her on the shoulder as she walked through the open door. "That's the spirit." Not so long ago she would have said time alone was worth its weight in gold. Now, company—Katie's company—was just as golden.

Five minutes after the ring of the doorbell had interrupted her plan of solitary drinking they were sitting on opposite ends of the sofa, each holding a glass of wine. "So, catch me up," Thea said. She was under no illusion that Katie's appearance here was just because Thea was such wonderful company.

Katie took a sip of the wine and grimaced. Thea wasn't sure if it was because her question made her uncomfortable or she didn't care for the wine. She was hoping for the latter. "I'd like to tell you it's good news, but it's not."

Thea's heart ached, yet she wasn't surprised. She nodded. "Go on. Tell me. Might as well get it over with. Today appears to be the day of bad news and worse news."

Katie didn't contradict her. "You recall I told you we found some cases of missing women in other counties?"

When Thea nodded again, Katie continued. "Well, we widened our search parameters even more to see if we might come across any other cases of missing women that match the MO in Alida's."

"You found more?" That possibility made her sick to her stomach.

This time Katie nodded, her eyes on the wineglass. "We found a disturbing pattern that for some reason slipped by all of us. More than likely we missed it because it was spread over not just different counties but four states as well."

"Four states?" Her heart ached even more, if that was possible. Some monster was out there stealing lives and destroying families, and no one was doing a thing to stop him. How could that happen? Why did it have to happen in her family?

Katie blew out a long breath. "Yeah, four damn states, and we just now noticed the similarities. We have women missing in Washington, Idaho, Montana, and Oregon. If I didn't know better I'd think someone buried the info."

A chill went straight to the bone. "Could someone have done that to all of them?"

With a grimace Katie finally met her eyes. "Anything's possible, but probable? It would be damn hard, and they'd have to have someone on the inside. Without law-enforcement connections it would be nearly impossible. Burying information in our system isn't easy. Too many checks and balances."

"But it's not impossible."

"No. Not likely either. Hopefully, this is more an instance of the cases being spread among small communities where the law-enforcement presence is likewise small. Most of the missing women lived on the fringe."

"But that's not the case with Alida. This is a big city with a large presence of law enforcement at all levels of government. She certainly didn't live on the fringe of anything."

"True enough. Alida's sudden and unexplained disappearance fits the pattern we discovered, but nothing else about her does. If the same guy is doing all this, he's getting cocky. He may have decided those woman weren't enough and moved on to someone a little riskier."

Thea set her glass on the low table in front of the sofa and ran her hands through her hair. Her head hurt. If it was the same person, he'd been practicing for a while, and the possibility frightened her more than anything she could imagine. She closed her eyes and rubbed her scalp with the tips of her fingers. It didn't help.

As if sensing her despair, Katie slid across the sofa and put an arm around her shoulders. "I know," she told her. "This is not good news."

The kindness of her gesture meant a lot to Thea. She opened her eyes and studied Katie. "Were you able to do anything with the plate number or the pickup truck?"

Katie shook her head. "Not yet. We're still working on it. Hopefully we'll come up with something soon. We have a huge inventory of Ford pickups in this area and don't have enough of a plate number to narrow it down to *the* truck. The guys working on it are good, and they'll get it if it's there to be found."

Tears pricked at the back of her eyes. Good wasn't anywhere in the conversation at all. Everything was bad and, instead of getting better, was getting worse. "I'm so scared."

Katie pulled her close and Thea let her. She welcomed the warmth of Katie's body because her own felt so incredibly cold. "I'll do everything I can to find her," Katie said against her hair.

Thea rested her head against Katie's shoulder and for the first time gave in to the tears that had been threatening since the very first call.

❖

Once the hotel room door closed behind her, Lorna grabbed Renee and pulled her close. Her mouth descended, and she kissed her as if it had been years since the last time they touched. The taste of her lips was so incredibly sweet. How she'd missed her. More than she could have ever imagined.

Lorna's hands slid down Renee's back, and all she could think of was getting rid of the fabric barrier between her and bare skin. Her need to touch Renee overpowered her. If she was under any illusion that her attraction to Renee was simple lust, she gave it up. Jeremy wasn't the only one in the family who was in deep.

"I love you," she whispered against Renee's hair, the catch in her throat impossible to stop.

Renee's hands came up to cup her face. She stared into her eyes, a smile on her lips. "You have no idea how much I love you too. It's been so lonely since you came over here. I'm awfully accustomed to waking up with you right next to me. The bed is big, lonely, and cold without you."

"I've only been gone a couple of days."

"It seems like an eternity."

"I missed you too," Lorna said and drew her close again. "And waking up next to you is the best."

Renee's hands slid beneath her shirt, then pulled it up and over her head. The heat of her hands on Lorna's skin was intoxicating. She couldn't wait and guided her to the bed.

Chills raced up her arms as Renee tossed her own shirt aside and slid out of her jeans. She wasn't wearing anything underneath. How incredibly hot was it to have a commando girl standing in her room? Her heart soared.

She still had on her jeans, and getting out of them was a chore. She very nearly toppled over trying to drag the stiff fabric off her legs. Renee lay stretched out on the bed watching her the whole time. She giggled. "Careful," she said in a low, sexy voice. "You don't want to hurt yourself 'cause then you'll miss out on all this." She ran a finger from her lips across her breasts and down her belly.

Jesus, she barely managed to stay upright. Her foot was caught in the hem of her jeans, and she was tugging trying to free it. "You're killing me here."

Renee's grin turned mischievous. "Me? Oh, sweetheart, that's nothing. I'm just getting started."

And she was. Lorna finally freed herself from the clinging jeans and launched herself to the bed. The second she stretched out beside her, Renee's hands slid over her breasts and down to where the heat pooled between her legs. Her gasp was loud as fingers whispered across the tender skin. It took every ounce of effort she could summon not to come right then.

"Not yet, beautiful. Not yet." Renee's mouth covered hers in a hot, demanding kiss before moving from her lips to her neck. The feather-soft touch of her lips against the skin of her neck made her shiver as though she was out in an ice storm. When Renee's lips found a nipple, Lorna's head fell back against the pillow. This was heaven, and she never wanted to come back down to earth.

The combination of warm lips against her breast and stroking fingers was more than she could take. She wanted to make it last, but she was powerless under Renee's loving touch. Her hips arched against Renee's hand, and she came in an explosion of sensation that left her panting.

Renee was laughing lightly as Lorna tried to catch her breath. "I'm sorry," Lorna said when she could put the two words together. "I didn't mean for that to happen."

On her side, with her head on one hand, Renee gazed down at her, smiling. "Sorry about what?"

"That was what? Two minutes? Three tops. I came as fast as if I were a virgin. You got nothing out of that, and that's not right. You deserve a lot more."

Renee was shaking her head. "You are so wrong. Do you have any idea how hot it makes me to know I can do that to you? Honey, you not only make me as horny as a teenager, but you do wonders for my ego."

"Really?" It was hard to believe she could have that kind of effect on anyone.

Leaning down, Renee kissed her, slowly and thoroughly. "Yes," she said when she raised her head. "I struggled for so long trying to find peace with myself and wondering if anyone would ever love me. I failed miserably as a straight woman, and even as attracted as I was...am...to women, until I met you, I wondered if I'd ever find a woman who could love me."

"I love you," Lorna said and knew she'd never meant those three words more than she did right now.

"That's what makes this thing we have so special. Every doubt disappeared the day I met you. Stupid as it probably sounds, you complete me. The fact I can make you feel like a horny teenager is icing on the cake. It makes me love you even more."

Lorna rolled over and covered Renee's body with hers. Everything she felt for Renee welled inside her, and her desire surged once more. "Well, then, it would be just plain rude to leave you both horny and unsatisfied. I'll just have to do something about that, won't I?"

"Promises, promises." Renee grabbed her head and pulled her close to kiss her.

Lorna made good on her promise.

❖

Really? Did he think he was so out of it he wouldn't notice him following...again? This was getting old. He had work to do, and his personal Peeping Tom was getting in the way. The adventure into the local gay bar should have sent him on his way, but apparently not.

Though he was loathe to admit it, he was curious what made him interested in him enough to start following. He hadn't left any trace of himself anywhere, and his behavior was nothing but boringly normal. As far as he was concerned, the mask he was forced to live behind was still in perfect condition. So what was different now?

He shook his head and smiled. It was really a rhetorical question. He knew exactly what was different this time. Each and every time before it was all about his important work. Then a most unexpected element pushed him outside the box. He still wasn't sorry. All things in life happen for a reason. It might have been nice if it had turned out a little different with her, but he also knew from experience that people didn't always respond to reason. They didn't take the path of least resistance. A subject that put up a little fight made it more fun.

Except for her. Even though it was hard to admit even to himself, he loved her. Or loved her in his own way. He was smart enough to realize his emotional makeup was a touch different from most other people's. He was fine with that. Comfortable in his own skin, as the saying went. It didn't, however, mean he was devoid of emotional attachment. On the contrary, he felt deeply, especially about her, and when she betrayed him, well, little choice was left to him. She picked the path, he simply followed it.

If his father taught him one thing, it was the undeniable right to hold onto the things that belonged to him. No one could take from him that which he was unwilling to relinquish. Or, in her case, who he was unwilling to let go of. Once his, always his was the motto he'd been taught. Thank you, Father.

Now, he had a different kind of problem on his hands: his unwelcome shadow. Usually disposing of a nuisance wasn't a big deal. Not so this time. This one could prove problematic for a variety of reasons. Not the least of which, all the wrong people would notice his disappearance fairly quickly. It didn't mean it couldn't happen; it just meant he needed to plan everything down to the tiniest detail to make sure nothing, absolutely nothing, came blowing back his way.

Actually, he welcomed the challenge. The unexpected ups and downs that came with each job were part of what made his work so enjoyable. Until things died down, he would need to stay quiet on the other front. So, planning the demise of the one who surely thought he was invisible was quite enticing. He could have a great deal of fun with it. By the time he finished, one problem would be eliminated, and enough time would have passed that he'd be able to commence once more with his good work.

Yes, the more he thought about it, the better it was. A plan was coming together in his head by the time he put his truck into drive and pulled away from the curb. As he knew it would, a dark-colored sedan also pulled into traffic several car lengths behind him. It kept pace without closing the distance. Vehicle Surveillance 101. Like he hadn't taken and passed that one himself. When it came right down to it, most people really were stupid. If it weren't for the blessed few like himself this truly would be a sad world to live in.

He was whistling as he pulled onto I-90 and kicked up his speed to seventy miles an hour as he joined the smooth flow of traffic.

Chapter Twenty

Katie, what the hell are you doing? The little voice in her head was screaming, yet Katie chose to ignore it. Thea was part of an active case. Even if Thea was ruled out as a suspect, a professional did not get involved with someone in a case. Especially not one as close to the investigation as Thea was.

But damn, holding her in her arms was like something out of a fantastic dream. Her despair was clear in her tears and trembling body, yet holding her felt more natural than anything Katie had done in a long time. Hell, it had been so long since she'd even wanted to be around another woman that this was crazy for a whole host of reasons.

After a few minutes Thea sat up and pushed hair away from her face. "I'm so sorry. That was uncalled for." Her face was streaked with tears, her eyes sad and watery.

With her thumbs, Katie wiped lingering tears from her face "Are you kidding? You're more than entitled to a good cry. Your twin sister is missing and we're not making much ground finding her. You should feel sad and, if it was me, pissed as hell at law enforcement for not bringing her home. You have every reason in the world to be upset, and you don't have to apologize for feeling that way."

"I'm not angry with you."

"You should be." She sure as hell would be if she were in Thea's shoes. In her mind they were doing a pretty crappy job so far and should be held accountable.

"Why?" Thea actually looked a little puzzled.

"Because I haven't done a very good job." Might as well be honest.

Thea studied her closely and then shook her head. "You've given us everything you have. I believe that."

Katie would love to believe it too, but in her heart of hearts, she felt that she was missing something. Not a little something either. No, it felt like a big, fat neon sign was flashing something that would break this thing wide open. Not just so they would be able to find Alida but the other missing women as well. Her gut instinct screamed they were all related, despite what Chad and Vince believed. For some reason she couldn't fathom, the two, who rarely saw eye to eye, seemed to think she was chasing her own tail. Then again, at least where Vince was concerned, if it wasn't his idea, it was a bad idea. Chad was a little more gracious and receptive most of the time, today not being one of those times.

When Vince had asked for her gut feeling, she'd thought he might finally have an open mind. So, she'd shared her initial thoughts with him and Chad, and then when she found herself mired in their skepticism, she'd kept the rest of it to herself. By and large, she seemed to be investigating this case by herself instead of with the help of the two guys who were supposed to have her back.

No big surprise, she was used to it. Things for women were way better than they used to be, but that didn't mean they were perfect. The good-old-boy mentality still made an appearance now and again. In this case, it was a now.

That Thea held faith in her meant a lot. It also spurred her to try harder. She knew she was on to something, and by God, she'd figure it out with or without help from the guys. It would be easier if they actually helped. She just couldn't count on it.

Of course, she and Thea also had Lorna in their corner, and strangely, she was pleased to have her there. Oddly, as the day wore on her feeling about Lorna's vision complemented her own research. The woman was on to something, and if they could put two and two together, they might find the answer.

Who would have thought she'd be happy to hang out with a so-called psychic? It was, however, the first time she'd ever allowed herself even the tiniest thread of belief. In this case, the thread was approaching more of a rope. She was buying in. Nothing about Lorna screamed deception or fake. The woman was real, sincere, and honest. That counted for a great deal, in her book. Maybe she was psychic. Maybe she wasn't. Katie only knew for certain that Lorna was here to help, and in this case, she was going to take Lorna's offer whatever she turned out to be.

She brought her thoughts back to Thea. "I have given you my all," she admitted. "Sadly, so far, it just hasn't been enough."

Thea touched a hand to her face, her dark eyes intense. "It will be. You and Lorna will find her. I feel it here." She took her hand away from Katie's face and laid it on her heart.

The trust she saw reflected in Thea's eyes made her all the more determined. "I can promise you I'll try."

For a moment Thea continued to stare into her eyes, and then she shocked Katie by leaning close. Thea's voice was as soft as she pressed her lips against Katie's. "I know you will."

❖

He taxied the small plane across the tarmac and into the hangar rented in the name of Johnson Valor. Of course, he was Johnson Valor, but he was the only one aware of that minor detail. The smucks here at the airport only needed a copy of his ID to complete the rental. It wasn't a fake ID either. No, it was the real deal. Easy enough to get when a person knew the right people, and he did.

The real Johnson Valor had died at the ripe old age of two in a little town called Connell. One birth certificate later and voila, he possessed exactly what he needed. Like the hangar, the plane belonged to Johnson. His plan worked flawlessly, and he could go about his business with no one the wiser.

True, he should be keeping a low profile, but the urge to hunt was too great. After he lost his tail, he planned to do nothing more than go home and work on the old place. But after an hour of sanding a table he wanted to restore, his restlessness got the better of him. The manual labor wasn't quieting the need rising inside his chest. In the end, Johnson needed to make a little trip, and so he did. Was a good one too. A little over an hour in the small plane and he landed in Boise. An hour after that, he had her. They were so easy. A couple drinks, an offer of a quick plane ride, and they were putty in his hands. So terribly predictable.

All it took once he buckled them in the plane was the offer of a drink. Nobody turned down the coffee and Irish cream. They all loved it, and not one of them ever noticed the oxy he laced it with. Enough of that crap combined with the alcohol in the Irish cream and they were lolling in the seat long before he ever made it back to Spokane. Oxy was a great drug and easy to get his hands on without breaking a sweat.

His latest conquest was no exception. She drank so much of the drug and alcohol-laced coffee he actually worried a little that she'd OD and his fun would be over before it even started. The only thing that let him know she hadn't checked out was the snoring. She was pretty hot, he'd give her that, but the snoring was far from appealing. How could a woman who looked that good sound like an old fat guy when she was passed out? Then again, given her line of work, sleep wasn't usually part of the package.

Getting his guests from the plane to the truck was generally quite easy too. Nobody paid him much attention, and if they did, his embarrassed explanation was simple: his companion overdid wine at dinner. That excuse worked every time, which so far hadn't been that often. In fact, it worked incredibly well because most looked away when they thought a woman was sloppy drunk.

Tonight was a good one, and no one was around by the time he returned with his prize. No explanations were required. He got the plane into the hangar, his toy out and into the truck, and then secured the hangar doors. She snored away the whole time, not stopping even when he hauled her out of the plane and deposited her into the pickup.

Traffic was light as he headed north. He'd like to think he was spontaneous and tonight was a lark. But he was smart enough to realize he was a creature of habit, and far from being a lark, this trip was a necessary part of his routine. The Northside was his comfort zone. He loved the mountains and the pine trees, the winding roads and star-studded sky. It was where he always felt most powerful.

No reason to think things would go wrong tonight. They never had before, and he'd been playing his games for a good long time now. If it ain't broke, why fix it?

When he reached his special place, he pulled the truck into the shadows. The big trees on the perimeter provided perfect cover, the low, overhanging branches casting deep shadows. It was ideal. In fact it was one of the things that made this place speak to his soul. The second his feet touched the grass, serenity washed over him.

From the back of the crew cab he hauled her out. She was warm and pliable, still heavily under the influence. In other words, perfect. Just the way he liked them. He kissed her cheek before laying her gently on the ground. She made a soft murmur. That was it.

Back at his truck, he took out the tools he needed for tonight's game. As always, they consisted of a tarp, a shovel, several lengths of rope, and a long cloth. Usually he didn't need a gag but better to have it close at hand, just in case things turned in a noisy direction. Another reason this was a special place: because of the silence. He liked silence.

"Hello, sunshine," he said as he kneeled beside her. She still didn't respond. He raised his arm and then brought his open hand down hard against her cheek. "Wakey wakey."

Lorna came straight up out of bed, sweat beading on her forehead, and not from the pleasure of making love to Renee. No, this moisture was cold and borne of pure fear. Her body was shaking, and as she held up a hand close to her face she could see how it trembled.

Renee slept peacefully next to her with her long hair splayed across the pillow and the covers pulled up to her glorious shoulders. It didn't matter how many times she woke up next to Renee, a flutter in the pit of her stomach happened each and every time. How she loved it.

Except right now it was tainted with the emotion that had jolted her from a deep and satisfying sleep. Something dark was walking in the night. Or as her grandmother probably would have said, someone had just walked across her grave.

Quietly she got up and slipped on some sweats. Then she went to her jacket where she'd tossed it across the back of a chair and slid her hand into the pocket. Earlier that day, she'd *borrowed* the keychain that held Alida's work-truck key. Actually it wasn't the whole keychain, just the fob, and as the keys were still in the ignition at the impound lot, no one had noticed and, the way she figured it, wouldn't for quite a while.

Holding the fob gingerly between two fingers, she padded into the bathroom and silently closed the door behind her. Only then did she turn on the light. Sitting on the closed toilet lid she took a deep breath and closed her entire hand around the fob. It was warm and getting warmer. Maybe it would only work in the truck. The whole seeing-into-another-dimension thing was inconsistent; what would or wouldn't happen was anybody's guess. Desperate as she was, anything was worth a try.

"Come on, Alida, talk to me," she whispered. "I need your help. Please."

For a few seconds nothing happened and she decided it wasn't going to work. Then the lights began to waver, and a sound something like the crash of the waves against the beach near her home filled her ears.

Stars were bright, like a thousand twinkling lights spreading across the night sky. The scent of freshly plowed fields wafted through the air, and a cool breeze kissed her cheek. She shivered and wrapped her arms across her breasts.

Where the hell was she? The earth was firm beneath her feet, her body alive with everything that whirled around her and touched every sense. Despite the sensory experience, she somehow knew she was a spectator, a visitor, and an interloper. She was not meant to be here.

At the sound of a vehicle she turned in time to see a dark pickup drive out of the cemetery and onto the dark country road that ran parallel to the spot where she stood. Shock rocked her when she realized she recognized that pickup.

The driver didn't see her, of that she was certain. Just as certain as she was that no one would or could see her. But she saw everything, even in the darkness punctuated only by the twinkling stars and the sliver of light from a crescent moon. It was as if her eyes possessed the power of an owl observing all that the night tried to hide and failed.

Around her, long and unkempt grass spread out, dotted by headstones old and often leaning. In the moonlight it was almost magical. Quiet, peaceful, and serene. For a long moment she stood and stared, wondering why she was here. What had brought her to this place?

As the red taillights of the truck faded so too did the sound of its powerful engine. Cool air brushed across her skin, and the tendrils of a weeping willow moved like the ripples of a curtain in a gentle breeze. She was surrounded by nothing but the silence of a country night. She couldn't even hear herself breathe. It was unnerving.

When a sound broke through the silence she whirled, trying to pinpoint where it came from. Sobs. Was that what she was hearing? She craned her head up. Was it coming from above? No, nothing was there.

She turned a full circle, scanning the lonely headstones. Still nothing. Slowly, she brought her gaze down until she stared at the ground. Bending one knee, she lowered herself to the rough grass. As she did, the sound of sobbing grew. It was still muffled, as if it was coming from a long way off, but definitely louder the closer she dropped to the ground.

Moisture soaked through her pants, the sensation icy cold against her skin. Gently, she stretched out on the grass until her head was against the earth, her ear pressed close. Feeling the cold and dampness against her ear, she closed her eyes and listened. There it was: a woman's sobs. At first it didn't make sense. This dream, or whatever it was, seemed to be playing games with her. Slowly realization dawned. This wasn't a trick or a game; truth was being horribly and vividly revealed to her. The sounds filling her head were not one woman's sobs; they were a chorus of many. Her eyes closed tightly as she listened, wondering if one voice was familiar.

The cries filling her ears broke her heart. She'd come looking for one, and yet suddenly it was glaringly clear that the lost was far more than a single soul. Slowly she opened her eyes, her ear still pressed against the cool earth. She was too saddened to move. Across the grass the lonely headstones that had stood for a long time in this almost-forgotten place were ghostly shadows. She started to rise and then dropped back down as something caught her attention. Again she stretched out on the cold grass and kept her vision parallel with the ground. The position gave her a unique perspective. Only then did she see what had been hidden from her as she'd stood gazing across the rows of headstones. Dotted around the edge of this old silent city were rectangular areas where the ground had sunk. The depressions were all the same: about three feet wide and five to six feet long.

❖

The Watcher dropped his hands and sighed. The energy it took to help her see through the veils separating the worlds depleted him. If he were physically closer, the task would be far easier. The sad reality of his life was that he could not. His penance was to stand on this land for as long as it took to complete his sentence on earth.

Once again his plight was repeated in a sad litany of repetition. She needed him and yet she was so far away. He could feel her need in his heart and soul. How he wanted to go to her, to hold her hand, to make her understand how special she was. He wanted to give her strength and courage, to show her the way.

He'd been lost so long ago and his price for taking the wrong path so very great. To earn his way home God had given him a mission, and after all these long years he finally understood the full import of the task he'd been graced with. Still, his path to redemption was not an easy one. So much was out of his control. She was his way home, though she would never know, for that was for him and God alone.

He must help her. Must make her see and understand. His struggle to find a way wore him down. To know and understand his mission, to feel so deeply and yet to be held back was akin to burning in the fires of hell. Perhaps such was part of the great plan and part of his penance.

All he could do was continue to try. His shoulders slumped and he lowered his giant body to the ground. Tonight the air was clear and filled with the familiar scent of the breeze coming off the ocean. No storms. No darkness. No companionship. The house on the bluff was silent, and only the old woman rested inside. The others who filled the home with light and goodness were far away. That he missed them all was an epiphany he didn't expect.

How he hoped she would find the way, for as she did, so too would he. His head lowered, his eyes closed, he whispered words in a language long since vanished from the world of the here and now. Then he was gone.

Chapter Twenty-one

Lorna dropped the key fob and put her hands to her face. She no longer heard the sobs of others. Instead, her own sobs were bouncing off the bathroom walls and filling her ears. The pain in her heart was white hot. How could she possibly make this right? The clarity that came now was far from welcome.

The bathroom door winged open, bounced off the wall, and nearly smacked Renee as she charged in. She took Lorna's face between her two hands. "What's wrong? What's happened?"

At her touch Lorna closed her eyes and took comfort in the simple feel of Renee's palms against her skin. Just her touch alone eased her aching heart. After a moment she opened her eyes and met Renee's worried ones. She blew out a long breath and said the words that were so painful. "Alida is dead."

"Oh, baby, you don't know that."

The truth made her voice shake. "Yeah, I do."

Renee's eyes narrowed and she studied her for what seemed like five minutes. Resignation made her shoulders slump. "Tell me." Her hands dropped from Lorna's face as she sat on the edge of the bathtub.

She blew out another breath as she tried to put it all in perspective. "I had another vision, except it wasn't like any of the others so far. Bizarre and scary."

Renee nodded. "I kind of figured that. Tell me about it."

Chills rolled up her spine as she pictured the view while she'd lain on the ground. It came back to her in vivid detail, as if she were still there. "She's buried in a cemetery." She didn't have to explain who she meant by *she*.

Renee stroked a hand across her hair. "Lorna, that doesn't make sense unless you're seeing the future, and so far everything you've witnessed are things from the past."

She put up a hand as if to physically ward off any more words. "I know it sounds weird, but stay with me. I held the key fob in my hand..."

"The key fob? What fob?"

"Oh yeah, forgot to mention I snagged it from Alida's truck. Anyway, I'm holding it between my hands, and the next thing I know I'm in an old cemetery somewhere out in the boonies. Around it on two sides are plowed fields ready for planting, and the other two sides are bordered by roads. It sits at the intersection of two country roads, and around the perimeter of the cemetery are graves."

"The perimeter?"

"That's what's so creepy about it. These aren't official graves. Someone has buried people around the edge of the cemetery, not in it like normal burials."

"I heard of something like that once. People years back couldn't afford a proper burial so they'd sneak in at night and bury their loved ones on the edges of a cemetery so they were on blessed ground."

"I don't think this has anything to do with consecrated ground. I think some sick sonofabitch is using this place as his personal burial garden. And the worst part is, she's there, I know it. I feel it."

"How could you tell there were graves? Were they marked somehow?"

She shook her head. "When I was standing I didn't see anything out of the ordinary. It was a regular old cemetery with little maintenance, big and small headstones, many of them leaning and near collapse. It was only when I was flat on the ground that I could see the distinctive impressions. And then I heard the cries."

"Oh, Lorna," she said and hugged her tight. The embrace gave her strength.

"My dear sweet friend is there beneath the shaggy grass. Renee, it was horrible and it wasn't just Alida. She's not alone. I don't know how many are there, and I'm terrified to find out. We have to locate the cemetery and bring them all home."

Renee was nodding. "I may not be from around here, but I have to think there are a good many of those old cemeteries around this area. How can we narrow it down to the one you saw?"

The same thought had already occurred to her. The area surrounding Spokane traditionally consisted of farmland populated by families that had worked the land for decades. Generations of families were buried throughout the county in the small, old cemeteries that dotted the landscape north, west, east, and south. The locations were different, the look of them pretty much the same.

"Yeah, ahead of you on that one."

"Any thoughts on how to narrow it down?" Renee asked.

"Two distinct features that caught my attention might help us. A big weeping willow grew in the corner of this one, and the entrance was a tall wrought-iron gate with a curved sign over the top."

"We'll find it. Your vision gives us the first real lead, and we'll be able to find it."

"I really hope so." As heartbreaking as it was to realize Alida was lost to them, she wanted to push hard to bring her home. No one deserved to be abandoned in anonymous graves. Not Alida and not any of the nameless others beside her.

"What do we do next?"

She sighed at the thought of what she was compelled to do. It wouldn't be fair or right not to. "I'll have to tell Thea."

Renee put a hand to her mouth. "Oh, God, that's not going to be easy."

"No. It's going to crush her." Her voice broke.

Renee took both her hands. "I think we should talk to that deputy first."

She started to shake her head and stopped. Perhaps Renee was right. Katie might be able to glean a little more information from what she'd seen. Before she said anything to Thea, she wanted to find Alida. Bringing her home was the least she could do for her friend. With Katie's help it could happen.

"That's a good idea. I'll call her." She got up, intending to go grab her cell phone. Renee didn't let loose of her hands.

"Baby, it's two a.m. Call in a few hours."

"But…"

"If what you've seen is what it sounds like, four or five hours won't make a difference."

Lorna paused and blinked back tears. Once again, Renee was right. It just hurt so much to finally accept that she wouldn't be able to bring Alida home alive.

❖

Katie woke up smiling for the first time in a long while. She jumped up and hit the shower. Though her mood was good, the seriousness of the promise she'd made last night still weighed heavy on her shoulders. The weight was all the heavier because of what had happened when she left Thea's. That thought brought a flush of warmth.

When she'd walked to the door to leave last night, she'd paused and turned to look at Thea. It was then she'd caught the reflection of her own feelings in her eyes. In them she glimpsed passion, attraction, and hope. Without giving herself a second to change her mind, she'd kissed her. She'd meant for it to be a gentle touch of the lips but failed miserably. It became hard and urgent, the kiss of a lover. The best part was, Thea responded in kind. She didn't pull away.

Her fingertips strayed to her lips. Even now, she could almost taste the sweetness of her lips and the promise they held. It spurred her on even more than before. She'd committed herself to this case from the moment it was assigned to her, and that was before it became personal. Now it was the *one*. The case every deputy encountered somewhere in their career and the one they wouldn't give up on… ever.

She was still smiling when her cell phone rang. It was barely seven, and so it surprised her when she heard Lorna's voice. By the time she finished talking with Lorna, she was even more motivated. At this point she wasn't sure if any of what Lorna told her would help, but she intended to follow up on it. She was still mulling it over when she reached the PSB.

At her desk, she started with the information she'd gleaned from the other states and counties reporting similar disappearances. She pushed back in her chair and looked around the room. Where the hell was Vince? He managed to show up every time she didn't need him, so the moment she wanted to see him, he was missing. She could use his help.

"Anybody see Vince this morning?"

She wasn't surprised to hear everyone say no. "Shit," she murmured under her breath.

Chad leaned against the wall, a fragrant cup of coffee in his hand, and said, "I heard him say something about heading north to follow up on a potential lead. Didn't quite catch what it was. Typical Vince, sucking down an expensive coffee and talking so fast nobody would be able to understand him."

Katie blew out her cheeks. Unfortunately she knew exactly what Chad meant. Vince was like a seventeen-year-old with a gun, most of the time. His clearance record was pretty impressive. On the other hand, he could be exceedingly annoying, and if he stopped at her desk to talk with a mouth full of food one more time, she'd scream or shoot him. And God help him if he called her "little woman" again. Still, she would like to talk to him this morning, and his not being here was incredibly inconvenient.

"Damn it," she muttered.

"Sorry, K. You could try his cell phone."

"Already did. Went straight to voice mail."

Chad shrugged and took a swig of his coffee. "He must be in a dead zone. Anything I can do for you?"

Maybe Chad could help, even if he'd initially been less than enthusiastic about this case. She preferred Vince simply because he had more years on the force, giving him a hell of a lot more experience. His attitude about the idea of Alida being abducted sucked, not that it mattered at the moment. If the guy was MIA, it was a good idea to take offered help, wherever it came from. She nodded and pointed to the empty chair. "Here's what I've got so far—"

"Roberts!"

Chad's head snapped around at the sound of the captain's voice. "Yeah, Chief, what's up?"

Don Garfield, six foot six with a full head of silver hair and a personality that could fill any room, nodded toward an open office door. "Need you in here."

With a roll of his eyes, Chad looked over at her. "Sorry, Carlisle. Apparently there's another fire with my name on it."

"Thanks anyway," she said dryly.

Before he walked off, he tapped his fingers on her desk. "I'll check back in later and see what I can do to help."

It was a nice offer, but she just didn't think it would matter. She had a feeling something was going to break, and soon. Where the hell was Vince? To Chad she said, "Appreciate the offer."

When he was gone, she tried Vince's cell once more. Nothing. Dumb ass, she thought as she dropped the phone onto the top of her desk.

"Learn anything interesting last night?"

"Excuse me?" Brandon stood at her desk holding a couple sheets of paper.

He smiled, all cheerful and bright-eyed. "You know, over at the sister's house last night?"

Unease made her slowly turn in her chair and stare up into his face. "How the hell would you know where I was last night?"

His gaze never wavered. "Ah, you know how it is. I get out and about. I see things."

So he saw her car at Thea's. It didn't mean a thing. Unless he saw them saying, kissing, good-bye. Keeping her voice level, she said, "Brought her up to date."

He nodded. "Yeah, good plan."

"What have you got for me?" Time to turn this conversation away from her activities last night.

If Brandon was aware of her blatant ploy to drive the conversation in a different direction, he didn't let on. "Wish I could tell you I came up with something good. Can't. Phone was a bust, if you get me. Only calls made were to another burner phone. No way to track who owns it. Or owned it. Probably in some trash can somewhere."

He was right, of course. The phone was undoubtedly long gone. "Thanks for trying."

Brandon dropped the papers on her desk and gave her shoulder a light squeeze. "No worries. I'm always here if you need me."

"Appreciate it." Sort of. He gave her a high wave as he headed back to his own space. The exchange left her feeling uncomfortable. The fact Brandon knew she was at Thea's house last night could be nothing more than simple coincidence. Or not. Dad always told her to be leery of so-called coincidences. True episodes were rare. This didn't feel like the real thing, but why would Brandon be following her?

With her fingertips she massaged her temple. First Vince was nowhere to be found, and now Brandon giving her the heebie-jeebies. Her earlier good vibes were fading fast.

"Let it go," she whispered to herself. She could deal with Brandon later. Right now her thoughts turned to the call from Lorna. She needed to figure out what to do with Lorna's info. Deep inside she had a feeling everything she'd discovered so far was all tied together, and this might be too.

Then another thought hit her. A little unconventional, but maybe that's exactly what this case needed. She picked her phone back up and punched in a number.

"Mom, I need to pick your brain."

Thea wanted to meet Lorna and Renee for breakfast but needed to work. For the first time since Alida disappeared, she couldn't ignore her job. With Renee, Jeremy, and Merry here, Lorna could still get a great deal done without her. In fact, she might actually do better without her filling the space with her nervous energy.

Still, it was hard not to be there. It took every ounce of effort she could dredge up to keep focused on the tasks needing her attention. Over all she thought she did a pretty decent job of attending to business, but it was the hardest morning she could recall since she started the company. Normally she loved the creative energy overflowing in the office. Today she couldn't embrace even an ounce of it.

By noon she was just about jumping out of her skin. At least now she felt okay about leaving again. Five hours of solid work had gotten the recent projects back on track, questions answered, and fires put out. By the time she left her people were briefed and fully capable of going forward without her. It was time to find Lorna.

A quick call and they were set to meet at Thea's house. Lorna seemed very intent on something, which made Thea's heart race. She just knew Lorna was going to break through the fog hiding her sister's whereabouts once and for all. Today was the day. She hoped.

Before she got her phone back in her pocket it rang again. "Hello?"

"Thea, this is Katie."

The warm sound of her voice sent a thrill sliding down her back. What was it about this cop that made her shiver? Whatever it was, it was good, and right now she very much appreciated anything good.

"Do you have news?" A sliver of something like hope flashed through her.

"Not exactly." The pause said more than the words.

She didn't want to feel so let down, yet she couldn't help it. Understanding at an intellectual level was one thing. Feeling it in her heart was something altogether different. "Oh." The word sounded flat, felt even worse.

Katie rushed on before Thea could say anything else. "Look, I got a call from Lorna this morning. You might have too."

She was the one who'd called Lorna, not the other way around. And it was this afternoon rather than this morning. "I talked to her, and I'm actually on my way to meet her right now."

"Okay, well, good, you've talked, and that's what's important. Here's the deal from my side of things. My mother happens to be a local historian. Actually, she's a professor out at Eastern Washington University, and part of her work is documenting the history of the area."

Maybe she wasn't paying very close attention because she wasn't hearing what she wanted to, and none of what Katie was saying made the least bit of sense to her. "What does this have to do with talking to Lorna?"

The tone of Katie's voice shifted from fast and furious to slow questioning. "Didn't Lorna tell you about what she saw in her dream or vision or whatever it was?"

She tightened her grip on the phone, afraid she'd throw up. "No, she didn't mention a vision."

Katie paused again. "Ah, I'm not sure why she didn't tell you. Maybe she wanted to fill you in face-to-face."

Tears started to fill her eyes. "Let's go with that." It was better than thinking her friend had shut her out of something important or, worse, something terrible.

"That's got to be what it was. Anyway, she had a vision, and it centered on one of the old pioneer cemeteries. So, with Mom having unique access to that kind of information, I ran all of it by her. She said it definitely sounds like it could be one of the old cemeteries on the outskirts of the city. According to Mom, a number of them match the description Lorna gave."

The hurt she'd experienced at realizing she'd been left out of the loop started to fade. If this was true, maybe they were finally getting somewhere. "So we need to check them all."

"Not all of them. Mom gave me a list of the ones she thought sounded as close as possible to Lorna's description. I thought we could work our way through them."

Honestly, the thought made Thea's heart hurt. She wanted to bring her twin home alive, but her mind told her the likelihood was pretty slim. Going to cemeteries to try to find Alida shattered that desire as if it were made of single-pane glass.

"Thea? You still there?"

She blinked and returned her focus to the conversation. She thought she'd been silent only a moment, but it must have been much longer. "Yes, I'm still here."

"Can I pick you up? I'd like you to come with me."

Rubbing a hand over her eyes, she willed herself not to cry. "I'd like that."

"Thea, we're going to find her."

That's exactly what she was afraid of.

Jesus Christ, it had been a long morning. He didn't think he was ever going to get out of there. And talk about a chicken-shit agenda.

Sometimes he wanted to jump up on the table and show them who he really was. To throw off the veneer and be the real man for once. They all underestimated him. Worse, they didn't really see him at all. It seemed as though no one took him seriously.

Well, one of these days he'd show them all. Oh, indeed he would show them exactly who and what he was. Then he'd see how serious they'd take him. Serious as the back of a shovel. That thought made him smile. He did so love his shovel.

He leaned back in his chair and looked around. Most of the people he worked with were okay in a bland, boring way. He didn't have anything against them, unless they looked a little too closely at what he was doing. Just like this morning. How the dumb ass ever thought he was invisible was a mystery. He'd picked up on him on the first day, tailing him like he was a newbie. Not even close. His skills were the best because he spent a lot of time honing them. Worked and worked and worked until perfection was within the palm of his hand. He was that good. Perfection wasn't luck, it was preparation.

Even the best faced off days, when things didn't quite go to plan. That fairly accurately described his morning. First he took care of his shadow and then endured the impromptu meeting that went on forever. The whole time he was itching to get back out to his truck and deal with his unintended passenger. Not that anyone would know he was in the truck. He'd made one hundred percent certain his secret remained precisely that.

He'd been anxious to get out of the meeting, and not because he feared exposure. It was more a case of hating loose ends. His world was tidy to the obsessive-compulsive degree. No big revelation there. He understood his own nature very well and was fine with it. In fact, the chaos other people lived in amazed him. He didn't understand how they functioned in such a loose way. To exist in such a manner would make him extremely uncomfortable. Tidiness soothed him, order and routine calmed his psyche, and that meant taking care of the visitor in his truck. Everything in its place was the credo of his life.

Finally he'd managed to extricate himself from the meeting and was back in his truck and back on the road. Calm settled over him as he drove up Division Street, despite the heavy traffic that forced him to stop at light after light. When he hit the intersection of Division and

Francis Avenue he made a split-second decision. Instead of heading straight north he took a left and drove west on Francis. Sometimes it was better to shake it up a little rather than contaminate what was already sacred to him.

He followed Francis as it curved around to the north and turned into State Highway 291. The drive took him past Suncrest and beyond Tum Tum to where it shifted from private ownership to tribal land. Out here, he was the only one on the road, and the landscape was hilly and spotted with outcroppings of ancient basalt rock. It wasn't the lush forested land just a few miles behind him, but it held its own special kind of beauty, with plateaus overlooking Long Lake and vast expanses of unspoiled fields dotted by unique stones carved by glaciers millions of years earlier.

It took him awhile to find a spot he liked. The area he chose was perfect for what he had in mind. He pulled the truck off the road and drove as far as he dared onto the rough land. It wasn't thick tree cover, though a fair amount of pine trees still provided what he deemed an appropriate visual barrier from the road. What made it workable for the plan he'd formulated on the drive out here was the abundance of small brush and downed branches. Nice and dry, and plenty of scrub.

When he finally managed to get his passenger out of the truck and on the ground, he grabbed his feet and dragged him a good twenty yards farther away from where he parked. This one was a mite heavier than his normal girls. No matter, a job was a job, and he got his passenger where he needed to be. Ten minutes later he stopped and studied his work. A massive pile of branches and dried brush now covered the motionless figure. Nodding, he decided it was just about perfection.

Back at the truck he grabbed the five-gallon can of gas he always kept topped off in the back of his truck. His always-be-prepared motto came in handy in more ways than one. Usually he used the gas to top off the truck tank. Today, he had something different in mind. The smell of the gasoline he poured onto the pile was pungent in the still afternoon air. When the can was empty, he returned it to the truck.

The gasoline fumes filled the air, and before he struck a match and tossed it into the pile he breathed in the scent. It made him smile. Tossing a match, he stepped back and waited only a second before his plan came to life. With a whoosh the flame caught, turning the mound into a raging funeral pyre. He allowed himself a full minute to stand and gaze upon the creative solution to his problem. It was good. It was right. He was happy.

As much as he longed to linger here and watch the fire do its work, it would be a very bad idea. He had to go. Turning his back on the blaze, he returned to his truck, got in, put it in reverse, and backed out onto the road, bumping through ruts as he went. Not wanting to risk the attention of either the Stevens County Sheriff's Department or the Washington State Patrol, both which patrolled SR291, he kept to the speed limit as he drove back to town.

Chapter Twenty-two

L orna was worried about Thea, who looked like shit. She was a beautiful woman who made both men and women stop and stare. But today her face was sallow, with dark circles under her eyes. Usually Lorna hated the stupid psychic thing, except at this moment she wished like hell she understood it enough to find Alida. Anything to erase the shadows that darkened Thea's face.

Before Lorna could walk through the open front door, Renee stepped forward and wrapped her arms around Thea, tight. "We're here for you."

If Lorna didn't already love Renee, that would have cinched it. Her way of knowing what people needed before they even realized it was magical, and she wasn't even remotely psychic. Renee did that for her every day. She should have known she'd pick up on the same thing for Thea.

Thea hugged Renee back and then stepped out of her embrace to motion them both in. "You don't know how much that means to me. Come on in. Katie will be here shortly."

Katie. Not Deputy Carlisle. *Katie*. This was undoubtedly the worst imaginable time to meet someone, yet Lorna sensed Thea was taken with the attractive officer. Honestly, who wouldn't be? She was striking and intelligent, and who could resist a woman with a badge and a gun?

She turned her gaze to Renee, and all thoughts of a hot cop disappeared. Nothing could make her heart soar like Renee did. She wasn't a tall, toned athlete. She didn't carry a badge or a gun. She didn't radiate power with every stride. None of it mattered, for she was pure magic, and Lorna didn't think she'd tire of her for one single day the rest of her life.

Renee caught her stare and gave her a small smile and a wink, which sent a rush of desire through her. Funny how that had never happened to her before she met this wonderful woman. How much her life had changed since she left for Aunt Bea's beautiful house on the shores of the Pacific Ocean. Like everyone else, a few of Lorna's friends were the eternally optimistic types who professed that life always worked out the way it was supposed to. When she was going through her ordeal with Anna she could have screamed each time one of them said that to her. She was glad she'd opted not to throw that particular tantrum because she'd be apologizing now. Seemed those sunny-natured friends of hers might be right.

"So Deputy Carlisle is on her way?" Lorna wondered if she could use anything she'd shared from the fob-inspired vision.

Thea nodded. "She has a list of cemeteries for us to check out."

"About that..." Lorna should have told Thea when she called earlier but just couldn't bring herself to say the words over the phone.

Thea waved her off. "You did what you thought was right."

It was typical for Thea to let her off easy even if she was mad. "I still should have told you so you didn't hear it from someone else."

"Katie isn't just someone else, so don't worry about it."

If Thea was pissed, she couldn't tell. She was calm and focused, her words sounding sincere. "What about Grant? Should we call him? He'll want to help."

This time Thea shook her head. "He probably would like to, but it's better we do this without him. Katie hasn't said as much, but I get the sense she still doesn't trust him."

"Do you?"

Though she paused for a second before answering, she was nodding as she spoke. "I do. I know he's kind of a butt. He's just not the kind of butt who'd kill his wife."

The grimace that crossed Thea's face as she spoke the words made Lorna sad. Thea was strong, but voicing the possibility of death had to hurt. No doubt she must have thought it. They all were certain to have considered it, but saying it out loud was different and far more painful.

A knock at the door made them all turn. Thea went to the door and pulled it open. Outside, Jeremy and Merry stood on the porch. "Hey, ladies. Thought you could use a gentleman's touch."

It still amazed her how quickly their little group had become a team. Out of disparate circumstances they'd come together and stayed together. In her wildest dreams she'd never imagined living with her brother—and his wife-to-be—at this point in her life. Nor did she imagine being in a relationship that filled her with love and hope every day. The four of them cohabitated in harmony inside the walls of the massive house, and it all worked.

It was more than just living together though. They seemed to be connected at a level beyond the sight and touch of man. Jeremy and Merry showing up now was an example. By herself, Lorna had possessed the power to see beyond the veil that separated the world of the living from the world of the spirits. With Renee, Jeremy, and Merry beside her, her power seemed to magnify. She didn't have to tell them either. They knew when they were needed, and they had her back each and every day.

One more time she heard a knock on the door, and again Thea went to it. No big surprise when she returned with Deputy Carlisle. Katie was primed and ready, and she didn't waste any time on pleasantries. "Here's the deal," she said as she handed each of them a standard-size piece of paper. "We're going to divide and conquer."

"But I'll need to see them to know." Lorna could describe the place all she wanted, but she was going to have to see it to know for certain.

"Got it covered." Katie held up her smart phone. "It's called picture messaging."

Why hadn't she thought of that? Technology really was her friend in this instance. "Good idea," Lorna said and tapped the phone in her pocket.

Katie gave her a pat on the back. "Hey, I didn't make deputy just because I'm cute."

❖

To say the afternoon was frustrating was putting it mildly. Katie wanted to stamp her feet and throw a tantrum like she used to when she was six years old and things didn't go her way. Opting for a more adult and dignified approach, she simply internalized like any good cop did. The plan was a good one. They would split up Mom's list and hit every cemetery on it. Thus far nothing seemed to jog Lorna's memory. So many of them looked alike: small and surrounded by fences of stone, wood, or wrought iron and with rows of headstones that varied in height from ground level to carved figures rising six feet in the air.

At least one of them should have triggered something, or so Katie thought, but Lorna looked sad and depressed as she gave the thumbs-down to every one of them. The afternoon had been a total waste of time, and they didn't have time to waste.

Now, the six of them sat in the back corner of a trendy pub on North Division drinking beer and mulling over their failure. If all else failed, drink. She didn't see a ray of hope on a single face. The reality of failure weighed heavy on every set of shoulders, and not one hand even bothered to pick up a beer. So much for the power of alcohol to dull pain and frustration.

"What now?" Thea asked as she held the dark brew between both hands and stared down into its murky depths.

Jeremy spoke up first at the same time he smacked his palm on the tabletop. "We start again tomorrow. We might not have found it today. We will in the morning. I feel it right here." He tapped his palm against his cheek.

Katie liked Lorna's brother. He seemed smart, and they really needed his optimism right now. His glass-half-full mentality might very well be misplaced, but she still appreciated it. Like his sister, he had a bit of a glow. He probably wasn't psychic like Lorna, yet something about him screamed *special* to Katie, and at this juncture, she'd use anything she could. If only their combined resources could have provided a better result.

"What's the point?" Thea asked, still not looking away from her beer.

Merry put a hand on Thea's. "We're going to find her, no matter how long it takes. That's why we're all here, and we're not leaving until we locate her. I promise."

Tears began to fall from Thea's downcast eyes. "It's too late, you know."

Katie couldn't help but put an arm around Thea's shoulders and hug her. "Thea, no matter what, we're going to find Alida, and we're going to bring her home."

She liked that Thea not only accepted her hug but actually leaned into her. The connection between them was powerful, and while she might be failing as a cop at the moment, she damned well wasn't going to fail as a friend. Maybe she'd known Thea for only a short time, and maybe they were just forging some kind of relationship, but they were definitely friends. The way she felt about Thea was as baffling as it was beautiful. She didn't usually fall for a woman so fast, especially someone involved in an open case, but none of it mattered because it was what it was.

For a long minute no one said a word, at least not until the server approached their table with a vase filled with pale roses. She set it in the middle of the table before taking out her notepad. "Can I get you folks anything to eat?"

Everyone but Lorna said no. Katie turned to look at Lorna, who was still silent and staring at the vase of roses. "We're all good," she said in a way she hoped was a polite dismissal. It seemed to work as the server gave them a smile and then went on to another table of guests.

"What is it, Lorna?" From the way she was staring at those flowers, Katie could almost see the wheels turning. Lorna's gaze was locked on the roses as if she'd never seen anything like them before.

"They look wild, don't they?" she asked in a breathless voice.

Maybe a little. What possible difference did it make what kind of flowers the server left on their table? "I suppose. Is that important?" Katie couldn't imagine why it would be.

Lorna's eyes were still glued to the roses as she nodded slowly. "Yeah. I think it's very important."

Jeremy put a hand on Lorna's shoulder. "What is it, Lorna? What are you seeing?"

Lorna held up a hand as her eyes narrowed. "Give me a sec."

Silence fell over their little group, and the only sounds were those of the other patrons, the low rumble of music from speakers high up on the walls, and the clatter of dishware and glasses. Finally, she looked up, her eyes bright and full of energy.

"Wild Rose," she declared triumphantly.

"Wild Rose?" Katie repeated. What the hell did that mean?

"Yup…Wild Rose. That's the name. It was over the top of the big wrought-iron gate leading into the cemetery. Until the waitress set the flowers down, I didn't remember it."

Katie was already pulling her phone out of her pocket. "Mom," she said when the call went through. "Do you know of a cemetery called Wild Rose?" As her mother spoke, she dug a pen from her pocket and started scribbling notes on a napkin. "Thanks." She punched the off button and slipped the phone back into her pocket.

"Mom says there's an old homestead cemetery out north called Wild Rose."

"Is it at an intersection of two roads?" Lorna was staring at her with a very eager expression.

Katie felt hope, real hope, for the first time in days. "Yes, it is." She looked around at them and nodded. "First thing in the morning, let's go up there."

"Fuck morning," Jeremy said as he stood up. "I say we check that mother out right now."

❖

The light of day was starting to fade by the time his truck was spic and span. He'd taken it to the car wash first to use the high-power spray. Then at home he'd pulled out his box of professional cleaning supplies and scrubbed every inch. Now it gleamed as though it had just come off the showroom floor. Not so much as a single hair was left anywhere.

He did appreciate good cleaning. It was another of the lessons the old man taught him. At the time of those excruciating lessons, he wanted to kill him. Especially when the bastard would kick the air out of him because he missed cleaning a millimeter of something. Didn't matter if it was his prized Corvette or the bathroom floor. The expectation was the same, as was the punishment, if he failed to meet the required standard. In the end, he came to appreciate the beauty of perfection. It had served him well over the years and brought him to this place of supreme satisfaction.

Now that he'd tidied up everything and handled all the loose ends, he wished he could hunt, just a little. So much out there would benefit from his vision and good work. It was frustrating to so often feel like his hands were tied. And, in fact, they were. He was forced to accomplish his work carefully so it took far more time than he cared for. If things were his way, he'd be like a tsunami roaring through the area and washing it clean.

But he exercised the patience drilled into him for as long as he could remember. One more of the old man's hated tutorials. There had been so many and they stood him well now. Another reminder that all things have a way of working out as they should if given enough time.

Of course that often left him feeling at loose ends. He wanted to work. No, he needed to work and right now he couldn't. It was too soon. The stakes were high, which was actually good because it showed how important the things he accomplished were. If they weren't, none of this would matter. He was creating a utopia that, given enough time, all would come to appreciate. The smart ones would realize what a hero he was.

He went to the refrigerator on the shop bench and pulled a soda from inside. He never stocked any alcohol in his fridge. Given the importance of his goals he had no place in his life for mood-altering substances. He couldn't afford to be off one iota. Not that booze had ever been a problem for him. It was a totally useless substance, and he didn't tolerate those who drank to excess. They were losers of the worst kind, right up there with drug addicts, abusers, and liars.

Leaning against the garage door and sipping on the ice-cold cola, he watched the sunset and appreciated the beauty of it. Deep reds and blues slashed across the horizon where the sky met the mountains. The air was cool and fresh, reminding him that while it wasn't summer yet, the promise of spring was abundant.

He liked it here, no question about it. Too bad he wouldn't be able to stay. In the long run, he would be compelled to move on, at least for a little while. It always worked this way. He could perform his work for a good time, and then it was wise to get along. He'd go somewhere new for a few years, and when it was safe, he'd come back home. There were always places that needed someone like him. He just packed up his belongings and flew away...literally.

Not just yet, however; he was still needed here, and regardless of anything to the contrary, this was home. It always would be, no matter where else he spent his time. Besides, he wasn't quite ready to leave her. She was special, not like the others. He wished deeply it could have worked out differently. In the end it had been her choice and she'd chosen badly. He couldn't help it. He didn't make the rules. He just followed them.

With one last swig, he polished off the soda and tossed the can into the recycle bin. Though he might not be able to work tonight, he could ease his restlessness. Pulling the keys out of his pocket, he climbed into his truck, breathing in the strong scent of the cleaner that still lingered. He backed out, hit the automatic garage-door remote to close the door, and then began to drive north.

"I'm coming, sweetheart," he whispered. "I'm coming."

Chapter Twenty-three

Halfway to the Wild Rose Cemetery, Katie's cell rang. She glanced at the caller ID and, seeing it was the boss, clicked on. "Carlisle."

"Katie, when was the last time you talked to Vince?" Don Garfield's voice was somber, more so than she'd ever heard it. A chill went up her back.

"Yesterday," she told him. "I called him a number of times today and it went to voice mail every time. When I asked if anyone had seen him, Chad mentioned he was going somewhere north to follow a lead. Not sure where or for what case. Going up north is pretty broad. No clue where he ended up."

Gruffly, he said, "He went north all right, but not on a lead."

The tone in his voice made the chills in her body go glacial. "What's happened?"

"He's dead."

She must have heard him wrong. Driving and having this kind of conversation wasn't happening, so she pulled to the shoulder and stopped. She needed to give this call her complete attention. "Say that again."

"Katie, he's dead," he said slowly, and the despair mixed with fury left no question about the truth of it.

"No. Fucking. Way. Pardon my French." She thought of cocky, arrogant Vince and couldn't picture him dead. Guys like him didn't die.

"It gets worse."

"Jesus, Don, how the hell can it get worse?"

"Whoever killed him tried to cover it up by torching him."

She lowered her head until her forehead rested on the steering wheel, the phone still pressed to her ear. He had been acting weird lately, and she'd wondered what the hell was up with him. Maybe she should have paid more attention or taken her concerns to Don. Maybe if she had, Vince would still be alive.

"How? Where?"

"Out past Tum Tum in Stevens County. A local resident trail-running with his dog discovered his body. Don't think the guy will be running that route again anytime soon."

She sat up and stared out the window, picturing the area. A good lot of space for someone who wanted to make a big fire. "How bad?"

"Pretty ugly. Body's in rough shape. Fucker used gasoline to make sure the fire was nice and hot. We'll have to get a positive dental match for confirmation, but from my standpoint, it's definitely him."

Don didn't jump to conclusions, so if he was sure the body was Vince's, it was. "Who would do something like that? I mean, I know better than anybody what a pain in the ass Vince could be, but to burn him? It takes a sick bastard to be that evil."

"Hard to say who hated him enough to be so brutal, Katie. He's put some bad people in jail, and you know as well as I do how far some will go to get revenge."

She did know. It was the reality of the profession they were in, and the suspect list was bound to be long. This was the first time, however, she'd experienced a loss like this, and it made her sick all over.

"What do you need me to do?" Regardless of whatever else she was working, an officer down took priority, and when that officer was in her unit, it zoomed to the top. Vince might have given her a hard time and pissed her off on a daily basis, but she'd do everything she could to bring in his killer.

"For tonight, nothing. I just wanted to give you a heads-up before it hit the news. We'll meet in the morning."

"Thanks, Don. I'll come to your office first thing."

"Sounds good. And, Katie—"

"Yeah?"

"Watch your back."

"Damn straight."

In silence, she put the car back into gear and pulled onto the road. Plain and simple, she was in shock. Nobody said a word the rest of the way out. Even when she parked at the outskirts of the cemetery, they seemed to be waiting for her, and she appreciated the respect and time they gave her to process what happened. She opened her mouth to try to explain when her cell rang again. What did Don want now? Surely there couldn't be more bad news. Then she glanced at the number on the display. It wasn't Don. She almost let it go to voice mail.

"Carlisle."

"Gotta know."

The voice threw her for a second. When she got it, she was still confused. "Brandon, why are you calling me?" Why the hell was the IT Tech getting ahold of her this late at night?

"Call me curious."

Had he heard what happened to Vince? "About Vince?"

"No, dude. I mean that's sick and all, but I'm more curious what you're up to out in the boonies."

Her heart started to pound, and a trickle of fear made the hair stand up on the back of her neck. "Brandon," she said slowly. "How do you know where I am?"

"Oops." With that single word she realized Brandon was, or had been, drinking. "Kinda forgot to mention I GPSed your phone." He giggled.

"You're tracking me?"

"Well, yeah, kinda. I am an IT God, you know. It's what we do."

A horrible thought jumped into her mind. "Were you tracking Vince too?"

"That butthead? Why would I want to do that? He's not near as awesome as you are. Oh, gotta go. Pizza's here. Be cool out there, Officer."

He was gone, and Katie was left with a dawning truth so bad it almost made her sick.

❖

Storm clouds were gathering in the east, growing darker and more menacing as the minutes passed. The Watcher stood at the edge of the water, staring as the waves grew more turbulent at his feet. The sea screamed its fury. Time was out for her, and he didn't know how else to help.

On the other side of the mountains, evil grew in strength and intent. She was the only one who could stop him, and he'd tried to give her the tools she needed. As if he hadn't already spent an eternity attempting to redeem himself, God had sent him a challenge seemingly impossible to meet.

Almost impossible, he reminded himself. So far, she had taken what he had sent her and made it work. His power was limited, and the limits reached, judging by the strength of the storm he watched rumble and roll in the distance. He kept his gaze on the clouds growing blacker, as if the evil that threatened her was gathering power.

Cold raindrops hit his face and he closed his eyes, feeling the cool wetness slide down his skin. They started slowly and built as the minutes ticked by until the rain turned into a downpour. Still he stood without moving, letting the rainstorm assail him. With his mind he searched for her spirit, at first finding nothing but a vast, empty expanse. His patience won, and slowly the thread of connection began to grow stronger.

With his face still turned upward and his eyes closed, he clasped his hands together and began to pray,

Father in Heaven, hear my words. Blessed is she who sees the souls of the hurt, the abused, the lost. Father in Heaven, give her the strength of the ages to save those souls and to bring them into your Kingdom. Father in Heaven, watch over her and lead her home safely. In your name, I pray. Amen.

And then he was gone and the rain continued to fall on the empty sands of the beach.

❖

The moment Lorna's feet touched the ground, a small earthquake seemed to rumble beneath her. Vibrations flowed from the soil, up her legs and into her shoulders. She glanced around to see if Thea, Katie, and Jeremy felt it too. Renee, who was usually in tune with her, was back at Thea's house with Merry. Months into her pregnancy, Merry wasn't feeling well so Renee stayed behind with her to make an herbal tea sure to settle her nausea. Just another thing about Renee that Lorna loved.

The three with her now didn't appear to notice anything out of the ordinary. Not the case for her. Tiny earthquakes weren't uncommon here, but she was convinced nature wasn't the cause of the trembles beneath her feet right now. Whatever was coursing through her body, it wasn't nature-made.

She gazed up at the cemetery entrance and was instantly plunged back into the vision. As she stood beneath the arching sign, the wind picked up and the trees began to sway. Overhead the moon was climbing in the sky, sending shafts of butter-gold light down on the rows of century-old headstones. Some of the headstones still stood straight while others leaned, and years of snow, rain, and hot sun had worn the names of the dead smooth.

"Is this it?" Katie asked as she turned full circle, taking in everything. "I can't see anything unusual. Even though it's getting dark, it looks just like all the others we went to today."

"Lorna," Jeremy said as he put a hand on her shoulder. "This is it, isn't it?" He didn't wait for an answer, asking instead, "What do you see?"

The second his hand touched her shoulder a roar began in her ears, and she dropped to her knees. For the first time she welcomed what came next. "Show me," she said under her breath,

A mist covered the ground, and the moon that just a moment ago had been so bright was now a muted glow that turned the mist pale gold. She looked around and realized she was alone.

Or was she?

She rose from the mist undefined and shadowy. The ghost of a figure, at least at first, before she began to take form. Petite, with long dark hair, she was beautiful and unfamiliar. A second woman appeared, young and pale, equally unknown. The first two were followed by a third, a fourth. They kept rising until seven stood in the silence, all eyes turned to her in an unspoken plea only she could understand, and indeed she did. Tears fell from her eyes.

She thought the veil had parted enough to show her all the secrets of this place. She was wrong. An eighth came to her feet from the mist that still swirled and pulsed. At first she was nothing more than a vague shape. Lorna's breath caught in her throat as the features became clear...and recognizable. Her heart broke.

Alida.

CHAPTER TWENTY-FOUR

No damn way. How was it possible? How could someone be here, of all places? This was his place, and he'd eliminated the one and only threat to his secret mission.

For a second, he thought about turning around and going home. Even if they found them, they'd never trace any of it back to him. But these were his women, and *she* was here. He would never, ever allow anyone to take her from him. Their bond would last forever.

Slowly, he drove down the quiet country road, fixated on the lights that spilled across the cemetery. Who would be here and at this time of night? It wasn't just his place; it was also his time. It had always been his time, when most of the community was tucked nice and warm in their beds, oblivious to what went on in the shadows and alleys of their cities. It always seemed to him that he, alone, cut through the darkness to reveal the truth. And he alone made the effort to wash the stain from the streets.

Right now, he needed to stop and think. Perhaps he was jumping to conclusions. It was certainly unusual for anyone to be here this time of night. In fact, it was rare that anyone came to this place to mourn for those who rested below the old headstones, for the residents of this silent city were no longer alive in the memories of those who were still breathing. Too many generations had come and gone since they were laid to rest to make this a place of frequent visitors.

That's what made the car parked at the edge, its lights on and sending a shaft of illumination across the small cemetery at the intersection of two country roads, so odd. And irritating as hell.

Like his home, he hated intrusions by those uninvited. They upset his sense of balance. Certainly he could work with the unanticipated, and he'd proved it in spades to himself earlier today. Still, this was a true blindside. He'd never seen it coming and it pissed him off.

He pulled up next to the car and studied what he realized now was a familiar vehicle. How did she get here? He'd been so incredibly careful, yet here she was sticking her nose into something she had no business being this close to. Not to mention the company she brought with her.

As he got out of the truck, he unclipped the rifle from its center console mount. His mind whirled with the possibilities for mitigating the potential damage of her discovery. No matter what direction he came at it, one solution kept coming to the forefront. Messy, yes, at least up front. In the end, it was surely the cleanest solution.

With his right arm he held the rifle against his back. He walked into the light and stopped at the edge of the cemetery. Four. Three women. One man. He liked those odds, with the possible exception of one member of the posse. She could be a problem. Not an insurmountable one, but a problem just the same.

He couldn't help smiling. At first he'd thought this would be a terrible inconvenience. Now, as he stood here watching them help one of the women up from the ground, he decided it was just what he needed tonight. He'd been bored and restless when he started his drive out here. Now everything had turned around. This was definitely not boring.

The work he did was important, and what he must do next was another element of that effort. In a way it was quite different, yet it was just as important. The day might have started out frustrating, but it was ending on a completely different note. In fact, it was turning out to be a really good night after all.

❖

Katie was holding one of Lorna's arms as she stared at the figure that walked into the lights of her car and the pickup parked next to hers. Moonlight glinted off the shiny diamond-plate toolbox mounted in the back of the dark truck. At first she thought she must be seeing things. It wasn't him, just someone who looked like him. Except her heart told her different. After Brandon's creepy call and his admission to tracking her through GPS she was half expecting to see him show up here. Everything felt out of sync, especially what she was seeing at this moment.

"Chad?" His name floated across the night air.

"Hey, Katie, what are you doing out here?"

"What are you doing out here?" she asked. Shock at seeing him was an understatement for a variety of reasons. First and foremost, Chad wasn't exactly the fieldwork kind of guy. He could do absolutely amazing computer research, and nobody came close to his skills in interviewing both victims and subjects. Out pounding the pavement just wasn't his strongest asset, so to see him out here now didn't sit well with her. Between the call from Don, the freaky call from Brandon, and now Chad, something was very off. For all her trash-talking about psychics, she'd give a whole lot to be one at this second so she'd know what the hell was going on.

He casually said, "Heard you were here and thought I'd come out and see if I could help."

Bells started going off in her head, and they weren't the pretty church-bell variety. "Heard we were here? From whom?" She narrowed her eyes and let her hand drift in the direction of her gun. He was good. Very smooth. Then again, he usually was except all of a sudden that smoothness took on a sinister feel.

"Got it straight from the lips of the guy in charge. Don, of course. Who else do you think would send me out here?"

That would be true if she'd actually told Don where they were going. "From Don?"

"Yeah," he drawled. "He called me, said you might need backup and suggested I come on out. Here I am."

Wrong answer. Only one other person knew where she was, and even he shouldn't. If her hunch about Brandon's obsession with her was correct, the last thing he'd do was tell Chad. Her senses screamed beware and her fingers itched to grab the gun at her waist. "Did he say if Vince is coming too?"

The question made her hold her breath. She already knew the answer. This man, whom she'd seen every day for the last three years, was suddenly a stranger. A cold-eyed and dangerous stranger who made the hairs on the back of her neck stand up.

Illuminated by the headlights, the look on his face made her cop senses go on hyper-alert. He was shaking his head slowly. "Katie, Katie, Katie, you and I both know Vince isn't going to make it. You're just trying to play me now."

The charade was up, for both of them. "Yes, Chad, we do both know that. But why would you hurt him? He was your friend."

He shrugged and smiled. "Trust me, Carlisle, he wasn't my friend, and he thought he was so flipping smart. Stupid bastard didn't think I'd notice him following me. He was trying to catch me making a mistake. You may not have noticed, but he was a nosy SOB." The sound of his laugh was terrifying. "He learned the hard way it doesn't pay to be nosy."

"You caught him instead, didn't you?" Her fingers tightened on her gun as she unsnapped it from the holster. She had to keep him talking until she had it at the ready.

"Of course I did. Pretty boy was no match for me. None of you are. You see me in the station every day and think to yourselves, good old Chad. A great guy to throw scraps at, but did you ever once think of me as a partner, someone you could depend on? No, all I was good for was to do your paperwork." His voice was full of bitterness and anger. This wasn't the Chad she saw in the office. She didn't know this man and didn't want to.

"I thought you were my friend." So far so good. She was keeping him talking and working her way as close as possible. Right now she was too far away to be able to stop him from hurting anyone else. It was critical to get closer.

His laughter turned loud and bitter, and it suddenly struck her he really was right. She'd never thought of him in the same way she did Vince or any of the other guys she worked with. He was okay, but in a pinch she'd have asked Vince to watch her back. Chad was part of the boring background.

"Fuck friendship," he said in an icy voice. "I don't need any of you. Never have and never will."

"Dive!" Katie screamed at the others at the same time she saw Chad pull a rifle from behind his back.

❖

In the quiet night, the shot sounded like a cannon going off, the roar echoing on the cool evening air. Lorna dove, and for the second time that night found herself facedown in the damp grass, or what passed for grass in this place. But this time it wasn't in a vision. It was real. For a moment everything was silent, and then she heard the groan.

"Jeremy?" She turned her head in the direction of his voice. There he was, sitting on the ground rocking from side to side while holding both his hands to his thigh. "Are you okay?" she asked in a desperate whisper.

"That fucker shot me," he ground out in a low, tight voice, "and it hurts like a sonofabitch."

On her stomach she crawled toward him. Before she got more than a foot, a shot hit the dirt inches in front of her face. "I wouldn't do that if I was you," a hard male voice said. "Stay right where you're at or I'll put a bullet in you too."

"Fuck you," Lorna returned, and his response was another shot, closer this time.

Movement to her left made her turn her head in time to see Katie scrambling to her feet. "Don't," Lorna whispered. "He'll hit you."

The lights of the vehicles shone on them like a spotlight on a Broadway stage. The term sitting duck took on a brand-new meaning. Katie didn't pause as she moved in a motion that was swift and precise, her arm coming up, and a gun was in her hand. In four swift shots, the cemetery was plunged into darkness. Smart thinking to take out the headlights.

The sick laughter came across the night air again. "Well played, lovely Katie. You've always been smarter than the brass gives you credit for."

"You're outnumbered, Chad. You can't possibly hope to take us all out," Katie cried.

"No hope about it, girlfriend. You signed your own death warrant the moment you stepped onto my hallowed ground."

"Why?" Thea's plea was wracked with sobs. "Why would you kill my sister?"

His voice seemed filled with genuine emotion as he answered. "I didn't kill her, my dear. I love your sister and want her by my side always. When she said she wanted to go back to her worthless husband, giving her a place of honor in my special garden was the right thing to do. Here, she and I can be together forever. I saved her from a lifetime of boredom with that no-good cheat she called her husband."

"She's dead," Thea screamed. "You killed her. There's no forever in that, you monster."

"No, I didn't kill her. I set her soul free. She's with me forever. That is a precious gift."

Lorna took the chance to crawl next to Jeremy as Chad's attention was focused on Thea. She didn't like that he could hear Thea clearly, even if he couldn't see her. Rationally she understood all cops weren't crack shots, but he'd already been accurate enough to hit her brother. She didn't want to see her friend hurt too.

"Give it up, Katie." His voice was hard and angry. "You can't win. This is my game, and I have a hell of a lot of practice. You have no idea who you're up against."

Lorna glanced up, her eyes starting to adjust to the darkness. He wasn't in sight, the vehicles presumably giving him coverage. Katie was a dark blur of movement, and with each step she took, Lorna's heart raced. Katie was their only hope, and Lorna was terrified he was going to kill her too.

Seconds after she reached Jeremy, her hands were covered with blood. "How bad is it?" she whispered while putting pressure on the open wound.

"Flesh wound," he answered just as quietly. "I'll be dancing again in the morning."

The pain in his voice didn't fool her. "You don't dance. How bad?"

He blew out a long breath. "Honestly, it hurts like a motherfucker. Looks a lot cooler on TV."

She slipped out of her shirt and tied it tight around his leg. If nothing else, she needed to stop the bleeding. "This should help."

As she tightened the shirt, he sucked in a breath. "911 would help," he said weakly. "Nice warm ambulance, hot lady EMT laying hands on me."

God, why hadn't she thought of that? Not the last part, just the calling-911 part. "Stay still," she warned him as she moved once more on her belly toward the big weeping-willow tree. It was the best cover she could ask for.

Once she was hidden among the overhanging willow branches, she pulled out her cell phone and hit 911. She would get Jeremy a nice warm ambulance, and she didn't care if the EMT was hot as long as they showed up.

"You killed all the women we found here, didn't you?" Katie's voice was more of a taunt than a question. Lorna had the feeling she was trying to make sure his attention was focused solely on her and as far away from the rest of them as possible. That was good. If he was listening to Katie, he wouldn't be paying attention to her.

His laughter pealed. It was so creepy. How could a man who seemed so normal and nice morph into something like this? "Of course I did, you stupid bitch. Have plane, will travel."

"Why, Chad? I don't understand. What did any of them ever do to you?"

Lorna dared a look in Katie's direction. She was inching slowly toward the place by the vehicles where Chad's voice was coming from. Though it was hard to see in the darkness, she was pretty sure Katie was still holding the gun. It worried her that Katie was so exposed and she wanted to yell at her to be careful, but she didn't dare.

She almost screamed when a hand clamped down on her shoulder. "Shhh," Thea whispered in her ear. "We have to help her."

"I just called in the cavalry."

"They won't get here in time."

Across the cemetery Chad's bitter voice made them both look his way. "Somebody has to clean things up, dear Katie. I mean none of you have been doing a damn thing. These women are trash. They pollute our streets. They spread disease and heartache to the good men of our community. The slaps all you liberal bleeding hearts deliver don't do jack shit. I'm the only one with enough balls to do anything meaningful. I make a difference while you sit around talking about rehabilitation and helping tragic women start over."

"You're sick," she snapped. "The only difference you've made is to bring heartache to families all over the Pacific Northwest. There's nothing noble in that."

"On the contrary, sweetheart, I've never felt better than I do right now. Those families you're worried about have to bear the responsibility for the poor excuse for women they put out on the street. They didn't just become trash one day. They had help, so if you expect me to feel sorry for their families, think again. The only thing I feel for them is contempt. They deserve the same fate."

As his words faded, a flash cut through the blackness. Then Katie screamed and fell to the ground and out of sight.

CHAPTER TWENTY-FIVE

One bitch down. Two to go, and two easy ones at that. Carlisle had been his primary concern. He'd seen her shoot out on the range, and the bitch could out-shoot just about any man in the sheriff's department. That was precisely why he had to take her out now. He wished he possessed her skill with firearms, because even though he'd hit her, the shot wasn't fatal. Her moans let him know he'd missed his mark. He'd meant for it to be a kill shot. She'd shifted at the last second, and it had become a wound instead of a kill.

No matter. She was down, and that was all he needed right at the moment. Once he killed the other two, he could come back and put a bullet right between her pretty eyes. He wasn't all that worried about the shots bringing anyone out. Around here, gunshots weren't exactly common. They weren't exactly uncommon either. With predators that threatened livestock, people used firearms now and again. It wasn't out of the ordinary for cougars to cause havoc in the vicinity, and locals were known to use lethal force with the impressive predators.

"Come out, come out, wherever you are." He taunted her as he stepped around the grill of his truck. Only silence met him. To his right Katie was down, and about twenty feet away the man was also down and unmoving. He loved it when a plan came together.

He swept his gaze over the cemetery, and it didn't take a rocket scientist to figure out where the other two were hiding, or attempting to hide anyway. Oh, a few of the headstones were big enough to hide a woman, but they weren't there. No, his eyes were on the big weeping willow that had stood in the northwest corner for the better part of a century. Every time he came here he wondered how much longer it would stand guard over the gifts he brought.

He left the rifle at the truck and instead pulled the gun at his waist. Up close and personal, he liked the feel of the Glock 22. The gun had felt right the first time he held it, and it still did. It was a quick and efficient tool for the administration of his special brand of justice. He planned to administer that justice right now. They couldn't blame anyone but themselves. They should have left things alone. The fact they decided to butt in meant they'd written their own fate. He was simply the one carrying out the sentence. Nothing personal about it. Pleasurable, yes. Personal, no.

The dry grass crunched under his feet as he walked between the headstones. "Come on out, ladies. It's not going to do you any good to hide behind the tree. I know you're there."

The fact that neither woman made a sound didn't particularly surprise him. They always thought they could hide from him. Through the years the women he'd hunted had tried it all. Running, hiding, silence, screams. None of it worked, and it wasn't going to work now.

"Seriously, ladies, you might as well come out from behind that tree. It's not going to do you any good to stay squirreled up in there."

He came around the tree expecting to see the two women cowering in fear. Except that's not what he saw. He stopped and tilted his head. What the hell were they doing? Both of them stood tall and straight and seemed to stare beyond him. No, that wasn't it. They were staring behind him. Slowly he turned, and then he froze.

What the hell? How was this possible? Standing there beautiful and alluring as ever was his only true love, Alida. She was just as she'd been on that last day, her dark hair shiny, her long legs encased in snug blue jeans. Even the hooded sweatshirt he hated couldn't hide her beauty.

He wanted to throw his gun aside and pull her into his arms. To touch her once more, to taste her kisses and feel the heat of her body pressed against his would be worth any price. A miracle had brought her back to him.

His rational mind was screaming that this was impossible. Despite what others might say, he wasn't crazy. He knew right from wrong, alive from dead. She was dead. He'd strangled the breath from her with his own two hands. With the same shovel that lay in the back of his truck now, he'd dug the grave where her body rested. No way could she be standing in front of him, yet there she was.

He let the hand holding his gun drop to his side as he took a step toward her. He had to touch her, to know she was as real and solid as she appeared. As he reached out with his free hand, a shot shattered the silence.

A sharp pain sliced through his chest and the gun fell from his hand, landing with a thump on the ground. Alida faded away as his knees gave and he toppled to the ground. Where had she gone? How could she leave him like this? He loved her with all his heart.

"Alida," he whispered as darkness began to crowd his vision.

"She's gone and you'll never see her again, you piece of shit," Katie said. The last thing he saw before his heart stopped beating was Katie standing over him, her gun in one hand, her other pressed against her blood-soaked shirt.

❖

The storm grew weaker until it faded away, replaced by clean air and the sound of the ocean gently lapping at the shore. The Watcher stood on the rocks jutting far out into the water and let the air blow softly across his skin.

The worst was over, and once more she had opened the door to heaven for the lost and, in some cases, forgotten souls. He sighed, and something like relief washed through his body. His faith in her was not misplaced. She was special, as he'd known she was the moment she came to this place. In her soul grace abounded, and in her he would find his own salvation.

Tonight she had found the lost, and in the days to come they would be reunited with those who'd searched for them, hoped for them, feared for them, and waited for the day they could bring them home. Evil had tried to stretch its wings and take more good souls to hell. She had spread her own wings and engulfed them all in her embrace of goodness. That was magic. That was faith.

With his eyes turned once more heavenward, he quietly prayed.

"Our Father, who art in heaven, hallowed be Thy name. Thy kingdom come, Thy will be done, on earth as it is in heaven. Give us this day our daily bread, and forgive us our trespasses as we forgive those who trespass against us. And lead us not into temptation, but deliver us from evil..."

CHAPTER TWENTY-SIX

Thea caught Katie before she hit the ground a second time. "You are one crazy woman, do you know that?" she asked as she held her. "Crazy." She said the last word with a sob.

"That bastard was going to shoot you. Couldn't let that happen now, could I?" Her voice was weak, tired.

Thea kissed the top of her head. "You didn't have to do that for me."

Katie's eyes fluttered and her voice grew weaker. "Yeah, I did. I've waited a long time for you, Theadora. I'm not losing you to some psychopath."

Thea pressed her face against Katie's hair and tears pricked at her eyes. "I don't want to lose you either. He already took my sister. Don't you dare die on me." Her shirt was wet, and she knew it was soaked with Katie's blood. "Please, don't leave me," she cried, her tears turning Katie's hair wet.

Katie's hand on her arm was cool. "I'm not going anywhere but I'm a little tired now." Her eyes fluttered closed.

"No!" Thea held her close. "Stay with me."

"Help is on the way," Lorna called from where she sat on the ground with Jeremy.

In the distance Thea could see the flash of lights and hear the sounds of sirens. Her relief nearly brought on another round of sobs. Instead she pulled Katie closer and tried to share her warmth. "Stay with me," she repeated over and over as she rocked her gently.

When the EMTs arrived and moved in to work on Katie, letting go of her was like losing a limb. The last thing she wanted was to be separated. Seeming to understand, the first responders let her ride in the ambulance when she told them she was Katie's girlfriend. It was a bit of a stretch, but under the circumstances she didn't feel one tiny bit bad. She planned to stay with her as long as she'd let her. They could sort out the girlfriend technicality later.

It was six hours before both Katie and Jeremy were in and out of surgery and finally in their rooms. Merry was with Jeremy now, while Lorna and Renee headed back to their hotel. Thea pulled a chair next to Katie's bed and rested her head on the mattress. Her eyes closed and sleep took her into its needed embrace.

A hand on the top of her head made her shoot up. Soft laughter brought her up short. "It's just me, beautiful."

Tears came into her eyes again as she met Katie's gaze. "You scared me," she said. "Don't do that again."

Katie's smile was the most beautiful thing she'd seen in a long time. "Scared myself, if you want to know the truth. I'll try very hard never to do that again."

This time tears flowed down her cheeks. "You kept your promise."

"My promise?"

"You said you'd bring Alida home, and you did."

Darkness flitted over her face. "I hoped for better."

"Better was gone the moment she met that man. I'll always love you for what you've done for my sister…for me." Thea said the words that filled her heart.

Katie turned her head toward the window. "It's my job," she said neutrally.

Thea put her hand on Katie's cheek and turned her face so their eyes met again. "Yes, it is your job, and you do it well. I get that, and it's another thing I love about you. I love so many things about you, and we have a lifetime to share them."

Katie's hand came up to cover hers. "I've never met anyone who makes me feel like you do, and I was afraid you wouldn't want to see me after this was over."

Thea smiled and held her hand up to her lips. "If you think you're going to get rid of me that easily, you need to think again."

The radiant smile on Katie's face made Thea glow inside.

EPILOGUE

It felt so good to be home, in her big house on the Pacific. Lorna would have to go back to Spokane in a few weeks for Alida's memorial service but would have some time to recover before that happened. Thea wanted to wait until Katie was up and mobile, which wouldn't be that long. The gunshot wound had been relatively minor, a through-and-through on her left side that missed anything important. Thank God for small favors.

It was still a little hard to wrap her head around all that had happened. One guy, supposedly one of the good guys, had killed her friend in the name of love. It was an old story that often ended tragically. If he couldn't have her, no one could.

But she wasn't his only victim. In some warped way he saw himself as an avenging angel set on a path cleaning the world of women he felt were unworthy. By the time the Spokane County Sheriff's Department finished at the Wild Rose Cemetery, they uncovered the bodies of eleven victims, Alida one of them. With the murder of Vince, Chad's total count was an even dozen...that they knew of. The very real possibility he could have killed even more gave her chills, and judging by what he'd said out in the cemetery she was afraid he had. They'd probably never know for certain because Chad wasn't saying a word.

At least he wouldn't have any more victims. Katie's shot had been true to its mark, and the deputy sheriff turned serial killer was as dead as his victims. The only silver lining to this horrible situation was that one evil man had been wiped from the face of the earth. She didn't feel bad about that.

The whole affair was a world changer for Katie. One colleague a serial killer, albeit a dead one now, another dead at said serial killer's hands, and a really good IT Tech out of a job when his unauthorized surveillance of Katie was uncovered. Poor Brandon was really more misguided than evil. Unfortunately, his infatuation with Katie had taken him over a line that couldn't be uncrossed.

All things considered, Lorna thought Katie was handling the entire episode with dignity and professionalism. Apparently so did the higher powers, for she was promoted to Vince's job of undersheriff.

Lorna's hair was still a little wet as she walked to the kitchen, and she had her mind on her training. Time was winding down, and her big test was coming up soon. She was looking forward to her race and to proving she could push through all 140.6 miles of the Ironman endurance test. Still, a few days of R&R here at home were an awesome treat. That trip to Spokane had taken its toll.

Even Jeremy looked better when he was able to relax in his own bed. As with Katie, the shot could have been far worse. A nasty wound in his thigh that was going to hurt for a while and require some physical therapy was the worst of it. All in all, though, both of them were lucky, really lucky. Oh, Merry would have to baby him a ton, and she sure as hell didn't envy her. That was the price Merry got to pay for saying yes when her brother asked her to marry him.

That thought made her smile. Actually, she couldn't wait for Jeremy and Merry's wedding. She loved them both and was thrilled they were going to be parents. It also meant she was going to be an aunt, which was pretty damned exciting too. A child always brought light and happiness to a home.

Family, it was all about family. At the window she paused and stared out at the view worth a million bucks. Every time she looked out this window she thanked Aunt Bea for giving her this place. It was her salvation in more ways than one, which was why more and more lately she wondered if Jeremy should be the only member of the family to get married. She'd never thought about marriage before, but she did now, and she knew why: Renee.

The thought of Renee brought a smile to her lips, and she turned to head to the kitchen. Here at the old homestead, no later than 7:30 every single morning, she would find a pot of fresh, wonderful coffee in the kitchen courtesy of Jolene. She was an incredible housekeeper and would definitely be an even better mother-in-law.

She winged it into the kitchen and came to an abrupt halt. At the table sat Jolene, Renee, Merry, and Jeremy, all staring at her.

"What?"

If she didn't know better she'd think she'd just stepped into an intervention. She didn't have a drinking problem, didn't do drugs, and wasn't a gambler. So, what exactly would they be intervening?

Renee smiled. "Sit. We have something to discuss with you."

Okay, so maybe this was an intervention. Gingerly she sat and accepted the mug of coffee Jolene brought her. "What? You guys are scaring me."

Leaning into her, Renee kissed her. "No worries, love."

"Okay, give it up. It feels like you're all getting ready to send me into rehab."

Jeremy laughed and then groaned. "Don't make me laugh. When I move it feels like someone just poked me with a hot iron."

"Tell me what you're up to or I *will* poke you with a hot iron."

Renee stroked her wet hair. "Here's the deal. Remember how I told you I'd been made an offer on my Seattle property I couldn't refuse?"

"Yeah…"

Jeremy jumped in, his voice excited. "We're going into business together."

"What?"

This time Renee's voice was filled with energy and excitement. "While you were in Spokane, the three of us got to talking. We all have different skill sets and expertise, and we figured out they all work together. That's when we came up with the idea to form the business."

"Business? What business?"

"We're going to rebuild the same business I had in Seattle, only do it web-based. I know the merchandising side, Jeremy is the business planner, and of course baby mama is our corporate attorney. It's perfect, and we keep it all in the family."

Jolene piped in. "I'm the corporate cafeteria."

They all laughed and then quieted as they looked at Lorna as she asked, "So you all are going into business together?"

Renee's face grew shadowed. "We thought you'd like our idea. Instead of three unemployed lumps living off your generosity, we all become contributing members of the household."

"It's a good idea," Jeremy added. "Renee has a great client base and awesome products. Merry and I have all the business skills she needs to make this big. We'll all be working again, Lorna, not just you."

Tears filled her eyes as she looked from one happy face to another. Renee took both of her hands. "If this doesn't work for you, we don't have to do it here."

Lorna smiled through the tears. "I'm not upset."

"You're not?" Merry still looked concerned. "Why are you crying?"

"I'm just amazed. It's like the old saying about making lemonade when life gives you lemons. That's what you all do, and you have no idea how that inspires me. I love you."

Renee hugged her tight and whispered in her ear, "I love you so much."

Lorna returned her hug as she looked over her shoulder at Jeremy and gave him a smile she felt all the way to her soul. "You guys are going to kick ass."

About the Author

Sheri Lewis Wohl grew up in Northeast Washington State and always thought she'd move away to somewhere exciting. Never happened. Now she happily writes surrounded by unspoiled nature, trying to capture a bit of that beauty in her work. No matter how hard she tries to write *normal*, though, it doesn't work—something of the preternatural variety always sneaks in. When not working or writing stories filled with things that go bump in the night, she trains for triathlons, acts as a zombie extra in a SyFy series, and is a member of a K9 Search & Rescue team.

Books Available from Bold Strokes Books

Break Point by Yolanda Wallace. In a world readying for war, can love find a way? (978-1-62639-5-688)

Countdown by Julie Cannon. Can two strong-willed, powerful women overcome their differences to save the lives of seven others and begin a life they never imagined together? (978-1-62639-4-711)

Heart of the Liliko'i by Dena Hankins. Secrets, sabotage, and grisly human remains stall construction on an ancient Hawaiian burial ground, but the sexual connection between Kerala and Ravi keeps building toward a volcanic explosion. (978-1-62639-5-565)

Keep Hold by Michelle Grubb. Claire knew some things should be left alone and some rules should never be broken, but the most forbidden, well, they are the most tempting. (978-1-62639-5-022)

The Courage to Try by C.A. Popovich. Finding love is worth getting past the fear of trying. (978-1-62639-5-282)

The Time Before Now by Missouri Vaun. Vivian flees a disastrous affair, embarking on an epic, transformative journey to escape her past, until destiny introduces her to Ida, who helps her rediscover trust, love and hope. (978-1-62639-4-469)

Twisted Whispers by Sheri Lewis Wohl. Betrayal, lies, and secrets—whispers of a friend lost to darkness. Can a reluctant psychic set things right or will an evil soul destroy those she loves? (978-1-62639-4-391)

Deadly Medicine by Jaime Maddox. Dr. Ward Thrasher's life is in turmoil. Her partner Jess has left her, and her job puts her in the path of a murderous physician who has Jess in his sights. (978-1-62639-4-247)

New Beginnings by KC Richardson. Can the connection and attraction between Jordan Roberts and Kirsten Murphy be enough for Jordan to trust Kirsten with her heart? (978-1-62639-4-506)

Officer Down by Erin Dutton. Can two women who've made careers out of being there for others in crisis find the strength to need each other? (978-1-62639-4-230)

Reasonable Doubt by Carsen Taite. Just when Sarah and Ellery think they've left dangerous careers behind, a new case sets them—and their hearts—on a collision course. (978-1-62639-4-421)

Tarnished Gold by Ann Aptaker. Cantor Gold must outsmart the Law, outrun New York's dockside gangsters, outplay a shady art dealer, his lover, and a beautiful curator, and stay out of a killer's gun sights. (978-1-62639-4-261)

The Renegade by Amy Dunne. Post-apocalyptic survivors Alex and Evelyn secretly find love while held captive by a deranged cult, but when their relationship is discovered, they must fight for their freedom—or die trying. (978-1-62639-4-278)

Thrall by Barbara Ann Wright. Four women in a warrior society must work together to lift an insidious curse while caught between their own desires, the will of their peoples, and an ancient evil. (978-1-62639-4-377)

White Horse in Winter by Franci McMahon. Love between two women collides with the inner poison of a closeted horse trainer in the green hills of Vermont. (978-1-62639-4-292)

The Chameleon by Andrea Bramhall. Two old friends must work through a web of lies and deceit to find themselves again, but in the search they discover far more than they ever went looking for. (978-1-62639-363-9)

Side Effects by VK Powell. Detective Jordan Bishop and Dr. Neela Sahjani must decide if it's easier to trust someone with your heart or your life as they face threatening protestors, corrupt politicians, and their increasing attraction. (978-1-62639-364-6)

Autumn Spring by Shelley Thrasher. Can Bree and Linda, two women in the autumn of their lives, put their hearts first and find the love they've never dared seize? (978-1-62639-365-3)

Warm November by Kathleen Knowles. What do you do if the one woman you want is the only one you can't have? (978-1-62639-366-0)

In Every Cloud by Tina Michele. When she finally leaves her shattered life behind, is Bree strong enough to salvage the remaining pieces of her heart and find the place where it truly fits? (978-1-62639-413-1)

Rise of the Gorgon by Tanai Walker. When independent Internet journalist Elle Pharell goes to Kuwait to investigate a veteran's mysterious suicide, she hires Cassandra Hunt, an interpreter with a covert agenda. (978-1-62639-367-7)

Crossed by Meredith Doench. Agent Luce Hansen returns home to catch a killer and risks everything to revisit the unsolved murder of her first girlfriend and confront the demons of her youth. (978-1-62639-361-5)

Making a Comeback by Julie Blair. Music and love take center stage when jazz pianist Liz Randall tries to make a comeback with the help of her reclusive, blind neighbor, Jac Winters. (978-1-62639-357-8)

Soul Unique by Gun Brooke. Self-proclaimed cynic Greer Landon falls for Hayden Rowe's paintings and the young woman shortly after, but will Hayden, who lives with Asperger syndrome, trust her and reciprocate her feelings? (978-1-62639-358-5)

The Price of Honor by Radclyffe. Honor and duty are not always black and white—and when self-styled patriots take up arms against the government, the price of honor may be a life. (978-1-62639-359-2)

Mounting Evidence by Karis Walsh. Lieutenant Abigail Hargrove and her mounted police unit need to solve a murder and protect wetland biologist Kira Lovell during the Washington State Fair. (978-1-62639-343-1)

Threads of the Heart by Jeannie Levig. Maggie and Addison Rae-McInnis share a love and a life, but are the threads that bind them together strong enough to withstand Addison's restlessness and the seductive Victoria Fontaine? (978-1-62639-410-0)

Sheltered Love by MJ Williamz. Boone Fairway and Grey Dawson—two women touched by abuse—overcome their pasts to find happiness in each other. (978-1-62639-362-2)

Asher's Out by Elizabeth Wheeler. Asher Price's candid photographs capture the truth, but when his success requires exposing an enemy, Asher discovers his only shot at happiness involves revealing secrets of his own. (978-1-62639-411-7)

The Ground Beneath by Missouri Vaun. An improbable barter deal involving a hope chest and dinners for a month places lovely Jessica Walker distractingly in the way of Sam Casey's bachelor lifestyle. (978-1-62639-606-7)

Hardwired by C.P. Rowlands. Award-winning teacher Clary Stone, and Leefe Ellis, manager of the homeless shelter for small children, stand together in a part of Clary's hometown that she never knew existed. (978-1-62639-351-6)

No Good Reason by Cari Hunter. A violent kidnapping in a Peak District village pushes Detective Sanne Jensen and lifelong friend Dr. Meg Fielding closer, just as it threatens to tear everything apart. (978-1-62639-352-3)

Romance by the Book by Jo Victor. If Cam didn't keep disrupting her life, maybe Alex could uncover the secret of a century-old love story, and solve the greatest mystery of all—her own heart. (978-1-62639-353-0)

Death's Doorway by Crin Claxton. Helping the dead can be deadly: Tony may be listening to the dead, but she needs to learn to listen to the living. (978-1-62639-354-7)

Searching for Celia by Elizabeth Ridley. As American spy novelist Dayle Salvesen investigates the mysterious disappearance of her ex-lover, Celia, in London, she begins questioning how well she knew Celia—and how well she knows herself. (978-1-62639-356-1)

The 45th Parallel by Lisa Girolami. Burying her mother isn't the worst thing that can happen to Val Montague when she returns to the woodsy but peculiar town of Hemlock, Oregon. (978-1-62639-342-4)

A Royal Romance by Jenny Frame. In a country where class still divides, can love topple the last social taboo and allow Queen Georgina and Beatrice Elliot, a working class girl, their happy ever after? (978-1-62639-360-8)

Bouncing by Jaime Maddox. Basketball Coach Alex Dalton has been bouncing from woman to woman, because no one ever held her interest, until she meets her new assistant, Britain Dodge. (978-1-62639-344-8)

Same Time Next Week by Emily Smith. A chance encounter between Alex Harris and the beautiful Michelle Masters leads to a whirlwind friendship, and causes Alex to question everything she's ever known—including her own marriage. (978-1-62639-345-5)

All Things Rise by Missouri Vaun. Cole rescues a striking pilot who crash-lands near her family's farm, setting in motion a chain of events that will forever alter the course of her life. (978-1-62639-346-2)

Riding Passion by D. Jackson Leigh. Mount up for the ride through a sizzling anthology of chance encounters, buried desires, romantic surprises, and blazing passion. (978-1-62639-349-3)

Love's Bounty by Yolanda Wallace. Lobster boat captain Jake Myers stopped living the day she cheated death, but meeting greenhorn Shy Silva stirs her back to life. (978-1-62639-334-9)

Just Three Words by Melissa Brayden. Sometimes the one you want is the one you least suspect. Accountant Samantha Ennis has her ordered life disrupted when heartbreaker Hunter Blair moves into her trendy Soho loft. (978-1-62639-335-6)

Lay Down the Law by Carsen Taite. Attorney Peyton Davis returns to her Texas roots to take on big oil and the Mexican Mafia, but will her investigation thwart her chance at true love? (978-1-62639-336-3)

Playing in Shadow by Lesley Davis. Survivor's guilt threatens to keep Bryce trapped in her nightmare world unless Scarlet's love can pull her out of the darkness and back into the light. (978-1-62639-337-0)

Soul Selecta by Gill McKnight. Soul mates are hell to work with. (978-1-62639-338-7)

The Revelation of Beatrice Darby by Jean Copeland. Adolescence is complicated, but Beatrice Darby is about to discover how impossible it can seem to a lesbian coming of age in conservative 1950s New England. (978-1-62639-339-4)

Twice Lucky by Mardi Alexander. For firefighter Mackenzie James and Dr. Sarah Macarthur, there's suddenly a whole lot more in life to understand, to consider, to risk…someone will need to fight for her life. (978-1-62639-325-7)

Shadow Hunt by L.L. Raand. With young to raise and her Pack under attack, Sylvan, Alpha of the wolf Weres, takes on her greatest challenge when she determines to uncover the faceless enemies known as the Shadow Lords. A Midnight Hunters novel. (978-1-62639-326-4)

Heart of the Game by Rachel Spangler. A baseball writer falls for a single mom, but can she ever love anything as much as she loves the game? (978-1-62639-327-1)

Getting Lost by Michelle Grubb. Twenty-eight days, thirteen European countries, a tour manager fighting attraction, and an accused murderer: Stella and Phoebe's journey of a lifetime begins here. (978-1-62639-328-8)

Prayer of the Handmaiden by Merry Shannon. Celibate priestess Kadrian must defend the kingdom of Ithyria from a dangerous enemy and ultimately choose between her duty to the Goddess and the love of her childhood sweetheart, Erinda. (978-1-62639-329-5)

boldstrokesbooks.com

Bold Strokes Books

Quality and Diversity in LGBTQ Literature

Drama

MATINEE BOOKS

SCI-FI

E-BOOKS

MYSTERY

EROTICA

YOUNG ADULT

Romance

W·E·B·S·T·O·R·E

PRINT AND EBOOKS